Jacqueline Carpenter is from Essex and is married with a grown-up son and daughter. These days she spends a lot of her time in Spain, where she adores the weather, the delicious healthy food and gorgeous people.

Her favourite pastimes are walking along the beach, chatting and dancing (badly!).

For all my lovely, unique family – those still with us and those sadly not.

Jacqueline Carpenter

LOUISA

AUSTIN MACAULEY PUBLISHERS™

LONDON • CAMBRIDGE • NEW YORK • SHARJAH

A CIP catalogue record for this title is available from the British Library.

ISBN 9781788484374 (Paperback)
ISBN 9781788484381 (E-Book)

www.austinmacauley.com

First Published (2019)
Austin Macauley Publishers Ltd
25 Canada Square
Canary Wharf
London
E14 5LQ

Louisa

A freezing fog was ambling itself across from the River Thames shrouding Bermondsey Walk and to Louisa it felt so cold it made her teeth actually ache. She scrunched the itchy, grey, woollen scarf tighter under her chin. She felt rigid with tension. She just HAD to walk faster, faster, faster. Her dainty feet stumbled along the uneven pavement where to the right of her lay the bombed remains of huge, eerie warehouses. Not so long ago they would have been bustling with dock workers, sorting and unloading goods brought here, to London, on vessels from all over the world. The River Thames on her left was dark and silent, sleeping under the dense fog.

Louisa silently prayed little Harry wasn't awake.

"Oh, please God, don't let him have woken Johnny," she pleaded to herself. She turned the corner, through the night-time fog she could just about see her home. She took a long, slow intake of breath. Her shoulders were hunched against the cold, harsh weather she thought she would never be able to unwind herself.

"Quick." She realised she was panting as she struggled to move her legs faster.

"Nearly there! Chin up, Lou Lou," she smiled to herself.

"Everyone's probably sound asleep and don't even know you've been out."

Chapter One

Nine Years Earlier

Louisa was so excited! Herself, her sister Gladys and her brother Stevie were all waiting in the sitting room of their cosy terraced house, No 12 Acacia Court, South London. Their home was built with rusty brown bricks and the dark green front door opened straight onto the street. Across the road from their home were three separate buildings each with three floors that contained flats. The flats stretched the length of Acacia Court and were called Peabody Buildings. Each flat had a balcony, on some there was washing flapping dry in the breeze, one balcony was piled high with crates and one had what looked like old furniture stacked up. The furniture had been there for as long as Louisa remembered and she wondered why they didn't get rid of it, she determined it was probably impossible to manhandle down the flights of stairs. The street was narrow and there were a few fluffy clouds floating across the sky. About a dozen children were playing football and hopscotch with a few of the girls giggling. Their sitting room window looked out onto Acacia Court and Louisa, Gladys and Stevie, were all craning their necks to look down the road to see if their dad was walking towards their house. Their mum Alice was busying herself in the kitchen from where mouth-watering smells were wafting.

"Oh, where is he?" Gladys pleaded, bouncing like a cute puppy, impatient with anticipation. Gladys, a year younger than Louisa was a real scatterbrain. She was as tall as Louisa and about the same weight but her hair was slightly redder and although she was usually happy her face was stuck in a frown. Louisa and Gladys shared a bedroom and irritated each other madly. Their brother, Stevie, was two years older than Louisa and to her, the most charming, handsome man in the world. He was wearing a crisp white shirt, navy tie and had that cheeky twinkle in his blue eyes. They could hear their mum singing to herself as she made steak and kidney pudding, her dad's favourite.

"Guess, who's home?!"

Tom Foster threw open the door and bound into the room, they all loved their dad and mum ran from the kitchen and clasped her hands together. Her handsome, hardworking husband was home from sea safe and well. The relief washed over her. Her family was complete again. "Thank you, God," she sighed closing her eyes.

Tom was a portly, cheery chap. Quite tall, 5 foot 10 inches, thirty four years old next birthday and had a shiny part of his head showing through his hair which Louisa was sure wasn't there last time she saw him and his tummy had shrunk a bit too but he was still cuddly and they all gathered around him hugging him.

"Got a cuppa for me, love? Nine months at sea and you're making me wait for a hot, sweet cup of tea?!" Tom bellowed. Gladys was skipping around the tiny room, Stevie was shaking his dad's hand and patting his shoulder and Louisa just hung onto his arm with her head leaning against his shoulder. Life was brilliant and Daddy had a bag of presents and a strange man, *a friend?* with him!

"And now, can you find it in your heart to make one of your hot sweet cups of tea for my mucker here too," Tom hooted in his rich, deep voice.

"I would appreciate you all to making him welcome. I'd like to introduce you my good friend James."

Tom announced sweeping his arm across the front of his companion.

"Now make sure you all mind your manners, you lot, as James is a posh toff from Kent!

Let's show him what a lovely bunch we South Londoners are!"

As Alice, Louisa and Gladys handed out the steaming hot cups of tea, Tom presented Stevie with a bottle of rum.

"Gordon Bennet!" Stevie yelled. "Rum! You've finally realised I'm a grown-up," he chortled.

Tom produced three brightly coloured patterned scarves and handed one each to Alice, Louisa and Gladys smiling as he did so. Alice was fortunate enough to be the recipient of two gifts and was given a small pack of handkerchiefs with a pink 'A' embroidered on one corner of each. Louisa's scarf felt so smooth, she stroked it against her cheek and suddenly became very conscious of their guest. He was looking at her and smiling, Oh, she worried he must think them all so rude they had been so wrapped up with their dad they had been practically ignoring him.

"Shift up, Lou Lou," her dad chuckled as he nudged Louisa along the brown cosy sofa, "let James take the weight off his feet." Tom proceeded to introduce James individually to his family. James was gorgeous! Louisa realised and started to feel very warm.

"Stop it," she berated silently, "Behave yourself, young lady!"

They all talked and sang and listened and the men drank very late into the night. James was pretty easy to speak to and he and Tom had them all roaring with laughter with their tales of the sea and strange people they had come across during the last few months.

The warm glowing memories of that evening would stay with them all for a very long time to come. Two weeks leave just flew by, twice a year they saw Tom Foster but his stories and money kept them fed and content while he was away working as a merchant seaman.

James had stayed three days at their house and promised to return soon. On his second evening at The Foster house, he had sat on the front doorstep, he said to get some cooler air, but Louisa suspected he was sitting there as their sitting room was so small he probably felt guilty taking a up a seat inside. She sat down on the doorstep next to him. The front door was open behind them and they could hear her chattering family.

Louisa told James all about their trip to Westminster Abbey earlier in the year to watch the coronation procession of King George VI. The way James gazed at her made her feel like royalty, her voice got higher and squeakier, she was so enjoying his attention to her storytelling. She recounted the day, it had been splendid.

"The last king had fallen in love with an American lady who had been married before and a king is not allowed to marry someone who has been wed before, so he had to choose! Her or his throne? I think it's very romantic that he chose her. Anyway, the new king, King George VI has a lovely wife, Queen Elizabeth and two princesses, Elizabeth and Margaret and they all rode down Pall Mall on horses and carriages and we lined up for seven hours to see them. It was like a fairy story, we all waved flags and cheered as the procession passed, I shall never forget it." Louisa felt like she was living it all again.

James's was mesmerised with this entertaining young girl, she made him feel so happy, she was so vibrant.

Louisa asked him, "Now how come you're in the merchant navy, James?"

"Well, my dad was in the merchant navy and I guess I just followed him," he replied looking down at his feet.

"My dad unfortunately died three years ago from tuberculosis which just left me and my mum."

Louisa tucked her arms around her knees.

"Oh, I'm so sorry," she offered, "that must have been awful for you." She stared at the flats opposite feeling awkward and wondering what to say next.

"Oh, it's not your fault!" laughed James.

He had such a gentle, kind manner about him, Louisa felt extremely easy in his company. They sat on the concrete doorstep in silence for a few moments, both staring ahead. Louisa looked casually sideways at James hoping he wouldn't notice her admiring his handsomeness. He was about six foot tall and quite skinny, he had lovely blue eyes and bony, chiselled cheeks. She had noticed that when he spoke to someone he had a habit of gently touching them for a split second on their hand or shoulder which endeared Louisa to him. He had a very thin nose and quite big ears but such a genuine smile which came really easily.

"I'm not really a 'Posh Toff' from Kent," he sniggered interrupting Louisa's teenage thoughts.

"We used to live in a tiny house over that way in 'The Thames Basin', James waved his right arm across Louisa's face pointing to the end of her street and intentionally nudged his elbow gently into her nose and laughed.

"Have you heard of it?"

"Oyee," she whacked him giggling.

"I had been with my dad on the ships for coming up to a year when he got well poorly, it was bad." James paused and took a deep breath. "He didn't want to die." He dropped his head.

"After he was gone, my mum got a job as a housekeeper in a small farmhouse in Kent to an elderly couple, they seem to like her, she's really good to my mum, the wife like, but my mum says the husband keeps himself to himself. He's not horrible like, just don't say much. It's dead quite down there and so pitch black at night you really cannot see a thing not even your hands in front of your face. It's all farms spread out, there are just no lights anywhere. She likes it down there, well, she seems content like, misses my dad like mad but at least she has no worries. I've been a couple of times and they always treat me well decent, well, she does he can be a bit distant but he might just be shy."

Louise had a gentle smile on her face.

"Actually, Mark, my best mate from schools down there as well now. He did three years in the army and learnt to be a motor car mechanic. Well, I knew he was wanting to leave the army when his time was up and the chap who mum works for said his friend owned the village motor car workshop. The owner has arthritis which was gradually getting worse and he was looking for someone to help him. My mum wrote to me and asked if Mark would like it, I wrote to Mark and Bobs your uncle! He's now a country bumpkin living in the middle of nowhere too!"

James had such a lovely way of telling stories, Louisa was laughing uncontrollably, the way he titled his head, threw his arms about, smiled whilst talking, he was so entertaining.

"They mend farm vehicles mostly but lot of people down there have got motor cars. They need them to get about really, it's such a long walk to anywhere, it's all pretty country lanes and also they've got loads more money than us South Londoner's to buy the cars with!"

Louisa realised it was starting to get dark and stood to go in, all the children that had been playing outside had disappeared into their homes.

"Oh, I had better see if my mum needs any more help," she explained, "I feel sad for your mum but it does sound lovely to be living in a farmhouse in the Kent countryside."

"Thanks, chuck," James winked at her. "It is pretty down there but the farm animals can't half pong," he laughed, "Come on, I can give you a hand with the chores too!"

Her mum worked hard whilst Tom was home to make his leave perfect but always had a smile on her face. Life was good and they all had so much to be grateful for. It was the autumn of 1937.

James returned from Kent three days before he and Tom were booked to embark on their vessel and sail off to India to collect Tea. He and Louisa had the same thoughts, sense of humour, ideas and just got on so well it was a pleasure for them to be in each other's company. They promised to write to each other. On his last evening, they were alone in the kitchen, James was drying the dishes from their evening meal and Louisa was taking them from him and stacking them away. James took Louisa's hand and smiled warmly at her, he whispered I just want to say to you that I can't wait to get back and see you again. Louisa smiled and they just gazed deeply into each other's eyes. They unlocked hands and after they had finished the chores joined the rest of the family in the sitting room.

The rain was bouncing off the dockside as they all hugged their dad as he and James prepared to board their ship again.

"Make sure there's some of that rum waiting when I get back in six months," Tom warned Stevie with his teasing manner. Alice dabbed her eyes as the men walked away. She hated this bit but Tom had the sea in his blood. His father and grandfather before him had both been seamen, the money was good, she still had to make meals last for days on end and God only knows how Stevie put away the amount of food he did into his tummy, looking at him you wouldn't believe it, so tall and lean, taller than his dad now by about five inches. The only money to be earned around here was from the sea, either away on a ship, unloading in the Thames Docks or working in shipping offices where Stevie had been lucky enough to land a job. Hayes Wharf employed hundreds of men, the ships came in most days laden with sugar, tea, cotton, fruit brought across the Atlantic mainly finishing up at the River Thames to be shared around 1930's United Kingdom and when the sailors disembarked after months away at sea they mostly headed straight into one of the many rowdy Inn's to enjoy their hard worked for cash. Luckily, for Alice her Tom was a family man who always came straight home then had a bottle of beer indoors. Alice was one of the lucky ones, had landed on her feet with Tom she had.

It was a hard life, London was a very busy, loud, city, there were good and bad like everywhere Alice guessed but there were so many people. The dock workers were mostly a cheeky lot, happy with their lot and just trying to make the most of their lives. Stevie used to play them up when he was younger. He would run around the dockside asking for 'anything going'. He knew most of the men, sometimes they would split open a sack of sugar and let Stevie and his friends grab a handful each. Pure treasure to young kids who never got any type of treats. They tried to squash the whole handful into their mouths all in one go but half the sugar would end up in their hair, their ears, all down their clothes and stuck in their nails.

The Foster family slowly walked back home, each quietly turning to see the huge ship departing looking ghostly through the smog, hoping it would miraculously turn around and return.

They knew it wouldn't but still looked anyway.

"Please, God," Louisa prayed to herself, "let James come back safe and sound... Oh, and my dad too, of course!"

Chapter Two

Ma Pritchard, as she was known to everyone, stood on her doorstep of No 13 Acacia Court. Her short, stocky arms were crossed under her bosom and wedged on top of her chubby tummy. She was wearing a green, flowery dress that was faded and a white apron over the top which had bulging pockets that drooped down like her bosom. The apron had splutters of food (or whatever else you could imagine) sprayed across it. Her hair was short and grey and stood upright resembling the texture of a scourer that you would use to clean your saucepans. She had a lit cigarette in her mouth and some wiry grey hairs sprouting from her chin.

Louisa could not ever remember seeing old Ma Pritchard without a dirty apron on and a cigarette stuck to her lips. She was a mother to four children, well, I say mother I think they brought themselves up, Joan was the eldest, she was quite tall with dark curly hair and a beautiful face, Phyllis was short with fair hair and a stern face, Tom was stocky like his mum but had ginger hair and was covered in freckles and June was petit with really blonde hair. There was no Mr Pritchard, never had been Louisa was sure. All the Pritchard children were so different to each other not only in looks but personality wise as well. When Ma Pritchard was younger she had worked in 'The Royal Blue' one of the lively public inns by Hayes Wharf docks. Alice had told Louisa that years ago never a year went by without Ma Pritchard's belly starting to swell and Alice would say,

"We will be hearing another baby crying before long you mark my words!"

Some of her babies had been taken away for adoption and two Louisa remembered had been born dead. That had been terrible.

Ma Pritchard was sacked about ten years ago from The Royal Blue and every time she recalled the story of her departure it was a different tale. Louisa's favourite version was that Ma Pritchard had stayed late to give the public bar a real good scrub over, but she had made it so clean the next day the patrons shoes all stuck to the floor and couldn't walk properly!

"Shall I come in, keep you company, have a cuppa with you?" Ma Pritchard spluttered through her cigarette, she then marched through their front door without even waiting for a reply. Alice didn't answer just went into the kitchen and filled the kettle from the tap.

"Just us women again looking after each other." Ma Pritchard pulled a lump of fluff off her apron and started to inspect it. "I suppose you heard my Joan's left me? Gone to live at her fellas house do all their cleaning instead of mine," she chuckled.

"Cleaning?" laughed Alice, "Where did Joan ever learn to clean?" The women walked into the front room and sat with their white cups of tea. Alice and Ma Pritchard couldn't be more different from each other but Alice was fond of Ma Pritchard, she made her laugh.

"Mum, I'm going to bed," Louisa interrupted their conversation, "but before I do, I have to ask you something."

For some reason Louisa didn't understand both Alice and Ma Pritchard looked up at her terrified.

"Rosie said there's a job going in Heart's Bakers factory if I want to apply?"

"Oh, my God! Oh, my God! How exciting! A job!" Alice put her cup of tea down and jumped up. "Phew, what a relief," she exclaimed, looking knowingly at Ma Pritchard.

"That's brilliant news, my darling, I will have to check with the school first but you have only got a couple of months left."

Louisa couldn't comprehend why her mum was so pleased.

Chapter Three

Rosie stood daydreaming in her bedroom at No 16 Acacia Court. It was 4 am and just getting light. She didn't mind getting up so early in the summer months. In fact, it was quite nice to hear the bird's singing and smell a new day dawning. But this was winter and still dark. She quickly splashed her face with water that she had poured into the china bowl the previous evening in preparation for the next day. The china bowl stood on top of a dark wooden chest of drawers which was in between two small windows in her bedroom. The windows over looked the Peabody Buildings opposite. There was a gas lamp glowing outside and making Acacia Court look hazy. The mist often rolled up their street from the River Thames. It looked clean mist today but normally in the winter it was grey fog and dirty looking and would deposit small black dots on everything outside. There was no sign of life in the flats opposite but a faint murmur could be heard in the distance of a new day's activities beginning at Hayes Wharf.

Rosie's sister Caren was asleep in the bed they shared. Her mouth was slightly open and she had flung her arm across the space Rosie had been occupying until ten minutes ago. Caren was a year younger than Rosie and Rosie thought, very cute. Both sisters had large, brown, lucid eyes but Caren's nose was daintier and her chin slightly smaller. Caren could sleep for hours like a baby. Unlike Rosie who had always been a busy bee and itching to go.

Rosie patted her face dry with the rough towel and lifted her hair brush. She tried to be as quiet as possible. Quickly, she pulled her dark, wavy hair into a high ponytail and secured it with a rubber band ready for the hair net she would soon don.

She dressed without thinking in a white nylon overall which had one pocket on each hip, picked up her small, black, satchel style bag and tiptoed from the room. Creeping down the stairs she winced at all the creeks they made. If her dad was woken he would begin shouting then her mum would be exasperated because her dad was awake. Her mum was always exasperated at her dad come to think of it.

At the bottom of the narrow dark staircase, she slipped her feet into the well-worn flat pumps she had been wearing since her last year at school. Rosie promised herself to buy a new pair this week. She was feeling excited and optimistic this Monday morning as her best friend Louisa was starting work with her at Hearts.

Rosie had started at Heart's Bakers when she was fifteen. Quite old to start work really some of their friends had left school at fourteen to get a job. Rosie had been quite puzzled as why her parents hadn't suggested she should get a job at fourteen, God knows they needed the money, but they hadn't and Rosie thought they just didn't realised that she could have been out earning. Her mum had too much else to worry about to even register that Rosie was fourteen.

There was only Rosie and Caren, no other brothers or sisters, but Betty, their mum was at 'her wits end' with their dad Ed. He was always drunk. That was the bottom line. If Betty thought she would ever be able to change him she was living in cloud cuckoo land thought Rosie.

Rosie watched Louisa close her front door and half walk half run the short distance between them. Louisa smiled but looked tired. Her eyes were puffy. Rosie looped her arm through Louisa's and twittered.

"Come on, poppet, you'll get used to the early mornings after a month of two."

"Errrrr," groaned Louisa, "I can hardly walk," as she gratefully leant into Rosie's supporting body.

"Cor blimey, this is going to wake me up good and proper," Louisa realised as they entered through the solid metal factory doors to Heart's Bakers. The noise was deafening. It was a great square area with lots of white overall dressed bodies milling about, every one donning a white net encasing their hair and each person busy going about their particular task. There was a long conveyor belt stretching from one end of the room inching slowly along to where two women wearing white gloves lifted, what looked like pies from a distance, and gently placing them into rectangular metal trays.

Across the back wall of the factory, behind the conveyor belt were three very imposing large grey ovens, two could be seen glowing as their doors were opened. In front of the ovens were three employees, of whom two skilfully manoeuvred long spatulas to remove golden loaves and artfully placed them onto waiting trays sitting upon the conveyor belt. The smell was divine and Louisa's tummy began to rumble.

A woman called Eve approached Rosie and Louisa from a desk to the right of the factory front doors. Louisa had met Eve the week before for a chat to see if she was the type that would fit in with the existing staff of Heart's Bakers. Eve had told her there and then she could have the position and Louisa had felt chuffed and very grown up. Eve now looked much more serious than she had at their 'chat'. A serious looking gentleman dressed in a black suit was sitting the desk looking at Louisa and Rosie. He didn't smile.

"Good morning, Louisa," Eve welcomed over the noise, "Pop this hair net on, love, look after it and bring it in washed every day as that's your very own net from now on."

Oh, well, thought Louisa, *this is it, my adult life has begun,* as she followed Eve towards the bustling factory workers.

One afternoon a couple of weeks after Louisa had started at Heart's Bakers her and Rosie were walking home from work together down Acacia Court when they spotted Betty coming out of her house all dressed up, with lipstick on, and even wearing high heeled shoes.

"Mum," called Rosie, Betty hadn't heard her name being called and was fumbling in a little purse she was carrying.

"Mum, where you going?" Rosie called again, louder this time, she had a very puzzled expression on her face. Louisa and Rosie hastened their step walk attempting to catch up with Betty.

"What you doing? Where you off to all dressed up?" Feelings of fear were beginning to build within Rosie.

"Don't laugh at me." Betty was tottering in her little pointed toe shoes with kitten heels.

"I'm going to The Seamaster's Arms," she whispered.

"Well, your Mum Alice," Betty nodded at Louisa, "well, she reckons I should get myself all togged up and go and sit in there, see what your dad makes of that, see how he likes it."

Betty had put her glossy auburn hair up in ringlets and was wearing a beautiful purple dress with a white fitted cardigan over the top, she looked really pretty, Some children playing in the street outside Rosie's house stopped and gawped as Betty, Rosie and Louisa walked past.

"No, really, no, oh, my God, Mum." Rosie and Louisa were laughing but nervous. "Are you sure that's a good idea?"

"Yes, why not?" Betty giggled. Rosie and Louisa walked Betty around the corner and into Hayes Wharf, frightened to let her go probably, not knowing if this was a good or bad idea and how it was all going to turn out. Rosie had a pained, embarrassed expression on her face which made her look like she's eaten something vile and Betty laughed at her. As they approached The Seamaster's Arms, Betty straightened her posture, raised her shoulders, pushed out her chest and glided as confidently as she could in her tottering heels straight through the saloon bar door. Rosie and Louisa stood on their tiptoes outside and strained to stretch themselves as high as possible so they could peer in through the etched glass window. They watched Betty sit herself on a bar stool and light a cigarette. There was a group of men at one end of the room sitting around a table but no sign of Ed, Rosie's dad. The door to the public bar suddenly burst open onto the street making Rosie and Louisa jump, out stumbled a tall young lad, obviously the worse for wear as he tried to walk his knees buckled and his head was wobbling, he collapsed on the floor and his head slowly went back as he fell onto the pavement. As Rosie and Louisa ran off laughing, Rosie declared,

"Oh, no! I'm going to wet myself laughing." They howled as only teenage girls can all the way home.

Louisa had posted two letters to James. She marvelled that her letters from London arrived on a ship somewhere in the middle of a sea! How did that happen? She must ask him. Anyway, she wrote and told him all about her new job, about Rosie and her crackpot family, of the other people working at Heart's Bakers and how her mum had been teaching her how to make an apple pie.

There seemed to be a lot of talk of some sort of conflict with Germany again and the government had said all of the United Kingdom has got to learn to eat home grown food, not food brought in from abroad. Her mum was very worried about this, what would happen to the jobs of most of the menfolk that she knew? They all worked in the business that brought food in from abroad. James had sent her a lovely letter back telling her about a strange land in Asia he was travelling to and how choppy the sea was. The weather was really hot and he was happy for her getting a job and asked her to write again very soon. Louisa read and reread his letter. She didn't tell her mum she was writing to him but knew she wouldn't be able to keep it quiet for long, not with Gladys around and her mum was bound to see any letters delivered by the postman anyway. Louisa didn't want them to know yet, she was worried they would think she really liked James, which she did, and look at her next time he came home and she would feel all self-conscious.

During their morning walk to work one day the following week Louisa enquired,

"By the way, what happened about your mum and her visit to The Seamaster's Arms?"

Rosie answered whilst raising her eyebrows.

"Well, my mum won't say but my dad has come straight home from work every night since and not had a drink, now my mum says she's fed up with him and wish he'd go back to the pub!"

Chapter Four

One dark evening, just before Christmas, while they were all sitting eating their evening meal suddenly Alice excitedly announced,

"Oh! By the way, on Saturday Ma Pritchard's invited us all in for tea. It's her birthday and she's going to treat us."

Louisa and her sister stared at each other, Louisa guessed Gladys was probably thinking the same as her, "how can we get out of this?" Stevie, Gladys and Louisa all chorused,

"Oh, that will be lovely."

About 4 o'clock on the following Saturday afternoon, they all stood outside Ma Pritchard's rotting door. It was covered in flaky paint and the bottom of it looked swollen up with moisture. Stevie looked very handsome as always and Alice had allowed Louisa and Gladys to use a tad of her pink lipstick. There was a horrid smell coming from somewhere like a hundred sailors had been using her doorstep as a toilet, Yuk! Louisa's shoes were sticking to the pavement. Alice banged on the door and quietly called, "Ma Pritchard." There was silence, no noise at all from in the house. They all stood there hoping she wasn't in and trying not to breathe so they could escape the awful smell.

"Ma Pritchard, are you in?" Alice shouted loudly this time, banging on the crumbling door again. When a shuffling was heard from inside they all sighed with disappointment.

"Agh," screamed Ma Pritchard as she flung open the door. "Love a duck, what a treat I forgot you were coming," as she threw her arms around Alice's neck.

"Come in, Come in." Ma Pritchard was so excited, they all inched hesitantly into the small dark sitting room, there was nothing on the bare floorboards and there was a wooden chair either side of a fireplace. In the hearth was a tiny ember just about glowing which was the only light in the room, they had all been in this house many times when younger but that was years ago and the most of furniture that had once adorned the room was nowhere to be seen. In the corner was a table with some bread on it, June, Ma Pritchard's youngest daughter was sitting on one of the chairs and mumbled something but her words were so hushed Louisa didn't know what she had said. Ma Pritchard made up for her quietness.

"Let me make you a cup of cha, Alice, so good of you all to come," Ma Pritchard shouted as she walked over to June and nudged her off her chair, she then proceeded to pick up the chair and really smashed it over her knee until it broke into about five pieces, Ma Pritchard then threw a piece of the broken chair onto the dying fire, all the time she was doing this she continued to shuffle about waffling on about this and that, who said what in the greengrocers and whose old man was drunk recently. Stevie, Gladys and Louisa just stood staring wide eyed in in disbelief and trying not to laugh. Ma Pritchard picked up a metal kettle off the table in the corner and put it on top of the newly stacked fire.

"Take a seat, Alice," Ma Pritchard offered and started to crush Stevie with a big hug and a dribble-laden kiss.

Eeeeeee, thought Louisa, *Oh no, she's coming at me now!*

Ma Pritchard wouldn't stop talking and it was so funny and so loud but they didn't get a crumb to eat just a cup of tea after what seemed like an age with the kettle heating on the fire. Louisa and Gladys pleaded with Alice on the way home, "please say we never have to go in there again," but Alice just laughed. Louisa couldn't wait to get home and sit on their cosy, clean sofa.

Louisa lay on her bed thinking of James, the five months since he had left had flown by, she had a letter in her hands from him! She had written to him four times now, she had told her mum as nonchalantly as she could manage and was really looking forward to seeing him again. So much had altered, she had changed, she was now working at Heart's Bakers, she had brought herself a couple of nice blouses, some rouge for her cheeks and some lipstick, her hair had grown. She was earning a weekly wage and felt five years older not five months. At Heart's Bakers, the early mornings were really hard but they did all have a good laugh while they were there and she got to bring rolls and sometimes sausage rolls home, much to Stevie's delight. James had written her the most beautiful long letters, they had discussed everything, he would be home next week and said he was dreaming of taking her for a picnic in Greenwich Park.

"A picnic! We'll freeze," envisaged Louisa. She fell back on her pillow.

"Will he still like me?"

Chapter Five

When she saw him she couldn't help but gasp, instantly feeling embarrassed in case the others had seen her reaction to this gorgeous, happy, strong man strolling towards her. He did look like a man. He looked older, taller, more sure of himself. She felt sick, all she could hear was the blood pounding through her body, her tummy started to throb and she felt she was going to burst. He looked straight at her, at no one else.

As always when her darling daddy was around, everyone was trying to talk at once, they all wanted to tell funny stories, more outrageous and louder and funnier than the last tale. Really they were all seeking Tom Foster's approval without realising, just to see his head fall back, hear his big laugh, see his belly shake. They ate egg and ham pie, mashed potatoes, braised apples and a huge sultana cake Alice had baked. The men drank the rum Stevie had saved and stout ale, the girls had tea and there was some talk about Adolph Hitler, Germany and Italy but not for long and they all went to bed that night laughing.

Louisa was the first person up the next morning, for her shift at the Bakery. Inside the Bakery it was very hot and the delicious smells just made your stomach rumble all day, even when you weren't hungry. Louisa earned £1 per week and gave her mum seventeen shillings for her keep. The other girls laughed at how naive Louisa was and kept telling her stories about their lives. Alice said they made them up when Louisa retold them at home (she didn't dare tell her mum all the stories! Some were just too rude) but Louisa was sure they were real.

One of the girls Clara was twenty years old, she had been working at the Bakery since she was fourteen. She lived not far from Louisa and Rosie an area of South London called Borough Market where Alice sometimes went to buy vegetables brought in from farms in Kent. Clara lived with her two older brothers who were very worried about the threatened war. Clara's mum had died when she was young and she had never known her dad. Clara's two brothers, Alan and Albert had brought her up. Alan must have been over six foot tall and had dark curly hair, he was very handsome and had big thick eyebrows that nearly met in the middle framing his beautiful brown eyes. Albert on the other hand was short and chubby and had a happy round face. Clara led a wild life, if her brothers had known what she got up to she would have been in for it. Clara used to meet boys and flirt like mad all the time. She said she was just practising 'so when she met her Mr Right she knew how to keep him happy!'

Louisa couldn't wait to get home later to see James, he was staying three days again before going to see his mum in Kent and as tomorrow was Saturday he was taking Louisa on the promised picnic to Greenwich Park.

"I've got some sausage rollies," Louisa called as she walked into their house. She had for the first time managed to force her way to the front of the 'left over' queue at the end of their shift and get six big fat juicy freshly baked 'unrequired' sausage rolls much to the disgust of her work pals who all jokingly booed her and Clara said, "Ogh! What you after tempting James with sausage rolls?"

The house seemed strangely empty. "Where is everyone?" Louisa enquired as she walked into the kitchen and saw her mum, she expected her dad and James to be sitting on the sofa or playing dominoes at the table and Stevie was usually home before her from his cushy job in the office at the docks where he was supposed to work all day but usually did about one hour grafting and yet still earned really good money, double what Louisa brought home.

"Gladys is helping Ma Pritchard with some bills," Alice looked up from the turnip she was struggling to peel.

"And James, Stevie and your dad have gone to The Seamaster's Arms to a meeting about a possible war."

"Oh." Louisa felt flat all of a sudden.

"Oh, well! At least I've got our planned picnic in Greenwich Park to look forward to," she fancied to herself as she walked slowly upstairs to her bedroom. She and James had talked for hours and hours but they had never been out all alone. She felt she knew him inside out and felt really comfortable with him but was now suddenly feeling anxious about the picnic.

"Say he thinks I'm too young all of a sudden or say I can't think of anything to say? It's all very well coming up with funny little snippets when you have ages to write a letter or your family are around but say I go completely dumb? Say it's really cold and I get a runny nose?" she spoke to herself as she emptied her work bag and took her white overall off.

"Can I borrow one of your new handkerchiefs please?" Louisa asked Alice later that night. Alice looked puzzlingly at Louise while shaking her head to say yes but didn't actually speak as she was listening to Tom.

"Well, what they're saying is three million Germans are now living in Czechoslovakia, they've somehow ended up there after the last war. Adolph Hitler wants the part of Czechoslovakia that all those Germans are now living in to become part of Germany. Well, obviously Czechoslovakia is saying no and Adolph Hitler's just threatening to go in and take it. Hitler has also voiced some desires to make the whole of Europe into one nation and be under his rule. I think myself that's what everyone is worried about, he seems a bit of a fanatic to me," Big Tom Foster announced as he tried to tune in the wireless.

"They say Hitler wants to rule Europe and he's going to poison us all, they say Italy has already started a war somewhere and Germany's going to join in."

"Oh, leave it out! Shut up! You're scaring us all, what a load of codswallop, who says?"

Alice marched up to Tom and jokingly hit him around the head with her tea towel.

"It's all gossip, its miles away and has nothing to do with us. How can someone just march in and take another country. Surely Czechoslovakia will just shoot them all?"

Alice and Tom had terrifying memories of the First World War, millions of lives were lost. Alice couldn't believe people could be as silly as to want to go through all that again, her own father had died fighting in the trenches, he was only twenty four, her mother had never got over the loss. Alice could remember her mother saying that she missed her father every day and still spoke to him. Tom only just escaped being called up to fight in it, if the war had gone on any longer he would have had to enlist.

Yes, the First World War was recent enough for people to recount the harrowing tales and terrors and they couldn't believe people would be silly enough to voluntarily enter another one. Tom was becoming very concerned though and tried to keep that from Alice. At The Seaman's Hut meeting, Adolph Hitler's threats were being taken seriously and Great Britain getting caught up in the conflict did now seem to be a possibility. Tom declared that from now on they were all to listen to the news on the wireless every night to keep up to date with events and see how everything was going. He switched the wireless on and it made lots of loud and shrill noises until eventually the whole family went quiet as they listened to a sombre, well-spoken voice telling them news that Italy had invaded a place called Ethiopia.

The next morning, Greenwich Park was stunning. The sky was a wishy, washy, hazy blue with soft puffs of white clouds floating lazily across. The sun had risen behind Greenwich Palace and was like a bright, clear, orange football coming out just to greet and heat them. It was really crisp but not raining which was a bonus. The grass was wet and shiny from the morning dew and Louisa was sure she could even smell the freshness of it. They walked holding hands, Louisa noticed that a few people walking past them were smiling in their direction. She was feeling extremely proud of herself, James had taken her hand as soon as they stepped off the bus. She was aware that the few people passing them were all mentioning 'Adolph Hitler'. James grumbled that's all that he had heard about for the past couple of months.

James and Louisa had left home early about 8 o'clock and got the bus from Tower Bridge. They sat upstairs and James leg was pressed against Louisa's the whole journey which made her tingle. She was sure she could feel heat coming through his grey trousers. The bus conductor smiled at them both as he took the bus fares from James and patted his shoulder. James carried the bag which was made of sacking which Louisa had packed earlier containing tomatoes, egg sandwiches, a thermos flask of hot tea, Louisa's sausage rolls, and some warm homemade cake Alice had presented them with as they left home that morning and a scratchy old tartan picnic blanket that had belonged to Alice's mum.

Louisa told James stories about Clara and her antics and Rosie's Ma, Betty, he was enjoying her amusing tales and seemed really interested. James squealed on Tom by telling Louisa how her dad had got so drunk one night at sea he spent the whole night passed out on the cabin floor with all his clothes on. He made her promise not to tell her mum, which she did, but secretly she thought her mum would probably have laughed. Or maybe not she may have said 'How much did that cost you?' Or she may have hit him over the head with a saucepan like Rosie said her mum sometimes did to her dad. The older Louisa got the more she realised how lucky she was, fortunate not to have a mad mum like Ma Pritchard. Her mum and dad were wonderful compared to some others she had met and seemed like best mates most of the time.

They walked for hours and Louisa felt like they'd been there days she didn't want the day to end.

"Would her ladyship like to partake in our delicacies?" James whispered into Louisa's ear and he took the picnic blanket from the bag and spread it onto the still slightly damp grass.

"Oh, my gawd! say me skirt gets wet and I end up with a big wet patch looking like I've wet me knickers," she fretted to herself and tried to sit on the ageing blanket as much like a ladyship as she could, whatever a ladyship was.

"Oh, I'm starving." The sausage rolls were delicious and they were really enjoying all the food. Today was perfect.

"I was wondering," James said serious all of a sudden.

Louise looked at his beautiful face with big wide eyes trying to quickly swallow a mouthful of egg sandwich.

"Can you wash me work clobber for me?" he laughed and rolled back onto the grass with his hands holding his ribs, Louisa jumped up and playfully smacked him, he gently took her wrists and pulled her slowly towards him as he put his lips to hers and kissed her slowly and firmly. She could feel his breath on her face, he smelt so of him, her heart was thumping, but why was he trying to prise her lips open with his tongue?

"Fancy getting wed?"

Chapter Six

"I don't know why you've got the hump with me, I should be getting married before you, I'm older than you and it means you'll get this bedroom to yourself what I think is what you've always wanted!"

Louisa was sitting at their tiny kidney shaped dressing table brushing her shiny brunette hair. It was getting quite long and looked really glossy. She was really pleased that it was forming large, round bouncy ringlets all on its own.

"How shall I wear it for my wedding day?" she questioned smiling at her reflection and completely drifting off in her own little world.

"I've never said I want this bedroom to myself," protested Gladys, "Are you sure you're not in the pudding club?"

Louisa rose from the chair with the hair brush in her hand as if to hit Gladys, then laughed and threw the brush onto her own bed as Alice opened their bedroom door. Nothing was going to spoil Louisa's happiness. She was so excited to be marrying James, to be a grown-up, to be a 'Mrs', Mrs Bishop she would be and Louisa decided Gladys was just jealous, she had been seeing a lad from their street called Daniel Booth for about four months but to be honest he wasn't the brightest star in the sky and he would probably never ask Gladys to marry him until Gladys told him to. Plus he spent all his wages on Fridays nights in the pub so if Gladys did end up married to him she would probably never even have enough money to buy food or anything. Why she stayed with him was a mystery to Louisa, she was such a pretty girl, could get any boy from their estate.

"And where's James going to stay if you can't get your own place or the council don't give you a place to live in? He's not sleeping in here, where am I supposed to go?"

Gladys went on and on like a broken record. Louisa was sure she was just carrying on like this to irritate her intentionally, for some sort of prank because she was bored and wanted to amuse herself.

Oh, gosh, thought Louisa, *Please let them someone give us a place, my own home and I can get away from groaning Gladys.*

"What time are you leaving on Saturday to go and meet James's Mum?" asked Alice bringing a soft calmness back to the room and obviously to put a spanner in the works of Gladys.

"Oh, well, about 8 o'clock from London Bridge station, James says we have to take the train to Ashford, it takes about an hour, where his best friend Mark is going to pick us up which I think is really very decent of him. Otherwise, we would have to walk miles because apparently the farmhouse is just in the middle of a load of fields.

"Never! Well, fancy that, a farmhouse in a middle of a load of fields! Where else do you think a farmhouse would be you big clot?" Alice chuckled and Gladys managed a smile instead of her usual frown, for the first time that day.

"Ogh, I am so excited." Louisa returned her gaze to the dressing table mirror, hunched her shoulders and confessed innocently 'and a weeny bit scared'.

Chapter Seven

Alice, Louisa and Ma Pritchard were all making the wedding dress. They had brought some fabric from new business in Petticoat Lane, which was run by an Indian Family who had just arrived to live in Great Britain. Petticoat Lane was in the east end of London and lots of foreigners from the Commonwealth Countries were moving into the area to try and start a new life in England. The father who was a small, slight man, spoke a little English and behind him stood who they had all assumed to be his wife and mother or maybe his mother-in-law. The women didn't speak any English at all, just stood there smiling and looking beautiful, their dresses were gorgeous, one in vivid orange and the other in a purple silky fabric, all flowing and decorated with hundreds of beads. They must have taken so long to create. Louisa wanted to look like them on her wedding day. Alice brought three yards of a white satin material and some very fine organza sort of fabric with tiny shiny circles on it. A nurse called Joey, who lived in Acacia Court, had kindly lent Alice the paper dress pattern that she had used years ago to create her own wedding dress. Alice had cut the fabric out, Ma Pritchard was tacking the pieces together for Alice to then sew properly by hand. So far it had taken hours and didn't resemble anything like a dress.

Alice had been buying some extra food and nuts for the 'wedding breakfast' every week. Tom had brought two barrels of stout and two bottles of rum from a man at the docks, they had some sherry indoors and James had asked the landlord at The Seamaster's Arms if he could borrow a few pint glasses for the beer. The wedding was set for Saturday, September 15th 1938 at Greenwich Registry Office.

Stevie bounced in from work one day brimming over with excitement. He was employed at Hayes Wharf as a Wages Clerk.

Every day he was locked in an office with four other men and no windows where they prepared all the wage packets for the staff of Hayes Wharf. That included the engineers who maintained the vessels and all the unloading equipment, the dock workers, the merchant seamen, the cleaners, the administration staff who arranged the import and exporting of all the goods, the personnel staff who were responsible for employing everybody, the canteen staff. It was a huge organisation and it added up to thousands of people. Their dad Tom was friendly with one of the personnel staff at Hayes Wharf, a fellow called Peter, Stevie had been really good at arithmetic at school and Peter arranged for him to have an interview when he was fourteen years old. Stevie didn't really give it any thought just went and did what his dad told him and fortunately got the junior payroll clerk position. It was only afterwards he thought, *I'm not sure I want to do this for the rest of my life!* He didn't like being locked in the room all day, the other men smoked heavily and it choked him. His clothes reeked of tobacco every night and he was sure it was turning his face grey. He also didn't like that he had to be let out to go to the toilet. It was like being ensnared in a prison cell. He did get on all right with the blokes he worked with though which was a plus, they did tease him a lot as he was the youngest in the office. They also amused themselves by playing quite a few pranks on him when he had first started working there, but they were generally a good natured lot, not nasty. He was earning good money for his age and he had to help with the household finances, he was the man of the house most of the time when his dad was away. But he craved a bit of adventure, he wanted to feel the wind in his hair, feel the sun on his face and meet girls. He only ever mixed with his family and neighbours how was he supposed to find a wife?

"I've enlisted in the navy if there's a war I can go to sea and give the Germans a what for," Stevie was beaming with delight.

"Oh, no, oh, no, oh, no," Alice wailed and she sat at the little table in the kitchen. "Oh, no, darling, what you gone and done that for? She was beside herself, so many young boys, like her poor dad had not returned from the First World War.

"No, you can't go off to fight, who will do the wages for the Dockers? That's a really important job, if there is ever any trouble then the docks will have to stay open, they will be needed, to continue operating and you won't be able to leave. No, No, they definitely won't let you go."

Alice was grabbing at straws, feeling desperate, this crazy idea of Stevie's had to be quashed straight away.

Stevie realised maybe he should have dealt with his news differently. He had been so excited, his chance to escape, see a bit of the world.

"What about your job, you pillock?" Gladys asked, "You'll never get another cushy job like that again."

"Your Dad will be heartbroken, he so wanted you not to follow him onto the ships." Alice was nearly in tears. "You'll have to go and take your name off, say you've got responsibilities at home and at work! And I mean whose going to look after us? We need you here!"

Stevie cuddled Alice. "Mum, I'm sorry but we have to keep the Nazis out if they ever invade and please don't worry, it may never happen, we may never go to war, and you should be proud of me! Your big brave son," he soothingly said as he tried to calm his Mum down.

Chapter Eight

London was getting a zoo.

Alice was in an absolute meltdown over it all. It was plastered all over the newspaper stands,

"LONDON IS TO HAVE ITS OWN ZOO – WILD ANIMALS IN THE CAPITAL!"

She had turned into a four-year-old, could speak of nothing else, she was going to see real animals! All types of creatures that she had examined in books on her mother's knee. Genuine, real life elephants and giraffes. You would have thought she had won the football pools. Ecstasy was an understatement. Louisa, Gladys and Stevie were swept up in her unbelievable anticipation of it all. Alice was even counting down the days until the grand opening ceremony.

"Oh, we will have to get up so early!"

"Oh, we can't be late, we need to try and get as close to the gates as possible!"

"Oh, there will be hundreds of people, people flocking from all over Great Britain."

"Oh, I don't care how long we have to wait about we must be there early, get right to the front of the queue."

"Oh, it will be so grand and just imagine all the animals we will see, with our own eyes, beasts that you will never see again, from all over the world, I can't wait."

Gladys wasn't that sold on the idea and Louisa was worried they would get eaten by an escaped tiger or something. But they all obeyed their mum and very early one sunny morning in June they got the bus to Regents Park in West London. It was amazing, they couldn't believe it, there was a giant tortoise, camels, giraffes, lions, monkeys, snakes, oh, so many animals all locked in cages. The chimpanzees were the funniest. They walked round and round, over and over again and must have watched the lions for a good hour. They had a cup of tea each in the daintiest cups Louisa had ever seen or held along with some delicious Victoria sponge cake. They were exhausted but stayed to watch two American men called Robert and Ted Kennedy perform the opening ceremony. They had funny accents and apparently were stand ins as their father was the ambassador of United States of America to Great Britain, he was meant to host the opening ceremony but couldn't so sent his sons instead. They were all nodding off to sleep on the bus ride home and Alice said the day had been history in the making.

Chapter Nine

On the 13th of September 1938, the Prime Minister, Neville Chamberlain had met Adolph Hitler in an attempt to placate the stormy situation brewing over Europe. Neville Chamberlain announced the talks were successful and good relations existed between The United Kingdom and Adolph Hitler's Germany.

Two days later, Louisa and James were married on the 15th of September 1938 at Greenwich Registry Office.

Louisa was magnificent in the white dress. It finished just below her knees and flared out from her slim waist. Underneath the skirt of the dress Alice and Ma Pritchard had attached some gathered lining to make it flow outwards. The top of the dress was in the latest fashion with a sweetheart neckline and the sleeves were slim down to her elbows which enabled her elegant wrists to be on show. Louisa wore a tiny silver cross necklace around her young smooth neck which Alice had presented her with. Her mother had worn it on her wedding day to Tom and had kept if safely wrapped in a small piece of tissue and a tiny orange cardboard box in the top drawer of her dresser where she also kept her hair brush, comb and Ponds face cream. Alice had often shown it to Louisa and Gladys as they had grown up saying, "you girls can wear this one day when you get married."

"Oh, Mum, thank you so much for making this, I could not be more pleased honestly, I know you and Ma Pritchard have broken your backs sewing it for me and I really do appreciate it." Louisa was so grateful.

Louisa had a pair of thin white gloves to wear which were borrowed from Joey the nurse down the road and a pale blue shawl for later in case it was chilly.

"Something old, something new, something borrowed, something blue."

Was all ticked off, the necklace was old, the dress was new, the gloves were borrowed and the shawl was, well that was borrowed as well but it was blue and she couldn't be expected to do everything perfect.

Her hair had been styled in ringlets by sleeping in hair clips all night and she had teased the crown of her hair up a bit higher than usual with a fine toothed comb. On the back of her hair, she had pinned a small white flower which Rosie had made from paper and Rosie had also made her and Louisa a posy of matching flowers to hold as Rosie was Louisa's flower girl.

Alice wore a navy dress and long jacket which she had kept for years and attached a gorgeous broach in the shape of a butterfly to the right lapel.

Gladys even looked good! She was wearing a black and white patterned dress which Alice had cleverly made from an old scarf and the bottom half was made from some blackout lining they had started to stock in the haberdashers, there was a big black ribbon bow sewn onto the waist and the colours of the dress suited Gladys's reddish hair.

It had been raining early in the day but now the sun was dappling through some soft white cotton wool clouds and they were ready to go!

Tom Fosters eyes welled up with tears as he gave his girls the 'once over'.

"Can't believe our girlies getting wed," he chuckled emotionally looking admiringly at Alice. "How did we produce such stunning ladies?" he marvelled.

Tom appraised Stevie

"And you, my son," he patted Stevie's right shoulder. "You look as handsome as your old man, make me feel really proud, all of you do."

Tom gently manoeuvred Louisa's arm through his and then puffing his chest out glided through their front door into Acacia Court. It was the proudest day of his life. Outside there were about twelve neighbours gathered. Some were actually going to the wedding ceremony, like Ma Pritchard and Joey, the nurse, others had been invited back to the house later to help celebrate. There were some children playing 'kiss chase' around the assembled crowd.

Their audience cheered and clapped. Their faces were truly happy and Louisa's nerves suddenly stopped and she began to feel extremely excited instead. Excited to look this good, excited to becoming Mrs James Bishop and excited at what may lay ahead in her life.

Tom Foster took a handful of half penny's and penny's from his suit pocket and scattered them gently across the pavement, the children screamed and ran scavenging on the ground to grasp the copper coins.

Tom had arranged for his friend Peter, who was the man who got Stevie the interview in Hayes Wharf, to drive them in his motor car to the registry office. He owned a Wolseley motor car that was his pride and joy. It was black and he must have spent all morning polishing it as it so shiny you could see your reflection in it. The Foster family and Rosie all squashed in the back with Tom sitting in the front. They were going to get the bus home after the ceremony but that was no problem. Louisa felt like a royal princess.

Peter drove very slowly out of Acacia Court into Thames Way, they drove a few hundred yards and Peter pulled the motor car over.

"I'll just wait here for five minutes to give the others a bit of time to get the tram or bus to the registry office," he bellowed from the driver's seat. Peter had been in the First World War and was a very lucky survivor. His ear drum had been burst in the trenches and he repeated,

"I'll just pull over here so your neighbours can get to the registry office on the tram or bus." All the girls in the back were busy chattering about what a surprise to see all the neighbours outside and what they had been wearing and the expressions on their faces. Louisa was worried her dress would crease up and was feeling very hot.

The shiny Wolseley pulled up outside the registry office gates at just past 11 am. The vicar was waiting at the huge double doors which were along a short path inside some metal gates. It was a large building but not all of it was the registry office. It was also home to council offices and offices where you recorded a death or birth in your family. It was constructed from the same colour bricks as Louisa's house and was on the edge of Greenwich Park in which Greenwich Palace stood.

The vicar smiled to welcome them, he turned around to look inside the building and raised his hand to signal to someone inside, Louisa's family all stepped slowly from the motor car. Gladys especially was extremely lady like, Louisa guessed she was hopefully practising for her own wedding one day. Louisa smiled coyly at the vicar. Tom and Louisa followed their family into the registry office and Tom guided Louisa to stand next to James. Louisa had noticed James mum Sylvia in the front row sitting next to her mum, Stevie and Gladys, she was relieved about that as Sylvia was coming directly to the registry office from Kent with Mark the best man who had offered to drive her in his motor car. Ma Pritchard was sitting in the row behind them. Clara was sitting there with Caren and her and Rosie's mum and dad, Betty and Ed who had all made it on public transport in time. Rosie stood behind Louisa then sat down with Alice and the others. James looked so handsome in a black suit, brilliant white shirt with thin black tie. He beamed proudly at Louisa and she felt the most fortunate girl in the world. Mark his friend was the Best Man and stood to the right of James, they all looked towards to the Vicar. Louisa noticed James's hands were slightly shaking as he forced himself upright and held his arms together tightly behind his back.

The ceremony was very short and concise but Louisa was glad because she couldn't really concentrate anyway, there were hundreds of thoughts flashing through her mind. James jitteringly slid the thin gold band onto the tiny third finger of her left hand and all the guests cheered. James pulled Louisa to him so tightly and they kissed. More cheers went up from the seats and all the guests stood. Everyone hurried swiftly from the registry office excitedly anticipating good food, drink and fun back at the Fosters!

Chapter Ten

As the wedding party laughed and strolled towards the bus stop heaving black clouds were rolling in across from the distant sky, Mark offered James and Louisa a lift back home in his car but wasn't sure where he had parked it and James thought it safer to go on the bus. They all laughed and wished James good luck on finding his motor car. Then it started to rain, great huge heavy blobs of water splashing down onto their heads and feet and anywhere else it could reach. The all started to run slowly, luckily, this bus stop had the shelter of a sloping roof which not all bus stops in London had. Louisa and the other females huddled under the shelter chattering and squealing as the big heavy bus homed towards them spraying big muddy puddles onto the pavement.

The wedding breakfast, as it was called, was such a success the neighbours spoke of it for months afterwards. They had rum, ale, sherry and some mead from Biddenden, Kent which Mark had brought with him. Alice also had her huge, grey metal kettle boiling constantly for endless pots of tea. She had recently started to use just one spoonful of tea leaves per pot as the government had been instructing them to cut down on everything in case of a war ahead. Alice couldn't imagine life without tea and was glad to be frugal with it. But today she was using two teaspoons of tea leaves per pot.

"Sod it," she laughed to Ma Pritchard who was standing next to her, "Not every day your daughter gets married," as she splashed the scalding water onto the tea leaves.

You didn't see many of the men drinking tea. The house was buzzing with laughter, unbelievable tales and very high spirits. They had a table laden with pork and aspic pies, sliced tinned spam, hard boiled eggs shelled and cut into quarters and some delicious buttered bread which Heart's Bakers had donated.

Rosie had recently started courting a boy called Frank, he was a friend of Carla's brothers and had come along with the brothers one afternoon to meet Carla after work and as soon as the girls walked out through the doors Frank had stood bolt upright and was just mesmerised by Rosie. They had all giggled and Rosie had blushed and lowered her thick dark eyelashes. But the next night he was there again and every night that week until the Friday when he asked Rosie if he could take her for a walk one evening. They had been for two walks since and one trip to the cinema. Rosie said she couldn't invite him to her home because her parents are mad but Louisa had insisted she invited him to the wedding. Surely her parents would be well-behaved and he would have other people talking to him so if they did act crazy he wouldn't notice as much. Yes that was the plan, Louisa had solved Rosie's dilemma, they could all be introduced to each other in a civilised situation.

Louisa had a funny feeling about Frank, she hated to admit it but she just wasn't sure about him she couldn't put her finger on it and would never dare say a word to Rosie but Louisa thought he was a bit shifty. He did look so gently at Rosie and yes, did nothing wrong but Louisa wasn't convinced he was a good chap! Frank shook Rosie's dad, Ed's, hand as he cleared his throat, the room quietened a bit as a lot of people stopped talking wondering who this stranger was?

"Pleased to meet you," Frank roared over confidently as Rosie introduced them nervously. Her eyes were wide with wonder at what her father was going to do. She saw from the corner of her eye her mother tottering over to get in the action and Ed shook Frank's hand vigorously up and down with a huge drunken grin across his face. Up and down it went, Ed just wouldn't let go. Louisa laughed as she guessed Ed was just using Frank as a means to remain standing upright. Betty whacked Ed across the temple and hollered,

"Let go, you'll have him bloody limbless, you drunken sot." And the whole room collapsed into loud laughter. Rosie let out a despondent sigh.

The afternoon was gone in a flash and Louisa felt guilty as herself, James, Sylvia and Mark all left about five in the evening to travel to Biddenden, where James and Louisa were going to stay for a two day honeymoon. The owners of Sylvia's farm had offered, which Louisa had thought was very generous of them, for the bride and groom to have a honeymoon at their farmhouse. Then unexpectedly at the last minute the owners said they had to go away. Louisa wasn't going to get to meet them, James had met them before. She thought that was probably better, if they were absent, they wouldn't have to tiptoe around if there was just the three of them. Sylvia still looked pristine in her grey dress and jacket with big fake yellow daffodil on the collar, she had mingled at the party and Louisa was a bit surprised about that. On their way out Rosie's dad was slumped up against the wall at the front of Louisa's house and looked like he was about to vomit. Betty aggressively nudged him with her foot, he started to gag.

"You bone idle good for nothing drunken useless layabout," she hissed at him then smiled and waved off the bride and groom along with all the other wedding guests.

Chapter Eleven

Louisa couldn't believe it was possible for her heart to be beating so fast and still be alive. Her legs were shaking, her whole body was twitching. "What was that?" Her underneath was pulsing and sweat was pouring down her neck.

"My God," she panted, in awe of James and married life!

He was standing now.

"Come back to bed," she pleaded seductively.

"Oh, my God, I want more, more, more!"

James lay beside her, slowly stroking down across her shoulder to her soft, plump breast. She closed her eyes and breathed in deeply. She could smell him and feel the heat from his body as he slowly moved his face towards her neck. Inhaling deeply, kissing her so gently even his smell aroused her, he wrapped her in his strong, muscular, warm arms and kissed her. She felt the heat rising up her whole body as he took her again, slow, slow, slowly until they couldn't get any closer.

James and Louisa had been married six months now. The flat was old and cold but Louisa didn't care, she cleaned it from floor to ceiling when they first moved in and now loved keeping it as clean and pretty as she could. There were drafts everywhere whistling when it was windy but she didn't care about anything except getting James into bed now they had their own place. He was home from sea for two weeks and had been up the docks every day asking for any jobs so he didn't have to be away from her all the time but so far had had no luck. Everyone was feeling worried there was so much talk about a looming war and the unsettledness in Europe. James earned good money at sea and Louisa had to give up her job at Heart's Bakers because married women were not allowed to work. She missed Rosie and Clara, she popped her head around the factory doors to shout, "Hello," whenever she walked past but only ever stayed a minute or so as she didn't want them to get into any trouble with Eve.

James was very quiet when he returned that evening after hours of job searching. They ate the tinned spam, mashed potatoes and peas Louisa had prepared in silence.

"Is something wrong?" Louisa eventually asked. She was worried he had gone off her as she had been acting so unladylike in the bedroom.

Louisa recognised the voice booming from their small black wireless on the sideboard. It was the voice of the Prime Minster Neville Chamberlain and he was talking about a person called Mussolini.

James slumped his shoulders.

"Oh, gosh, Lou Lou, I'm just feeling a bit despondent, I really didn't want to say anything to you, I don't want you to worry but I got chatting to some of the Dockers after they had clocked off and all this talk about what Germany's up to is quite distressing. Old Neville Chamberlain has gone and told Poland that if Germany or Italy ever invade them then we, us, Great Britain will go and fight and help them get their country back! I mean I just don't understand why we have gone and got involved, I mean there's loads of country's closer to Poland than us and none of them have offered to help, well, I think France has. It's all right these members of parliament offering our services, they are not the ones that will have to lay their lives on the line and go and leave their families and fight, no, it will be us idiots!"

Louisa thought she was going to be sick, she had heard so much now of this Germany, this Adolph Hitler and we all had to bring him to a stop but quite honestly it had all gone in one ear and out the other, her life was perfect and she didn't want it to change one bit. Now James was worried it was all suddenly becoming very real.

"It said in the *Daily Express* the other day that there's not going to be any war, My mum had it, I read it, they said it's just people all getting worked up about nothing, just scare mongering, got nothing else going on in their lives," Louisa appealed to James.

"Please, James, please say no, you won't have to go and fight, will you? You are needed to bring all the tea and sugar into the country." Louisa was trying to laugh it off, make it all go away, she thought if she didn't take it seriously then it wouldn't happen.

James stood up and pulled her up from her chair.

"Well, I reckon we will all have to do our bit, Lou Lou, if the worst comes to the worst."

Squeezing her tight he added, "We will just have to cross that bridge if it does ever come to it, now what can we do to take our minds of it?"

Smiling mischievously he pulled her into his chest with his muscular arms, that smell he had filled her head and she closed her eyes. *Why has he this effect on me*, she wondered. James started to undo the top button of her blouse with one hand whilst his other strong arm remained around her shoulders.

"You don't think I would rather be off fighting than here with you do you?" he grinned.

"Here with you, undressing you and…?" His breath was like a slow, warm summer breeze caressing her ears. Her head was spinning, her tummy was throbbing and her legs were shaky. He pulled her closer and guided her to the cosy haven of their bed.

Chapter Twelve

Eight hours later, elsewhere in south London Rosie's mum Betty lay in bed too. But in a completely different scenario. She was staring at the ceiling.

"What am I going to do?" she asked herself, "I just can't stand this for the rest of my days!"

She and Ed's confined bedroom stank of alcohol. Ed was lying next to her on his back and snoring really loudly with his mouth gaping wide open, he had many teeth missing and the ones he did have were not pleasant to look at. The stench coming from him was unbearable. His legs were splayed and he had one hand down his trousers holding his manhood.

"Yuk, yuk, yuk." Betty closed her eyes. "God help me escape," she spoke in her head as she inched the brown blanket off and slipped as gently as she could from the bed. Ed was taking up nearly all of it as usual and she had to sleep on a tiny narrow section which made her feel as if she was going to fall out of the bed flat onto the floor every night. She tiptoed out of the room, she wanted him to stay asleep for as long as possible. She knew the minute he woke up his groping, dirt stained hands would be pawing and pulling at her roughly. If she could just get dressed without rousing him she had more chance of escaping his advances, appeal to any common sense the old goat, who was unfortunately her husband, had left in his shrivelled pea sized brain that he had to go to work. It was the same every morning.

Betty sighed as she thought back to their courting days, they were so happy, always laughing and kissing. Ed was gorgeous then. Always clean smelling and freshly shaved. Not like now always reeking of vile body odour and with a rough, bristly chin. Betty was surprised he hadn't lost his job at Hayes Wharf, surely they noticed his stumbling walk? His shaky hands? His red bulbous nose and bloodshot eyes?

"Mind you it probably wouldn't make much difference if he did get the shove from work," she mused to herself silently, "Spends most of his dosh in The Seamaster's Arms now anyway."

Betty clasped her hands together and looked towards the ceiling.

"Oh, please I pray please help me," she pleaded. She was tired of being angry. If only the government would make him go and do six months compulsory service training in the Navy, Army or Air Force, they had just brought in a new law saying that all twenty and twenty-one-year-old men had to, why couldn't they make all men under thirty five do it? They're still strong, well not her man but most men under thirty five were still strong and fit. Now that would be a result, he wouldn't be able to drink and they could have some money come into the house for a change instead of going straight in the landlords till at the pub.

Betty could hear Caren moving about in the girl's bedroom but she didn't pop her head around the door, she continued down the narrow stairs through the sitting room and into the kitchen. She had heard Rosie leave not long before and she lit a lamp and a flame for the kettle on her stove. She put some tea leaves into her teapot and quietly laid some cups and saucers out. She poured a big cupful of porridge into a saucepan, added half a cup of milk, half of cup of water and a pinch of salt then gave it all a stir with her wooden spoon. The sun was bright on her back and it felt good.

She was constantly thinking, going over everything, looking for an answer. Even in her sleep she was sure her brain didn't switch off. She needed a sign, somebody to point her in the right direction, anything to solve her wretched situation.

Standing up straight she turned to face the bright sun dappled window. Spring was coming. She would get away. As soon as Caren was working too, Betty would get away from him. Hopefully, Caren would get into Heart's Bakers factory as well, her Rosie was a good girl so there was no need for her to worry, she knew Rosie would be appreciated at Heart's Baker's for as long as she wanted to be there and there was no reason to suspect they would refuse Rosie's sister a job now was there? As soon as they had a vacant place, Betty was sure Caren would get it. Then she could be free. Free as a bird. Free from his snoring and his smelling and his prying hands.

Chapter Thirteen

Over the next few weeks, air raid shelters called Anderson Shelters were delivered to all the houses in Acacia Court.

The government announced that it was just a precautionary measure. But Louisa and everybody knew that they wouldn't shell out a lot of money manufacturing air raid shelters, delivering them and putting adverts in the newspapers instructing the public what they were for unless this threat hanging over all their heads was pretty real.

"They must think we are blinking stupid," James groaned.

Tom attempted to assemble the shelter without reading the instructions and swearing for all the street to hear. He laughed as he cursed and Ma Pritchard thought it was hilarious, he was so upset the only place for the Anderson Shelter to go was where he grew his green beans. He'd planted lots of seeds for potatoes, tomatoes, green runner beans (his favourite) and onions. "Now we won't starve!" He gave Alice strict instructions how to water them all when he was away and now he had to move them to make way for the air raid shelter.

"Bloody Hitler!" he shouted. The government were also now delivering gas masks and they were terrifying! Like something from outer space, the youngsters in Acacia Court thought they were hilarious and invented a new game wearing the gas masks and chasing each other. Everyone had to attend meetings in various locations to hear what to do and how to act when and if the Germans did arrive. It was all seeming inevitable. There were instructions everywhere. If you heard a siren it meant you had to get to safety as soon as possible. You had to go to your air raid shelter, if you were out and about then you were to dash to the nearest safe haven and take refuge. Even advising the public to hide in the closest underground station if they could find nowhere else. Everybody was so busy preparing, there was so much to do, but generally the belief on the street was that it will all blow over, be solved by the politicians.

Every evening on the radio, they would all listen to instructions on how to survive a war. How to cook meals from just a few measly ingredients, how to make clothes last longer, how to blackout your windows, it went on and on like a class teaching them all how to live a very different life to the one they were all accustomed to.

The next commission for Tom and James was aboard a Royal Navy vessel called HMS Victoria. It was much larger than the ships they usually waved off and the quayside resembled a party, it was like a celebration, everybody cheering and waving flags, mothers crying and couples kissing passionately. Louisa was intrigued. Alice was concerned.

"You going to be all right," she asked her portly husband as they had one final embrace.

"Who me?" guffawed Tom, "Course, I will, don't you go fretting yourself, my lovely!" he chuckled as they parted company. Alice blew her nose all the way back home.

"Are you OK, Mum?" chorused Louisa, Gladys and Stevie.

Chapter Fourteen

Oh, my God! Could I be? The thought suddenly screamed in to Louisa's brain one day while she was visiting Heart's Bakers factory, she had popped in to say hello to Rosie and the other girls on the way home from collecting some groceries one morning. She timed it to coincide with their lunch break hoping that Eve would let her stay five minutes. Louisa always had lots to do, visiting her mum and cleaning their little flat. It was only two rooms but lots of dust seemed to blow in through the draughty windows, she had to wash clothes, do the cooking, but with James away it didn't take that long and she got so bored just sitting indoors. She missed having a laugh like she used to have at work, she was feeling a bit lonely really. There was no one to talk to at home.

She had no idea why, all of a sudden she would suddenly think about periods in the middle of a Bakers factory but she did and said her farewells, dashed home as fast as she could and looked at her little calendar she had received as a Christmas present and which she kept on her sideboard.

"Oh, my God," Louisa screeched to herself, she was two weeks late! How had she not noticed before now? How did she think she couldn't be pregnant with the amount of time her and James had spent discovering each other! She was pleased, ecstatic, scared, worried, tearful and felt sick.

"Well, married life is certainly suiting you, my love," Alice cooed over her daughter, "Your skin is glowing and your eyes are a twinkling." Louisa had popped into her mum's the next morning on her way to the shops. She didn't even need to buy anything, she would if she saw something cheap she could store, but she had to get out of the flat, get some fresh air, have a chat with people. Her mum's kitchen was all warm and steamy, there was washing hanging on the wooden dryer rack dangling from the ceiling and a big saucepan boiling on the stove erupting more steam.

"Fancy a sweet cup of tea, darling? I could do with a sit down for five minutes. Oh, I haven't stopped all morning, been shopping, done the washing, watered the vegetables I'm done in."

Alice chuckled, continuing to potter around the small space as she spoke,

"Oh, Ma Pritchard was in last night until late, oh, we did laugh; honestly, she makes me split my sides sometimes, Joan's come back home, apparently she can't live with the new boyfriend, she thinks his family are a bunch of odd bods!" "Would you believe it? His family are odd bods!" Alice chuckled then suddenly looked at Louisa.

"You alright? You've hardly said a word since you walked through the door, Oh, my gosh, nothing's wrong, is it? Are you coming back here to live? Like Joan next door?"

Alice was joking but inside she was starting to panic.

Louisa's neck began to burn, she felt the colour slowly spreading to her cheeks, the more she tried to stop it the hotter she became. She moved her hand slightly to the right to steady herself on her mum's wooden table.

Alice babbled, "What is it? Please tell me what's the matter, love? You can tell me anything you know that." She patted Louisa's back.

"If you would just let me get a word in Mum I will tell you," Louisa jibed, she felt even sicker now with nerves and anxiety.

"You are going to be a grandmother," she blurted out.

Alice fell backwards against the sitting room door which wasn't closed and she nearly ended up flat out.

"Get away with you! I'm too young," she giggled clasping Louisa's tiny hands.

"Oh, my gosh, me a grandmother, oh, how fantastic, I'm in shock, make us that cup of tea, no, on second thoughts, you had better sit there and rest, I'll make it. Blimey, what a shock! I can't believe it, how long have you known? How did you keep that to yourself? Blimey, you haven't wasted much time! Oh, my gosh," she screamed dancing on the spot, "I'm going to be a granny, I'm going to be a granny, oh, congratulations by the way!"

Chapter Fifteen

A couple of weeks later Louisa was sitting at her little second hand table reading an old copy of the Daily Mirror her mum had passed on to her. There was an article on the front page and some pictures of King George VI and The Queen Elizabeth who had earlier in the year visited Quebec in Canada and then they had gone on to New York City in the United States of America. Louisa just loved reading about the Royal Family, she idolised the princesses, Elizabeth and Margaret, they were younger than Louisa but always looked so glamorous and well-dressed. They had such elegant posture. Louisa sat up straight. King George had been on the wireless the other night broadcasting to the nation. Louisa was daydreaming about the grandness of Buckingham Palace, where the Royal family live, when a letter popped through her front door, she stooped to pick it up, the postmark was 'Ashford, Kent' and she sat back down to read the letter instead of swooning over the royal pictures.

"Right," Alice bellowed as soon as Louisa walked through the door the next morning.

"I've got it all sussed out, you move back in here, we can all look after one another whilst the men are away at sea or…" Alice stroked Louisa's hair, she could see there were tears welling up in her eyes. "We can all muck in together whilst the men are away especially, now you have my grandchild in there." Alice was clucking like a hen she felt so protective towards her daughter and would do anything, bend over backwards, to keep her safe and healthy. Alice was smiling and patting Louisa's tummy.

"Oh, Mum, thank you so much you really are a diamond," Louisa replied slowly.

This wasn't the reaction Alice had anticipated, why wasn't Louisa excited to be coming back home?

"I received a letter yesterday from Sylvia."

"She couldn't look her mum in the eyes as she handed Alice two sheets of pale blue paper.

"I've been awake all night worrying about what to do."

Alice gently accepted the letter and walked heavily into the sitting room, she sat herself slowly on the sofa, she was feeling a bit concerned as she peeled the pale blue sheets apart, what could Sylvia be saying that had upset her Lou-Lou?

She tilted the first sheet towards the window so she could see the writing more clearly.

'Dear Louisa,

I hope you have been enjoying married life. I'm guessing James will have set sail by the time you read this letter. I told Mrs French your happy news and she said you are more than welcome to come and stay here with us. You can help out with light duties whilst you are able to and in exchange Mrs French has offered you free board and lodgings. You can stay as long as you would like to and you will have your own bedroom.

With all this talk of conflict I think it's best to be out of London for the safety of you and my first grandchild! Also you can save the rent on your flat which will save you and James lots of money. I think Mrs French is quite excited actually as I am and I do hope you accept her offer and I look forward to your reply.

Please give my best wishes to your family.

Love
Sylvia xxx'

Louisa watched her mum through her big tearful eyes awaiting a response. She had been awake all night pondering about how she was going to break this news to her mum. They were so close now, since she got married and had given up work she saw her mum most days. But James had mentioned before he set sail that if we did go to war, he would be happier if Louisa could somehow be out of London, all the talk was the Germans would attack London first. But Louisa had let it go over her head as she didn't want the war to interfere with their perfect life. He said he wanted to protect Louisa, but had no choice, he couldn't be there. It had been so emotional and draining the past few weeks, knowing James was going, trying to carry on as normal, everyone terrified, all the gossip and horror stories, Adolph Hitler will do this, the Germans are here already. All this worrying about everything, was it because she was pregnant she wondered and feeling constantly sick.

And now both her mum and Sylvia want her to live with them. She did feel bad, it wasn't a case of liking Sylvia more, her mum must know that surely. James was right it would be safer to be out of London, she had a baby to consider now.

The next two weeks whizzed by, what should she take? She didn't have much but she needed clothes for her expanding tummy and knew she wouldn't be able to get anything at all where she was going. It was in the middle of nowhere! The sky was so dark at night you couldn't see your hand in front of your face and they even spoke a bit differently. Alice helped her choose, she packed three outfits into a small brown suitcase and they both stood looking at it, it had two nighties and some toiletries too. The girls at the bakery had given her some scones to take as a gift for Sylvia and Mr and Mrs French. She wondered what James would say? Would he be happy? Would he be a bit puzzled like Louisa felt herself? Anyway, she had decided to go now. She had nothing to lose it would save them money as well as she was going to be fed in Kent for nothing! I wonder if I will get lots? She hoped so to herself, she was eating for two now and always felt starving. Her life was so happy and perfect she was worried this dreaded war would come and spoil things but felt confident it would never happen. Nothing could burst her bubble. Every time you went out the door all you could hear were gossipers spreading doom and gloom, they gave you the hebeegeebees about Adolph Hitler and what he was going to do to the whole of Europe. James would be back soon and they could be a perfect little family together.

Alice was clinging to Louisa, even Ma Pritchard came to see her off.

"You'll be back next week," Ma Pritchard laughed, "all that country air and cows dung is no good for a London lassie!" They all waved and cheered as she walked off down the road with her cute case. The train from London Bridge station was so busy, she could hear more talk of the war from the other passengers, 'Hitler's going to poison us all, take our country and fill it with Germans,' and 'You mark my words we will all be dead before

Christmas,' all the usual scare stories. A small hard faced lady sitting opposite Louisa kept nudging the lady next to her to keep her awake. It wasn't working the ladies head kept lolling backwards and her mouth falling wide open. Louisa had to look elsewhere to stop herself from laughing, further down the carriage there was a man sitting with his back towards her, he reminded her of her James, he was about the same height, had the same dark hair and his stance was identical. Louisa settled back and watched the lush green fields as they made their way out of London and wound through little picturesque villages towards Ashford. She felt a bit nauseous and prayed she wasn't going to start gagging in front of all these strangers. How embarrassing that would be.

Sylvia had written to Louisa, another soft letter, cheered Louisa up no end.

"Perhaps Sylvia just warms up as she gets to know you more," Louisa had commented to her mum.

In Sylvia's letter, she said her employers, Mr and Mrs French, the owners of the farmhouse where she lived and worked, were very kindly going to collect Louisa from Ashford Station in their motor car. They would wait for her by the ticket office.

"You're like royalty being picked up in a car," teased Alice, "won't be talking to us soon if you get too snooty."

Louisa felt homesick already, she would never stop loving her family, they were perfect and meant the world to her even Gladys wasn't so bad now they didn't share a bedroom. Anyway, what an adventure she bucked herself up and admired the sheep and green fields out the window. Her mum would have liked looking at the sheep. It was a beautiful sunny day, the train had emptied in Faversham, Louisa wondered where all those people were going, then a few more people got off with Louisa at Ashford Station. She slowly walked towards the exit sign and noticed straight away how lovely Ashford smelt, at the end of the platform she could see a man on his own with a walking stick , Louisa felt dizzy and slowed her pace, a very elegant looking lady joined the man with the stick and Louisa felt very nervous.

"Louisa?" asked the lady, she looked like a ballerina as she approached her and her smile was warm and her eyes too. Louisa grinned from ear to ear and goodness knows why but she curtsied. Mrs French laughed and clasped Louisa's hand. Louisa was so relieved, when sitting on the train, she thought about what she was actually doing, it was a bit of a risk, going to stay with people she had never met and an old lady she'd only met twice, even if she was her mother-in-law. The sun seemed hotter than in London, she couldn't get over the fresh smell it was so clean and everything on the car journey was so pretty. The roads were narrow and winding with tall, green bushes along the edges of fields. Occasionally, they passed a stone house with a red roof and they passed a couple of other motor cars going in the opposite direction. Eventually, they pulled onto an area covered in tiny pebbles at the front of a large red brick house. It had a round canopy hanging above a shiny red front door. To the right of the door was a big bay window with a little lawn in front of it which was edged with tall, red rose bushes. It was beautiful sight.

"Welcome to Biddenden, Louisa," Mrs French laughed.

Chapter Sixteen

Mr French carried Louisa's twee suitcase round the side entrance of the fine looking house, Louisa trailed after him. He didn't speak so she kept silent and she noticed he didn't use his stick and appeared to be walking fine. Louisa followed him into a kitchen where Sylvia was waiting, she hugged Louisa for what seemed like ages and Mr French said, "We will see you both later, we have an appointment to attend to." Louisa had no idea where Mrs French had gone.

"My dear girl." Sylvia held Louisa in her arms. "I'm so happy you are here safe with me, I've had the wireless on," Sylvia whispered and checked over her shoulder to see if anybody was in earshot, "and they said Germany had invaded Poland."

Louisa couldn't understand why she had to whisper.

"What does that mean?" Louisa pouted her lips at Sylvia.

"Well, I don't think it's very good, my dear, now let me show you where you will be sleeping and then we can sit down and go over rules etcetera," Sylvia said in a loud authoritative voice as she steered Louisa across the large square kitchen. There was a rectangular window over the sink which looked out onto, what seemed, a never ending garden. There were some white lacy curtains at the sides of the window tied back with yellow ribbon. Sun was streaming through. On one wall, stood a large solid-looking stove with wooden logs piled in the bottom and a grey, metal kettle on the top next to a saucepan with some purple berries in it. High above the stove some clothes were drying on an oblong shaped wooden hanging frame. To the left of the stove was a dresser with two drawers and two cupboards underneath. Louise couldn't take it all in, it was gorgeous. "I hope one day James and me will have a house like this in Biddenden," she gushed at Sylvia. They walked into a hallway that was dark and long. It had stairs on the right, a door on the left which was closed and ahead was the big red front door Louisa had admired from the front. The floor was tiled and there was a thin green and red patterned rug running from the front door.

"This is the sitting room," Sylvia waved towards the closed door, "Mr and Mrs French sit in there most evenings between seven and ten and I clean it every morning at seven am, you can help me whilst you are here."

Sylvia started to climb the stairs, the whole house looked spotless not a speck of dust anywhere. On the left nearly at the top of the stairs was a window, which Louisa glanced out of quickly as she passed. All she could see was green, green and more green fields. Oh, and the odd sheep and building. Up three more steps they reached a large landing with four closed doors. On the wall opposite the window hung a large painting of more fields encased in a lavish ornate gold coloured frame.

"Mrs French painted this," Sylvia explained, "She's very creative, now here is your bedroom." Sylvia pushed the end door open to reveal a room measuring about ten foot long by eight foot wide, it had a comfy looking double bed with a quilted cover in pink and cream, there was a chest of drawers on the right wall with a china washbasin and jug. Straight ahead over the bed was a window overlooking the front garden with the rose trees. Louisa felt very relieved and lucky.

"We shall get up at five thirty every morning and return to this room about seven in the evening after we have eaten supper and cleared up. We will also get the breakfast items prepared before we go to bed as it makes it so much easier in the mornings."

Louisa placed her case on the bed to start unpacking, Sylvia slowly picked it up and put it on the floor brushing down the bedspread.

"I shall go and make us some tea and you can empty your case now. Do you know how to make jam?"

"Erm, I think I made some gooseberry jam ages ago when my dad was given a big sack of gooseberries from one of his friends in the docks, but I didn't make it all on my own, Gladys and me helped my mum."

"Come down in ten minutes for a cup of tea," Sylvia ordered and left the room. Louisa looked out the window and noticed that too had white lacy curtains this time tied back with pink ribbons.

She felt like she had joined the armed forces all these orders Sylvia was dishing out. When she got downstairs, Mark, James's best man at their wedding, was in the kitchen.

"Oh, Mark, it's so lovely to see you again, I forgot you were working down here, do you live close by?" He looked bigger and browner than when she'd seen him last, he had grey overalls on and he nodded at her.

"Hope everything goes well down here in the Garden of England for you Louisa," Mark hugged her laughing.

"And I hear congratulations are in order!" He shook her hand. "James is going to be a daddy! How's he going to do that? That man can't even look after himself," Mark chortled.

"And if there's anything I can do or you need anything, love, just ask," Mark kindly offered.

"I'd better get back to work now, see you soon," he waved as he left the sweet smelling kitchen.

That evening much to Louisa's surprise they all sat together at a big wooden table in the middle of the kitchen floor. Mrs French insisted Louisa call them 'Cyril and June' and told her all about a card game called cribbage, that they had been playing that afternoon at a friend's house locally. June seemed very happy but Cyril didn't contribute much to the conversation and Louisa got the impression that they didn't have any children. June was born in the house and when she married Cyril he came to join her in the family home. Her parents had lived there also until they both died peacefully in their sleep, her mother seven years ago then her dad died a year later. June was very chatty but Louisa did notice Sylvia didn't say anything at all and Cyril only made a couple of comments. They ate a huge serving of steak and kidney pie, mashed swede and boiled potatoes that Sylvia and Louisa had prepared that afternoon. It had been like a cookery lesson. Louisa felt exhausted it had been a long day, she felt like she had left London a week ago.

The next day after cleaning the whole house from bottom to top, Sylvia showed Louisa around the garden, it was full of trees and vegetables, there were berry bushes and green beans and tomatoes, they ate bread and pickles for lunch and made blackberry jam.

At 11 am, on the 3rd of September 1939, two days after' Louisa had arrived in Biddenden, Neville Chamberlain made an announcement on the wireless that Great Britain along with France was now in a state of war with Germany.

The Second World War had begun.

Chapter Seventeen

The weeks went by slowly, every day was the same, Louisa had trouble keeping track what day it was. Cyril and June went out most afternoons to visit friends or go shopping in Tenterden, a nearby village and they all ate supper together at night except on Sundays when they had a main meal at midday. About once every two weeks, Cyril and June would entertain friends in the sitting room during the evening and there was always June's laughter coming from the room. Only a few times did Louisa hear the 'war' mentioned. A gentleman guest boomed that Soviet troops had invaded Poland now from the West. It seemed a million miles away from Biddenden.

"I had an inkling, you know, love, before you told me, I woke up one morning and thought Louisa's in the family way!" Sylvia had said patting Louisa's growing belly, she laughed. My grandma used to read neighbours tea leaves you know, she was always right, but sometimes she saw tragedy in the leaves if she did she didn't tell anybody about the impending doom!"

Sylvia seemed quite pleased Louisa was expecting but she was a funny one, Louisa thought, she didn't show any feelings, could be quite aloof sometimes, although she did seem to be fussing a bit more lately saying Louisa couldn't carry anything heavy or stand on any stools.

In the evenings, Sylvia and Louisa sometimes sewed or read Junes old magazines or wrote letters. Sylvia had knitted some pink and blue cardigans for the baby and they spent time going through the little kit Louisa had accumulated for 'Junior' which she kept in her bedroom. She was getting very excited, she was worried about James, was he okay? Was there any trouble near him? Where even was he? She hadn't heard anything so assumed he was safe. In Acacia Court, you could just walk up the road and see the newspaper stand to find out the latest news but here she didn't see any newspapers and the wireless was in the lounge where she and Sylvia rarely went. Cyril and June didn't tell them anything and all Louisa had seen were a few planes flying overhead. She had watched them in the garden one day whilst standing alongside Cyril who was also watching them whizz across the cloudy sky.

Sylvia stayed in the bedroom next door to Louisa and would tap gently on the wall every morning at five thirty to make sure Louisa was awake. Not once had Louisa not already been up. She seemed to have an inbuilt alarm telling her what time to wake up every day. Most days she lay in bed stroking her growing belly. It was getting quite plump now. She spoke in a hushed voice to her unborn child telling him or her about James, her family and the two cats that lived behind Cyril's shed at the bottom of the garden. She just could not wait to meet junior! The baby seemed to know she was talking and wriggled and kicked as if to say 'hello mummy'.

Mark came in the garden or kitchen most days and Louisa was always so pleased to see him, it was refreshing to have someone else to speak to, Louisa didn't know how Sylvia had stood this life for so long, it was lovely and she was very grateful but it could be so boring, it was so different to all the noise and people swarming around you in London. Sylvia never saw anyone or went out anywhere. There was no pavement along their road so they couldn't walk anywhere and anyway, where would you walk to? To look at more fields or more sheep? There didn't seem to be many people around.

They grew so much fruit and vegetables in the garden which somehow tasted nicer than the fruit and vegetables Louisa was used to in London. They also had chickens which laid eggs most days, you had to be careful when collecting the eggs as there were two stray cats that hung about the bottom of the garden. They were like little lions hiding behind shrubs and Cyril's shed, wagging their tails and watching the chickens hoping to pounce on them. It was quite funny to watch. The chickens lived in a big mesh hut but if they saw the cats close up they all started squawking and flapping their wings and jumping on top of one another. The local farmers sold Cyril and June meat and flour. Everything else they just made for themselves, they were always busy and Louisa thought it was a lot of work for Sylvia on her own.

Then all of a sudden their peace was shattered, hundreds of planes flew over dropping bombs everywhere, you could see the fires they had caused, not that far away from them either, surely that was still Kent, it couldn't have been London, it looked too near. How they didn't get hit she couldn't understand, They were from the Luftwaffe, the German Air Force and it was relentless, must have come over every night for about three weeks, you couldn't sleep, they droned on all night, back and forth with explosions going off every minute or two. Louisa vowed to ask Mark if he knew what was going on in the war, she would tell him that no one in this house seems to want to talk about it. She would have thought that Cyril or June would have told Sylvia out of politeness, I mean they know she has a son out on a ship somewhere who could be in danger.

She received letters from her mum and Gladys about once a week, they missed her and the letters really made her laugh, stories of the neighbours, the dock workers in Hayes Wharf, how London had gone mad going over the top about the war. Louisa was always so pleased to receive the letters but after reading them just wanted to go home. She felt so far away from everything she knew. Rosie also wrote, her letters were hilarious, made Louisa laugh out loud, lots of tales about Rosie's mum and dad, Betty and Ed and their marriage woes. What Carla and everybody at Heart's Bakers were getting up to. Rosie was still courting Frank and Louisa was hoping he would not propose to her. James had written twice and was hoping he would be able to dock for a few days leave at some point. He was sworn to secrecy couldn't say where he was, where he was headed, what they were doing it was all top secret in case the German's stole his letter. Louisa laughed and shook her head. His letters were so beautifully written and contained lots of bossy instructions on how to keep healthy, what she had to do for the welfare of their first born. Louisa read and reread them over and over again, she smoothed them over, kissed them, held them to her heart and closed her eyes. They just made her feel a bit closer to him, he had touched the paper. She was really worried about him but if she had a letter that must mean he was all right.

The war seemed to have moved up a notch or two and there were planes flying over every day in all directions. The bombing nearby seemed to have calmed down. Cyril was always out there watching and Louisa wondered why he hadn't been called up to help in the war effort, she asked Sylvia discreetly why when they were hanging out the washed clothes one day but Sylvia just shook her head and nodded towards Cyril's shed. Oh, God, Louisa hoped he hadn't heard her, she didn't know whether he was in the shed or not, Louisa felt bad, he was quite old and probably too old to do anything around here for the war. Before she had left London, the older men had offered themselves to be air raid wardens or part of the local defence force in the event of a war, but they probably didn't need too many of them around here, perhaps they hadn't even recruited any, I mean it was just so quiet only a couple of farm houses to each street. Louisa couldn't seem to stop asking herself questions. 'Where was the air raid shelter?' and 'Do they have any gas masks?' She hadn't noticed any. Instruction leaflets were delivered to the residents in Biddenden about what to do if the Germans did invade or if you smelt funny gas, surely they needed gas masks if they did? Cyril was told if he wanted to go out in the dark he would have to cover his motor car headlights with paper, to stop the lights being seen from enemy aircraft flying overhead. He went out straight away and taped brown paper over his headlights. *What's the point of that?* thought Louisa, *It might rain tonight.* But come to think of it she did hear him start his car up when she was in bed quite regularly but had never given it much thought before. *I wonder where he gets off to late at night. Very odd!* There was just so much to think about and plan for this war and every night, she prayed in bed, "Please keep my family and James safe, please, please, please."

Chapter Eighteen

Unbeknown to Louisa, there was actually a lot of action occurring. In September 1939, there was a huge battle in the Atlantic Ocean involving submarines, battleships, destroyers and air craft carriers. All trying to protect the cargo vessels England bound across the sea hoping to deliver food to the United Kingdom. Trying to protect the cargo vessels her dad and husband were on. Germany had an enormous navy compared to Great Britain who at that point of time massively needed to increase their naval equipment rapidly.

The odd shaped building next to Cyril and June's house was apparently a hop farm. They grew hops to make beer and it had a triangular shape on the roof with a funnel at the top. One morning, Sylvia and Louisa were washing the breakfast dishes and they could hear a lot of noise coming from the direction of the hop farm, female voices, car engines revving and men shouting. They looked at each other with puzzled expressions, Louisa stood on tiptoes at the back door but couldn't see what all the commotion was, Sylvia washed the last dish and shook her head to Louisa signalling for her to follow her. They ran to the window up the stairs and looked out. There were people streaming all over the farm. About thirty women and a few men, some cars, a Land Rover type vehicle and a tractor with a trailer on the back. The women looked very glamorous, with scarves tied around their heads and vivid red lipstick but they were all wearing what looked like Marks overalls. They were laughing, some were even smoking cigarettes and the men looked like they were flirting with them all.

"They must be Land girls," Sylvia announced all animated, I read about them in the newspaper, they were advertising for women to join the 'Women's Land Army' and help grow food in case we run out during the war.

"Blimey," said Louisa, "they look like American film stars."

Sylvia continued, "It said in the advertisement they needed women to plough fields, dig up potatoes, harvest crops, all sorts of heavy manual tasks."

As they watched from the window a chap climbed from the tractor and started to take from the trailer hoes and rakes and lay them on the field.

"I wonder where they will all live?" Louisa queried out loud.

"Well, they won't be able to all stay in that Hop's house."

"No, well, they've come from somewhere this morning, how exciting!" Sylvia said as she started to go down back to the kitchen.

Chapter Nineteen

One evening while they were eating supper, Cyril had been praising the president of the United States, Franklin D. Roosevelt, when he suddenly said,

"I hope you don't mind," he paused and took a deep breath, "We have been talking, June and I and we feel we are too old to have a baby in the house! We wondered if you have made any plans for when the baby arrives? Are to going to return to your mother's or?" Cyril shrugged his shoulders.

Louisa was completely in shock, totally puzzled, she thought they liked her and that the offer had been for her to stay as long as she wanted to be safe in the country. The government were sending hundreds of thousands of children and women out cities and towns all across the United Kingdom. Evacuating them out to the countryside, to couples like Cyril and June, and here they were going to send her back to London. Louisa looked at Sylvia who was obviously as taken back as Louisa. June's lips tightened and she looked quite angry.

After a few minutes, Louisa replied,

"Well I can go as soon as the baby's born if that's okay with you? I think I have about three weeks left if my maths is right! If you don't mind that is, I don't really want to travel home so close to my due date."

Louisa felt she had no choice, the conversation ended there, nobody said another word, they all just sat there looking at their plates, she felt very upset and unwanted.

But after a couple of weeks, she had got over the shock and she was looking forward to going home. To be going where she was wanted. She had written and told her mum and also to James, she thought James would be annoyed, he had wanted her out of London to keep safe. All Sylvia said was that she was very sorry and that they had initially said she could stay for as long as she wanted. The letters she had been receiving from London hadn't said anything about bombings so maybe it wasn't that bad in London, maybe they had all gone over the top expecting the worst. The only things mentioned were that France had been occupied by German soldiers and that the United Kingdom had a new prime minster, Winston Churchill, the old one Neville Chamberlain had lost the election because Winston Churchill had got masses more votes than him. Louisa had seen a picture of Winston Churchill ages ago in The Daily Mirror, she liked the look of him, he looked a bit like her dad, all cuddly and soft.

"Why did Mark not enlist for the army?" Louisa wondered out loud one day to Sylvia as they prepared dinner in the kitchen.

"Well, he has a protected job looking after the farm vehicles, if they don't service then we don't eat! So he's needed here," was all Sylvia replied. Louisa was going to ask some more but stopped herself as an enormous bolt of pain went through her back.

Later that evening her labour pains really kicked in.

No, thought Louisa, *can it be a week early?* she was worried something had gone wrong, was her new best friend okay in there? She looked at her huge belly as she lay on the bed. The pains got more and more severe until she screamed out, she couldn't help it, this monster noise just came roaring from her lips. *Oh Jesus, God and Mary, this hurts!* she thought. Sylvia tapped on the door and opened it.

"Oh, my word… you're having my grandchild," she screamed before leaping into action. The next few hours were a complete blur to Louisa, she kept lapsing in and out of consciousness, puffing, screaming and being so embarrassingly unladylike whilst June and Sylvia flapped around her. She had a faint recollection of hearing Cyril and Mark's voices outside on the landing or was it James? She felt delirious and her hair was stuck to her forehead. She heard animal like noises that surely weren't coming from her? And was worried about the cream and pink bedspread. Her legs were all over the place, the pains were enormous and then, what seemed like all of a sudden, there he was! She had a big, fat, round screaming baby on the bed and Sylvia was crying with happiness. Handsome little Harry! Named after her mum's dad who had been called Harry, he had died in First World War but Louisa had heard lots of tales about him and decided he sounded a lovely fellow and her son would be 'Little Harry' named after his granddad, a war hero.

At some point a village nurse had arrived but Louisa didn't even notice her until Harry was wrapped up and lying beside her. She felt in a sort of trance, she was absolutely elated and absolutely shattered, felt like she could sleep for a week but that still didn't stop her praying,

"Please God keep James, Harry and my family safe please, please, please.

It was a challenge getting used to less food, especially when they had been eating whatever they wanted. The ration books had arrived and June and Cyril had to go collect little bits of chicken and ham, eight ounces of butter between the lot of them, no more fruit pies as the butter couldn't be used for pastry and a few tea bags per week. Mark actually brought some rabbits over that somebody had caught, but there was no way Louisa could help skin them. She pretended Harry needed feeding and escaped to her room and Sylvia said she would make a rabbit pie with lard instead. Louisa skipped supper that night and looked forward to going home to Acacia Court and her mum's dinners.

Cyril spoke of 'wringing the chicken's necks' and eating them but June gave him such a filthy look and it wasn't mentioned again.

In the dark, in the distance at night, you could sometimes see light illuminating the sky, you could hear the airplanes flying overhead. Cyril said the Biddenden and Tenterden village signs had been painted over so the Germans won't know where they are when they invaded. That made Louisa have a fit of giggles.

Cyril and June continued to go out in the afternoons but not at often as petrol was rationed as well. One morning, Cyril drove Louisa and Harry to the Office of Births, Deaths and Marriages at Tenterden. All the fields they passed had women working on them, The Land Army.

"They must be growing so much food," Louisa exclaimed.

They passed women driving Land Rovers along the country lanes. They even passed an ambulance being driven by female too.

"There's a lot a women have come down to work in Ashford Hospital," Cyril advised Louisa nodding his head.

So when little Harry Bishop was just four weeks old, Louisa felt she had better be back off to good old home. Her returning to London hadn't been mentioned again but they also hadn't said they could stay so she was feeling a bit stronger and getting in a routine and started to plan her return and was actually looking forward to showing off her handsome little Harry and seeing everyone again. She did understood about Cyril and June not wanting a baby in the house, he did cry a lot during the night and I mean there was her, Sylvia and Harry and only two of them and it was their house. Sylvia had mentioned one day that Cyril had refused to accept any evacuees from London as he didn't like children so he probably hated having Harry in his house. But Louisa was still baffled as to why they had offered her a home in the first place. She was guessing now it was a way of getting out of having the evacuees, saying they didn't have enough space if she was living with them. Anyway, Louisa had enough to think about, she was a feeling anxious about Harry's safety now that England was involved in a war.

There were thousands of soldiers not only British but from Belgium, Holland and lots of commonwealth countries too, all trapped in a corner of France called Dunkirk, Mark told Louisa and Sylvia one afternoon while June and Cyril were out. The German Army were beating the Allied Forces and had driven them nearer and nearer to the coast. He said hundreds and hundreds of boats from Great Britain, from the Royal Navy, even some little private fishing boats, they had all gone over the English Channel to rescue all the trapped soldiers, it had taken days to get the troops safely out of Dunkirk in France. Over three hundred thousand soldiers were rescued. Picked up and ferried back to our shores, Heroes they all were. Winston Churchill said it was all a great success and Louisa hoped it meant they were winning the war, not losing and everything would soon return to normal. But Mark said all the troops were needed back in England because Germany was sure to invade us next. Then what would happen? They had already invaded a small island off France which belonged to Great Britain called Jersey and all the people who lived on Jersey now had to take orders from German soldiers.

Chapter Twenty

Louisa couldn't believe the devastation that awaited her as she travelled on the train from Ashford Station through the beautiful countryside to London Bridge. In Kent, it was all red and golden leaves on trees, beautiful golden fields swaying with hay waiting to be harvested by the glamorous Women's Land Army or vivid green meadows with sheep dotted about grazing. Every station they stopped at more passengers got on, it had been quite empty when the train started at Ashford but by the time they reached London Bridge Station the carriage was crammed full with people standing as well. The lady sitting opposite was reading The *Daily Express* newspaper and on the front page was splashed 'Churchill officially becomes Prime Minister'. There were lots of soldiers in uniform, all going to join up Louisa guessed then thought no they must have already have joined up and be going to war? She was shocked at how loud and noisy everything seemed. On every station platform there were wives, girlfriends, mums, children all cheering and waving little union jack flags to see their beloveds off to combat. It was a mixture of fear and a party atmosphere. Very strange. Handsome Harry was awake the whole journey but quiet and when they eventually reached London Bridge, Louisa let everyone else get off then struggled up the platform with Harry in one arm and her case in the other which kept bashing her ankles. Sylvia had insisted she take an apple pie home for her family which she had made the day before with apples picked from the garden and Mark had given her a pack of cooked beef from a local farm. He had very kindly taken her to Ashford Station in his motor car, carried her luggage onto the platform where he pressed the pack of meat into her hand.

"Give my regards to James and tell him to get a proper job," he grinned, ruffled his large hands gently through the sides of her hair and smiled as he waved her onto the train. He was still standing there grinning as the train chugged out of Ashford.

"Ta-ta, Louisa," he waved from the station platform.

"Ta-ta, Garden of England, thanks for a lovely time!" Louisa replied, chuckling; she was pleased to be going home.

Even before Louisa had walked out of London Bridge station she could smell the burning and the first thing that struck her was how light it seemed, then she realised why it was light, half the buildings were missing. Where there had been warehouses there was now the odd unsteady brick wall sticking out on its own. Everything else was just rubble at street level. Some rubble even seemed to be smoking. Also there were hundreds, yes, it must have been hundreds of people everywhere, young pretty women, children running about, handsome soldiers flirting with the young pretty women, mothers shouting for their children to stop running about, old ladies flirting with the handsome soldiers. Even a group of small children all clutching miniature suitcases with cardboard nametags tied around their necks with string. It was manic, at the end of her street there was nothing. Louisa didn't recognise this as the same London she had left, there were tin air raid shelters everywhere and children running up the street in gas masks and that dreadful smell of burning. *No one had mentioned this in their letters,* Louisa thought. "My poor Harry had better not get a bad chest with all this smoke floating about in the air," she said to herself.

As she neared her front door she noticed two men sitting on next doors doorstep smoking cigarettes.

Where's Ma Pritchard, Louisa wondered, *and what's that red light hanging outside for?*

Her mum looked amazing, she was crying with happiness to see Louisa and meet Harry for the first time.

"Oh, he's so big," Alice couldn't wait to get him off Louisa and just sat down cuddling him for ages. Louisa made them all a pot of tea, chatted to Gladys and asked questions but she was sure her mum didn't once divert her gaze from Harry.

"My first grandchild – you are beautiful and I will love you forever," she whispered to him and then, "Oh, we've got so much to catch up on, love," to Louisa as an afterthought.

Chapter Twenty-One

Oh, my gosh! Louise thought to herself, stretching the words out, as she looked at her reflection upstairs in her bedroom later that day.

Why did I eat all those blinking pies?

Her memories of what she looked like in this mirror were of a smaller Louisa! Much slimmer and younger. Years younger. She looked down at Harry gurgling and kicking his legs on her bed. He was adorable and his eyes followed her as she tried to make herself look better. She turned to her left, held her tummy in as much as she could, arched her back, stood on her tiptoes, turning to the right she tried to breath in again,

"Oh, cripes, I still look pregnant. Oh gosh, even my cheeks seem the colour of blackberries!"

"Why did I eat all that jam?" she asked Harry shaking her head.

James threw open the bedroom door.

"Aggggggghhhhhhhhhhhhhhh."

Louisa exhaled an enormous screech, she thought she was having a heart attack. She tried to stop screaming but couldn't, James gave her the biggest hug ever but still she couldn't shut up! Her legs were like jelly. James bent and picked up Harry, Louisa thought she would treasure that image until the day she died.

"Oh, my gosh." Louisa couldn't stand up properly. "I am just so glad you are safe, my darling, I didn't know it was as bad as it all is, I heard nothing down in Kent. They're in another world down there! How comes you're here, where's my dad? Is he home too?" Louisa knew she was rambling, she couldn't stop herself, it was probably shock.

James and Harry just stared at each other for what seemed like ages, James was taking in every single part of his son.

"Hello, Harry," James cooed in an 'in love' voice. Louisa was so happy.

"That I do not know, my love."

"What? How comes you're here if my dad's not coming home?" Louisa hugged him tightly around his waist. She was pleased as punch and more.

"I was allowed to be transferred to another ship as you had given birth, given special license for two days off, I wrote and told our mum's but wanted to surprise you! I will have to go back on another vessel that they are finding me while we speak."

"I don't believe my mum and your mum both knew you were coming home! How? And how did my mum keep a secret? Must be the first time ever! She could never keep anything quiet!" It was a long-standing joke that if you wanted anyone to know something, just tell Alice and ask her to keep it quiet, she was so excitable she'd just blurt it out then say, "Oops a daisy," with both hands over her mouth!

"I'm only home for two days, love, I'm sure it will soon be over, won't be long now, we'll give them bloody Jerries a 'what-for', I'm needed, every man has to do his duty, then I'll be able to look after my beautiful wife and gorgeous son forever. James wistfully looked back at Harry, sitting still in his arms and enjoying the attention.

"Happy, happy, happy ever after!"

Louisa scrutinised her husband's face, he looked haggard, drawn and older. She wanted to believe him but wondered if he even believed himself.

Later that night after tea of boiled beef and beans, sherry and beer, two hours in the air raid shelter and a lot of laughter, James put Harry into his crib and fell into bed beside Louisa. Louisa didn't want to sleep she just wanted to cherish these precious hours together.

"I can sleep next week," she screamed to herself in her head as she fought to keep her eyelids open. There was one part of her she didn't have any trouble opening though! James made the sweetest, tenderest love to her for what seemed like hours and she felt young and alive again.

The next morning Louisa asked James, "Why does Cyril not fight or even do anything for the war effort?" as James blew raspberries at Harry, he shrugged his shoulders,

"I didn't know he didn't help with anything."

Harry was hysterical with laughter.

"And why has Ma Pritchard got a red light outside her door for, is it some sort of safety light that planes can't see?"

Alice burst out laughing. "You could say it is a sort of help with the war effort I suppose," she joked as she winked at James.

"You're a seaman," Alice waved her finger at James, "don't pretend to me you don't know what a red light means! James you going all innocent in front of your mother-in-law," she chuckled.

"What! Ma Pritchard's got a red light outside her front door," James shouted screwing up his face in mock revolution.

"No, you silly apeth, Ma Pritchard ran off with a retired sailor and she's living somewhere in Dagenham, she still pops around for a cup of tea now and then but has to be careful as she did a runner and owes lots of rent – we have a new neighbour now – Penny and she's very friendly if you know what I mean!" Alice taped the side of her nose.

"Oh, my gosh! A brothel next door, I don't believe it!" James gawped.

"You are going back to live in Kent," he ordered Louisa jokingly at the same time as Louisa asked, "what's a brothel?"

That night they were in and out of the air raid shelter four times, as soon as the all clear siren sounded they would all trample back up the stairs, get all comfortable in bed then off the air raid siren went, up and down all night they were.

"Might be better to just stay in the shelter all night from now on, girls," James advised them all.

Chapter Twenty-Two

The noise was unbelievable. Louisa felt like she had just closed her eyes. She wasn't getting much sleep since having Harry as he wanted feeding constantly and now just as she had finally settled him back to sleep the air raid sirens started, the whole house shook, everything went black, the sirens were still going off somewhere in the distance but her home seemed to be in slow motion. Louisa grabbed Harry was out the bedroom door and down the stairs before she knew what she was doing. Her instincts told her to go and that's what she did, no screams or fuss just survival instincts taking over. This was a bad one. Her heart was pounding, the blood inside the head was gushing, her breathing was calm but rapid, Harry was silent she ran barefooted into the Anderson shelter and grabbed a space on the bench. She did notice without looking that the London skyline was ablaze with fires and airplanes. It was a black sky but there was noise all around them as if it was the middle of the day, she could hear people in the distance panicking getting to their shelters, people shouting in the street, pandemonium everywhere. The air was thick with smoke and her eyes started to water immediately. She couldn't see the other end of the hut although it was only a few feet away. She could feel the ground shaking and the rumble of airplanes nearing them. Her heart filled with terror. Her mum flew through the door, sat down, then immediately jumped up.

"Where's our Gladys?" she screamed as she bolted out of the shelter door.

A hot, yellow thundering, what can only be described as a lightning strike, crashed down onto the entrance to their 'safe' shelter and then silence. Silence so eerie it deafened her.

For what felt like hours, but was probably only a few seconds, Louisa sat clutching Harry on her own in the shelter. She could hear screams and muffled cries for help from her neighbours but her whole body seemed frozen stiff, she couldn't open her mouth to call for help, she was shaking all over, the door was flapping slowly against something on the floor, she pondered if it was her mum's leg but everything was hazy and shrouded in dense dust. Her jaw felt solid. As she weakly stood she saw a torch beam moving quickly in her direction then another following and could faintly make out English (thank goodness) male voices, amongst the thundering din in the distance, the whole world was just carrying on at war but she had a dread that her whole world had just changed forever. She wanted to get out of the hut and run away, she wasn't strong enough for this, her legs wouldn't hold her, her head was spinning, she was going to be sick, she mustn't drop Harry.

When Louise woke the room was light, her first thought was, *Oh, my gosh, I had the most terrifying nightmare last night.* She peeped slowly to her left to check Harry but his crib was empty. It was then that she realised she had tears streaming down her cheeks, it wasn't a nightmare. It had happened, hell had arrived in her life. She screamed.

"Harry, Harry, where's my baby?!" hysterically sobbing, still shaking violently, getting from her bed, shoving her feet into slippers, barely able to breath, her legs felt as heavy as lead when Ma Pritchard opened the door and in her arms was a cuddly, chuckling, contented beautiful baby called Harry . He was totally oblivious to all the heartache around him. Louisa just threw her arms over them both and cried and cried until she fell back onto the bed.

"Are they both dead?" She was too scared to ask, too terrified to look up into Ma Pritchard's face, too anxious that she knew the answer already.

"I'm so sorry, I came as soon as I heard love," Ma Pritchard was sobbing now. "I'm so, so sorry."

Chapter Twenty-Three

Louisa felt like she was watching one of the movies at the Greenwich Odeon. Everybody was so dressed up. So dandy for her mum and sister. They would be flattered, there were so many people at their funerals, so popular was her darling mum and her beautiful sister Gladys.

"Look how liked we are!" Louisa could just imagine her mum saying with a wry grin whilst patting her hair.

Louise felt sick. Sick, sick, sick to her stomach. This didn't seem real. The crowd were chattering all around her but she couldn't hear what they were saying. People were coming up to her squeezing her hand, patting her shoulder, stroking her face but she couldn't see properly, there was a pink haze clouding her vision. Ma Pritchard stood strong and upright beside her, the complete opposite to how Louisa felt, Louisa hung on to her arm, so heavily but Ma Pritchard didn't flinch. Louisa had sent letters to her dad, James and Stevie explaining the horrors of that night two weeks ago but didn't know if they had received them or ever would. She didn't know what to write, how do you write a letter like that? So she kept it short and sweet, or not so sweet. Ma Pritchard's daughter Joan stood next to her and was holding Harry. Louisa could not contain the pain. Every part of her body physically hurt with the heartache. People kept telling her, "Be strong, Louisa. Alice would want that," but she wasn't strong, she knew they only meant well but she felt so weak and feeble and her mum wouldn't want her to be strong, they were wrong, Alice would want to be holding Louisa and Gladys's hands and be blowing bubbles to Little Harry.

The neighbours had a bit of street party to 'remember amazing Alice and gorgeous Gladys', they drank ale and some rum and jigged a bit. Penny the new neighbour introduced herself but apart from that Louisa didn't remember much of the service or even the whole day actually. They had a very quick funeral service, you couldn't be out for long as you never knew what was going to happen. They were buried in cardboard coffins as wood was needed for the war effort. They were buried together at Greenwich graveyard in view of the church where not so long ago they had all been happily together at her and James's wedding. Louisa felt as if she was up in heaven with her mum and sister watching over everybody down here on earth. Louisa wasn't allowed to see her mum or Gladys after they'd died as they were too badly injured. That was just too horrific to dwell on. She wanted her mum and sister, it was all too painful.

After about an hour, the mourners went back into their own homes, night was falling and they all had to be get inside, draw the blackout curtains, listen for more air raid sirens, just wait to see what another night in war-torn London brought. It wasn't only London, cities and towns all across Great Britain had similar streets where scenes of absolute devastation had occurred, in Liverpool, Manchester, and Coventry to name a few, huge craters created by bombs where people had been and homes and business. All wiped out, gone forever.

The bombing went on for the whole of that night and for over seventy days and nights more. It was horrendous, how their house had remained standing or she and Harry had survived she'll never know. The blast that had taken her mum and sister had hit the house three doors away. There was no house now, not there or all the way down to the end of the road. All the homes had gone. The air raid wardens couldn't even see who was buried under the huge piles of smoking bricks, charred blackout curtains ripped and ragged blowing in the wind. Rags scattered the streets, lumps of wood and chunks of broken china. The families that had lived there couldn't be found, that was their lot. Buried under a pile of bricks never to walk in Greenwich Park and watch the' River Thames again. Just gone in a flash.

At least they were all together, Louisa thought, *Not left here like me all on my own with a baby to look after*. There was one small mercy felt by Louisa though and that was that her mum and sister were buried at a funeral. A place where she could visit and place daisies and talk to them. Not under a demolished house. In the weeks that followed there were sad tales every day, some people had simply disappeared and their relatives were out looking for them, searching hospitals, schools, everywhere I mean where would you start? Sometimes, Louisa heard stories of items of clothing like coats or a shoe being found but no person or body to be seen. Now that must be even more heart breaking.

One of the Peabody Buildings containing the flats opposite Louisa but down a bit to the left had also been hit but those families had already fled to the underground station to sleep. The building was half knocked away and the remaining half was eerie just standing there exposing a mirror still hanging on one wall and half the staircase.

Hundreds of people, children, whole families were now going to the underground stations every night like it was their bedrooms. They ate, played cards, chatted and tried to sleep on wooden benches or hammocks hung across the railway tracks. It must have been awful, where did you go to the Lavatory? How did you wash your hands? How did you even sleep with all those strangers around you, some probably even snoring loudly like Tom Foster did. Rosie told Louisa that Clara and her two brothers were going to the underground at Holborn every night. Clara said it was actually good fun, there were some nice looking boys down there and she had been chatting to two of them.

Heart's Bakers factory took a direct hit on day thirty of The Blitz and was totally obliterated. The ovens were still there, standing proud and solid struggling to be seen amongst the mound of concrete, machinery and broken bricks that was once her workplace.

In November, the German Air force annihilated Coventry City with nine hundred bombs.

The newspapers named the relentless bombing 'The Blitz', the German word for 'lightning'. After a few nights Louisa made her and little Harry a bed each in the air raid shelter, there was just no end to it, you couldn't sleep the sirens were going constantly. The bombing was flattening London, she could see that. One night they bombed St Pauls Cathedral which was about four miles from her as the crow flies and the pictures were in the newspapers the next day, the flames were so ferocious they illuminated nearly the whole of London. Thousands of people lost their lives, everyone had lost someone, many lost their whole family, all their belongings, their homes. London was just a pile of rubble, smoking. The poor, brave emergency services were working flat out but just couldn't cope.

Louisa suspected they would all eventually be killed by the German army and Britain would lose the war, but when she listened on the wireless to King George VI saying they must be all brave and muster through she felt stronger. The Queen even visited Hayes Wharf and clambered across a bomb site which had once been a warehouse.

On Christmas Eve 1940, Louisa even decorated the inside of the Anderson Shelter with some of her mum's Christmas paper chain decorations. Louisa cocked her head to one side as she remembered sitting at the little kitchen table with Gladys making them, how old would they have been she wondered? Probably about nine and ten years then. She held them to her heart then draped them down the back wall of the Shelter. She put a small green woollen stocking out for Harry which contained some knitted animals which Sylvia had made and posted to her, and a small book about ships which had been Stevie's and she would read to him when he was a bit older. His first Christmas and we've got to sleep in here. She blew a kiss to the paper chain.

"Merry Christmas, Mum and Gladys, wish you were here," she whispered before going back indoors.

Chapter Twenty-Four

One spring day, a few months after the funerals, Louisa woke up feeling happy and optimistic. She cleaned the whole house from top to bottom, humming a Vera Lynn song as she dusted. She scrubbed some clothes, hung them on the wooden dryer then made a big pot of vegetable and mutton stew. She would mash Harry's up, all squidgy for him. He had some teeth now. Penny next door popped in for a cup of tea, Louisa thought she seemed nice enough, a kind nature although quite secretive, her daughter Violet was just over a year old and a sweet little gentle girl. Louisa hadn't seen much of anybody recently as the bombing had been happening in the daytime as well so she felt like they lived in the air raid shelter. Penny had tried to get a house in a new place called Dagenham, she said it was the modern place to live, but the council refused her and said she could have No 13 Acacia Court or nothing.

Louisa did ask Penny if one of the two men she'd seen sitting on her doorstep was her brother but realised later that Penny hadn't answered. Maybe all the bombs have made her deaf.

Next day, Louisa got a lovely sympathetic letter from Sylvia in Biddenden, June and Mark also had all written little notes on it to her. She cried. Still no word from her dad, Stevie or James though but it might be a bit soon to expect a letter from James already. Louisa just prayed every night in bed that they were all right and to keep everybody safe. The post lady had tears in her eyes as she handed Louisa her letter.

"I just get so upset every day when I try to deliver these letters and the addresses don't exist anymore," she confided shaking her head.

"Last night was the first night in months we didn't hear a siren," answered Louisa puzzled, "I can't believe it! I wonder why?"

"Please, God, it's all over," replied the post lady trying to sound convincing but from the expression on her face Louisa could tell that she didn't hold out much hope.

One morning, Ma Pritchard turned up early banging on the door. Louisa hadn't even washed or dressed, she was just finishing feeding Harry his favourite breakfast of rusk biscuits mashed up with dried milk mixed with cooled boiled water. She had not been sleeping well recently, night after night she was having nightmares of bombings, sirens, screaming everywhere. Night after night dreaming of sitting in that awful shelter trying to feed Harry, keep him warm, shaking with fear, seeing her mum, hearing her scream 'Where's our Gladys' over and over again.

"Bananas! What are Bananas?" Louisa screamed, "I don't think I've ever seen them! Or did we have them when we were little?" Louisa wondered out loud. "Where did you get all this from Ma Pritchard? I'm so grateful surely you didn't carry it all' on the bus?"

Ma Pritchard had brought a box of food with jam in and sugar and some rice. Louisa hadn't seen any jam since she was in Biddenden. They sat and drank tea and Ma Pritchard entertained Louisa with stories about her when she and Gladys were young, tales of Ma Pritchard and her mum dancing and getting up to all sorts. Louisa was sure half of it was made up but it was good to laugh. Ma Pritchard had a new home in Dagenham, it sounded lovely, she told Louisa the address and Louisa wrote it down. They also spoke of the latest stories about thousands of people being evacuated out of cities, sent to the countryside, to relatives or anybody who would have them.

"Well, I never," Ma Pritchard exclaimed, "have you heard about all this evacuating malarkey? I mean fancy sending your four-year-old off on a train with a bit of card around his neck to a place where he or she don't know anyone, not a soul, you don't know where they're going, don't even know the people who they're going to live with."

"They could do anything to your child," Louisa agreed.

"Where did you get all this fancy food from?" Louisa repeated prodding Ma Pritchard's stomach.

"You still haven't told me – you're a dark horse you are."

"My friend at the East London Docks sees me all right," Ma Pritchard said with a wink.

"Don't go asking how I pay him back though," she laughed to herself as she headed towards the front door.

"And don't you go telling anyone about my black market goodies or they'll be no more for you young lady and handsome Harry," she whispered cheekily as she patted Louisa's face and smothered Harry with slobbering kisses. It had been a lovely day.

Another lovely day was when Penny and Louisa went to Greenwich on the bus. It had a lady bus driver! Now that the government had sent all the men away to fight in the war the females had taken over 'men's jobs'. Apparently, according to The Daily Mirror, all the women were doing fantastic. Not only in the newspapers but there was so much admiration for how fabulous the women were doing, up and down the United Kingdom they had risen to the challenge and were working in factories, driving tanks, building ships, learning how to be plumbers and motor car mechanics. There were posters up on any wall that may be standing with pictures of glamorous women with scarves tied around their heads and spanners in their hands saying things like 'Look Lovely for the war effort' and 'Give our boys a boost with your beauty'.

On the bus journey there, they couldn't believe how many buildings were missing. Great big holes in streets and areas, it looked like more than half of London had gone. It was so sad. When will it ever end? Suddenly Louisa had a fright, she hadn't had a period for ages, when was it? Surely before her mum and Gladys had died. Penny said shock can stop periods but Louisa thought it was more likely to be James and his 'hours long love making that night' Louisa smiled to herself. But seriously how will she cope if she is pregnant again?

"Has your mother-in-law invited you down there again?" Penny asked Louisa on the bus journey home. Violet and Harry were both asleep in their mother's arms.

"Now there's this mass evacuation surely they'll let you go and stay there. It's got to be safer and at least you know them, they're not strangers, you know who you'd be going to, wouldn't you?" Penny chattered away but Louisa wasn't really concentrating just trying to remember when her last period was.

"You never know they might even let me and Violet bunk in with you," Penny teased.

Louisa and Penny had taken a very meagre picnic for them all, Violet ran around on the grass with no socks on and a funny little hat that she refused to share even with Harry, she was giggling with delight and Harry was trying to follow her half walking half falling on his bottom laughing hysterically. He was trying to walk now but it was painful to watch, he tottered like a little torpedo from Louisa to Penny just making it before collapsing into his chubby legs. He was so wobbly. It was very amusing to watch.

"No, it's a bit of a mystery really, I don't understand but they said they were too old to have a baby keeping them all awake all night," laughed Louisa.

"Oh, how selfish, I mean it's all right for all us to be bombed to death and kept awake all night by the Luftwaffe but they can't even lose a bit of sleep to a baby," Penny said whilst pouting her vivid red lips at the bus conductor.

The bus conductor winked at Penny, laughed then let them off their fares! Louisa whacked Penny across the arm. "You hussy," she laughed and then thought, *I must try and get some of that red lipstick before James comes home again!*

"Well, blimey, it's the first bloke we've seen all day," explained Penny then added sheepishly, "Sorry, didn't mean to say 'bombed to death!' Not very tactful am I?"

The bus journey seemed like it took ages, Louisa was worried, they had been advised over the radio not to go far and although Greenwich was only a few miles away she was starting to feel anxious. The journey took three times as long as it used to, the poor driver was avoiding holes in the road and there was bomb debris strewn everywhere. A group of firemen were working on a building that looked like it was about to collapse so that caused a big traffic jam which added even more time to their journey. Everybody on the bus was talking about the fall of Belgium, Holland and Luxembourg to Germany. German soldiers had actually marched into their countries, their homes, their town halls and said, "We're in charge now, do as we say or we will shoot you."

"What a cheek, they just want to try and march in to my flat," a tall, very glamorous red-haired lady squealed.

"It will be us next," added an old lady who was sitting in the seat in front of her with her arms tightly folded, as if she was going to keep the enemy at bay with her body language.

"I think we should all just go dancing and drinking while we can," continued the glamorous red head looking directly at the bus conductor, "I mean what you got to lose, look at all them poor buggers up in Clydebank in Scotland, hundreds of them got bombed, Belfast and Liverpool too, they lost even more lives up there, I bet all those poor buggers wished they had gone out dancing more, bloody Germans they don't care who they drop them on, churches, schools, even hospitals they haven't got any morals!"

When they eventually did get back to their homes a man was standing on Penny's doorstep.

"Oh, gosh," Penny muttered, "Can Violet come in with you and Harry for half hour?"

"Of course, love," Louisa replied, "Is everything all right? Who is he?"

Penny didn't answer Louisa, just shyly smiled and walked up to her front door, he was a very handsome, tall chap about thirty years old and looked very well-dressed. Violet was so excited to be coming in with Louisa and Harry, she was such a little dolly she even gave Harry her precious hat.

If I ever have a daughter, I hope she's just like Violet, Louisa was daydreaming, her and James would have a child each, he would have his son Harry, she could have her Dolly, yes that's what she would call her daughter 'Dolly' and tie pretty ribbons in her hair.

A lovely day are not the words Stevie would use to describe his life at that moment. He opened his eyes, his head was banging viciously, his lips was as dry as cardboard, he couldn't lift himself up, he was laying on something hard, hard and cold, he inched his head very slowly to the right. He was on a rock solid mud floor. The room smelt disgusting, there were other people in the room, a great many of them but he couldn't make any of them out, his vision was blurry. He was conscious of them speaking amongst themselves but it was very hushed. He tried to lick his lips but his tongue felt like a barber's razor, he didn't know where he was, he couldn't feel the trembling of his ship, the thumping in his head was unbearable, he couldn't keep his eyes open, his head slipped sideways and he slumped back into unconsciousness.

Chapter Twenty-Five

Rosie lay in her bed staring at the yellowing ceiling, her sister wasn't beside her, if she was already up and out then it must be quite late. Rosie tried to muster up some enthusiasm to get out of bed. Since Heart's Bakers factory had been bombed she missed her job so much she could cry. She went to the labour exchange most days and the queue was enormous. The ladies in there had put her name on the waiting list for any job, Rosie had stressed she would accept any position. All this advertising for women to join the workforce yet when you try they can't get you a job.

"Now get a grip, young lady, chin up, I might get a bit of good news today," she mused as she kicked her blankets off and made her way to the wash bowl on her chest of drawers. She mixed some bicarbonate of soda with a little splash of water from her jug and created a thick paste, rubbing it gently onto her chin then spreading upward to her nose and forehead she looked out the window into the street. It seemed so light now half the buildings had gone, she would never get used to it. She massaged the mixture over her top lip, put a few inches of water into the bowl and splashed her face clean. Fifty splashes Penny had advised her that was the amount needed to make your skin fresh and clear. But you weren't allowed to use too much water, that was rationed too. Patting her face with the towel she eyed her modest make up collection. One poppy red lipstick which she meant to keep for special occasions but could never resist the urge to put on, one brown eyebrow pencil which she also used to draw lines down the back of her legs to create the illusion of stockings and tripled up as an eyeliner pencil too. She had a small blue tin of Vaseline petroleum jelly which she swept onto her eyelashes to help them grow and on to her lips at night before going to bed to keep them soft and dewy. Beside her make up collection perched a grey pumice stone, that little godsend removed dry skin from the soles of her feet and if she rubbed it fast enough it took the hairs off her legs as well, there was no such luxury as a ladies razor in the Second Word War.

Stockings needed Nylon and that Great Britain didn't have so all the girls were faking them with eyebrow pencilled lines down the back centre of their legs. Apparently Nylon was used for parachutes and other necessities for the war effort and there was no Nylon left for sexy stockings.

Opening her cupboard, she eyed her outfits, there wasn't many, whilst she was working at Heart's Bakers it didn't bother her as she could wear her white overall every day. But now she had to think about what to get dressed in and it was coming monotonous donning the same old clothes. If only she could be a Land girl and get an attractive overall to wear with her poppy red lipstick, pencilled on eyebrows and a headscarf worn in a beguiling fashion.

"Stop feeling miserable," she chided herself again, "Today something great is going to happen, I'm going to get a job and I may even get a letter from Frank."

Rosie decided after she was dressed to nip in to see Louisa, perhaps Louisa would walk with her to the labour exchange. Even perhaps Louisa might like to be a Land girl herself, then it would be like the good old days working together. Harry could either walk with them to the labour exchange or go in his pram although he was far too big for that now.

Louisa was in her kitchen preparing breakfast when she looked at her tummy and just knew she was expecting again, she danced all around the table with Harry in her arms giggling, he loved it! There was a loud banging on the door. It was Rosie.

"Oh, come in, sugar plum it's so good to see you," Louisa said putting Harry down and hugging Rosie, "I miss you so much, fancy a cuppa?"

After chatting for ages and feeding Harry Louisa rushed upstairs to quickly get washed and dressed. She felt excited about going to the labour exchange with Rosie. Rosie had suggested she may get a job and Louisa thought, *Why not?* She hoped they may have some suggestions for a vacancy where Harry could go along with her.

"Harry do you want to go for a long walk with Mummy and Rosie?" Louisa asked Harry.

"You can wear your hat!"

As they strolled down Acacia Court towards Bermondsey Walk, everyone they passed wanted to stop at chat, tell them all the latest news and gossip. They finally arrived at the labour exchange and there were only two women in front of them. There was a kind looking lady with short fair hair and gold-framed glasses behind the desk who smiled at Rosie and said she should definitely receive a letter offering her a position of employment during this week. Rosie couldn't stop grinning. The lady would not give any more information and turned her attention to Louisa. She seemed quite optimistic that they could find a position for Louisa that would accommodate Harry and the girls both felt like skipping out into the sunny London street.

Rosie filled Louisa in on the state of her mum and dad's marriage all the way home and the girls parted at Rosie's front door promising to let each other know if they had any news of a job.

Finally, when they got indoors, Harry took his hat off, Louisa sat on the sofa thinking about James and their new baby caressing the hat. As she turned it over she had to look twice, inside was written 'Frank Butcher' Louisa was sure she had heard that name before and made a mental note to ask Penny who had given the hat to Violet.

Chapter Twenty-Six

The following Monday morning Louisa answered the door to the post lady. The females of Great Britain were gradually taking over all the 'men's jobs' and so now they had a 'post lady' instead of the pre-war 'postman'. They had to keep the country going. All the talk was of how fabulous the women were doing, from John o' Groats to Land's End, women had risen to the challenge and were working in ammunitions factories making bombs! Driving tanks, building ships, learning how to be plumbers and even engineers And to top it all they were doing an amazing job, even better than the men could!

The post lady smiled sheepishly and handed Louisa two letters, Louisa thanked her and went to the sofa to sit down and open them. Louisa's heart was thumping as she looked at them both to see if one was from James, she recognised Sylvia's handwriting and tore at the envelope.

'Laburnham Farm
Biddenden Village
Near Ashford
Kent
June 1941
Dear Louisa

I hope this letter finds you and Little Harry safe and well? Please give him a big hug from Granma Sylvia.

I haven't heard from James for a while and was wondering if you have had any letters from him lately? I know it's difficult for the Royal Post Office to manage and transport the mail but I do worry about him. Have you heard how your dad and brother are too? Has there been any news from anyone?

Mr French asked me to politely request Mark not to visit so frequently, he didn't give an explanation. When I relayed the message to Mark he didn't seem upset but I bet he won't be bring him any more rabbits! I wonder if Mr French is suffering from the miseries, he just seems to sit in his shed by the chicken hut all day every day not saying much to anybody even to June.

I trust you are coping fine on your own my dear? I know you are a strong girl. These are tough times.

I have been very busy here, do you remember the Land Army girls whom we watched from the landing window just after you had Little Harry? Well, we have two of them lodging here in your old bedroom. Maureen and Carol. They are funny but it's so much more work for me. They pay rent and I now have to prepare their lunch for them to take to work and prepare them an evening meal as well as June, Cyril and myself. I do all their washing too! They do work really long hours, about fifty a week although Maureen did say they won't have to work so long in the winter months because it will be darker and they earn nearly two pounds per week! Good money isn't it! Although Carol said they have to kill rats if they see them! She said the Hop Farm is swarming with them. I hope the rats don't start coming from the Hop farm into our garden! I would scream and run in the opposite direction! I could not kill one!

If there was any way I could get you down here to be a Land Army girl I would but I just do not have the time to look after Little Harry if you were at work, I think June would probably help but not sure Cyril would agree to you living here again even though Harry's older now and hopefully sleeping right through the night. Sorry, my dear.

Anyway, we also have lots of planes flying over us all day and night now. There is an airfield at Headcorn which is about six miles away and the Air Force is using it. It' so noisy! Also, although I haven't seen them, Ashford is really busy with nurses and doctors and all sorts of medical staff as they are bringing back many of the injured to the hospital there. I've heard all sorts of terrible stories about the most horrific injuries, men losing legs and arms. Oh, I, just like everybody else, can't wait for this war to finish. Please let us win. I'm worried June said the other day that if Germany does move into England they will land at Dover first and invade Kent! I think I will move back to London!

Please give Harry more cuddles from me and if you hear from James can you let me know if you have time. Keep strong, my dear.

Love Sylvia

"Oh, bang goes our evacuation to Biddenden," Louisa told Harry.

Harry ran around the room shouting,

"Bang, bang, bang."

"In actual fact," thought Louisa out loud, "that's quite a chatty letter for Sylvia and in actual fact everybody is quite chatty lately aren't they Harry? Nobody seems to be grumbling, it's just as if it's a big party, everybody seems really cheerful and excited."

Harry agreed with her nodding his head and chanting,

"Mum, mum, mum, mum," whilst leaning against her knees.

Louisa mused over Sylvia's comments, would that have been the reason for Cyril asking her to leave. Had he heard the Land girls needed rooms and could pay him rent? Louisa nodded to herself, she was sure that was the real reason it all made sense.

The second letter was from H.M. War Office. Oh, no, Louisa felt sick, sick and numb. At first glance she thought it was from the labour exchange. She was shaking so much she took Harry's hand and slowly walked him next door to Penny's house.

"Can you come in a minute," Louisa asked whilst handing the letter to Penny.

"I couldn't open it on my own, I was just too scared of what's going to be inside?

"Oh," said Penny, she was just as worried as Louisa, "it's addressed to your mum." "

Penny made them a pot of strong tea and took a sharp knife from the cutlery drawer to slice open the envelope with. She cleared her throat and didn't make any eye contact with Louisa as she read the contents.

'The War Office
Ministry of Defence
Westminster
London
W1

Dear Mrs Foster

It is with our great regret that we write to inform you Mr Thomas Foster passed away after suffering from Tuberculosis in Asia whilst serving for the Royal Navy as a Merchant Seaman.

We have given him a respectable burial at sea and send you and your family our deepest sympathy.

A Royal Navy representative will call upon you in the near future.

Yours sincerely

Mr E. Skecher

Ministry of Defence'

After the first line Louisa couldn't hear properly any more. Her eyes were covered in a red fog. Her head was pounding as loud as someone banging on a door. Her darling, darling daddy. Tuberculosis? When? She looked at the letter, there was no date on it, how long had he been dead? He's been dead and I was dancing around the kitchen table this morning.

"Oh, my god, I can't deal with any more pain, my world has gone," she sobbed into Penny's shoulder. It only seemed like five minutes ago she had been picking gooseberries in Biddenden with the sun burning her back and all her loved ones were alive. Penny was so kind, she guided her up the stairs and sweetly ordered her to rest on the bed.

"The shock is not good for you if you are having a new baby, your dad is with your mum and Gladys now and they're all up in heaven together, I'll keep an eye on Harry and Violet downstairs, you lay here and just breath slowly, I'll bring you up another cup of tea in an hour or so."

Louisa tried to sleep but just couldn't, she spread herself out across the bed looking at the ceiling, she was so scared her heart was fluttering, *Oh, god, when will it all end, what's going to happen to us all, why did I have to have a life with a war in it?*

Chapter Twenty-Seven

The chatter in the street was 'Great Britain' was winning and the Second World War will soon be over, Louisa desperately wanted that to be right, she'd even sit with Penny and Rosie at night and listen to Winston Churchill broadcasting on the radio telling them the latest situation, Britain had attacked Italy earlier in the year and it was going to be a 'Long Slog'. It didn't sound like it would be over soon to Louisa, Rosie and Penny. Winston Churchill said he was a British Bulldog and would lead them all to victory. But when you looked out of Louisa's window and saw the bomb sites with children playing on them that didn't look like victory.

They also listened to broadcasts of how to make delicious recipes from practically nothing. Harry was eating quite a lot now and Louisa was having to eat less so he could have her rations. She would have to start cooking more vegetables because that could fill him up and they were not rationed and they're good for you. Also she had found some of the runner beans growing in the garden that her dad had planted long ago. It comforted her that her Little Harry was eating runner beans planted by her darling daddy. How they had survived The Blitz was anyone's guess! A miracle sent from heaven!

"Why don't we look if we can get a job?" Penny suggested one day, "Maybe we could work opposite hours and then I could mind Harry while you work and you could have Violet while I work?

"Oh, my gosh," exclaimed Louisa, "What a brilliant idea! I just can't believe I didn't think of that earlier, I've fancied getting some work for ages, I just can't make ends meet lately and Rosie and I even went to The labour exchange but I haven't heard anything back from them yet."

She wrote letters to James, Stevie, Sylvia and Ma Pritchard to tell them about her dad. They were very short notes she didn't know what else to write about, felt so numb, she didn't want to tell them about the new baby in the same letter so left that bit of information out. She did answer Sylvia's questions saying she was fine and hadn't heard from James, she hadn't heard from her brother once since he'd joined up and prayed he was okay. She didn't mention anything else, it would have felt too inappropriate to discuss farms and hospitals in a letter about her dad dying.

Her belly was growing, she thought it looked bigger this time around, must be all those bananas from Ma Pritchard or was it to be a girl? A little Dolly?!

One day Louisa and Harry went out long walk, they were out a couple of hours, they walked along the River Thames and watched a boat having crates unloaded, Louisa gave Harry a running commentary as to what was happening, she reckoned that would help his vocabulary and stop her going mad from having no one to talk to. They looked at all the bombed buildings and Louisa explained how they had looked previously and why they were now piles of rubble. They sat on a wall for a while watching the seagulls with Louisa holding Harry's hand very tightly.

She was thinking about Sylvia's letter, she couldn't be a Land Army girl, now she was expecting again; anyway, the work would probably be too strenuous.

"We are lucky, we are lucky, we are lucky, there is always someone worse off." Louisa didn't know what she would do without Harry, she was bursting with love for him, she was lonely at night and couldn't wait for James to come home, also the money he had left her last time was running out, she told herself she must be a spendthrift from then on but she was so grateful to have her lovely son. She did receive a payment from the Royal Navy which she had to collect from the post office every week but it just didn't seem to be going very far these days.

"I know, Harry," she exclaimed looking into his beautiful blue eyes, "let's go down the labour exchange again see if they have got any good news for us yet." Louisa stood up from the wall purposefully and walked Harry as fast as his little legs would go.

98

"Shall we go and get your pram first, Harry?" Louisa knew he was too big for it now but they had been out walking for a good two hours and he was so slow she wanted to get to the labour exchange as quickly as possible. They stopped off at home and popped Harry into his pram, she picked a bottle of cooled boiled water that she had prepared earlier from the wooden draining board in the kitchen and bumped the pram out of the front door.

Harry looked tired and lay back drinking his water, he was squashed and Louisa laughed. They headed off up Acacia Court and on the corner passed the newspaper stand which had its usual wooden easel on the pavement on which they displayed a poster with the latest news story written across it in bold black ink. Today's poster said,

'WE SINK BISMARK.'

Louisa felt sick she had no idea what ship James was on, say he was on the Bismarck and has been sunk?

"Oh, Mummy is a silly girl, Harry! As if we would sink our own ship, The Bismarck must be a German ship! Louisa twittered and bounced herself and Harry's pram happily in the direction of the labour exchange.

As they turned into Commercial Road she thought she could see Eve, her old boss from Heart's Bakers walking ahead of her.

"Eve," Louisa called quickening her pace.

Eve obviously hadn't heard her.

"Eve," Louisa shouted as loud as she could.

"Oh, watcha, Louisa!" Eve turned around and waited. "How are you and little Harry?" Eve smiled at Harry who was just about to nod off. "Ah, bless him, he's got so big!"

"I'm fine, thanks, Eve, just off to labour exchange to see if I can get another job, you must miss working, what are you doing now all day?" Louisa was pleased to have an adult to talk to.

"Love a duck, I've just been to John Heart's house, ogh, it's' so lovely over in Stepney, East of the river, his house stands facing a lovely little park with trees in so green over there. Anyway, well, it's not official yet but he's got somewhere to open another bakery and has asked me to go back and run it and see if I can get any of the old staff back!"

"No, love a duck! What a coincidence!" "It must be fate my mum and dad arranged this," Louisa laughed.

"Well, I was just going see what the old factory looks like, see if I can see anything laying about that we can use, of course I won't go onto the rubble and then I was going to see Rosie, you can tell her now! If you tell her and then I'll pop around tomorrow morning to her house about 10 o'clock, is that okay? The new site is just by the Tower of London so we only have to walk over Tower Bridge I know it's a bit further but it's better than having no job at all."

Louisa stopped walking, Eve turned to her.

"Well, I am supposed to get women, married or single, to work 40 hours a week and the government will help me with the wages. You'll get one pound, five shillings and sixpence,

I'm sure you could use the money and that's more than I used to pay! Fancy it, Love?" Eve asked with a hopeful look on her face.

"Oh." Louisa was suddenly disappointed. "I can't do 40 hours as I've got no one to look after Harry all that time." Louisa was aware Eve knew about her mum and Gladys and Louisa hoped she hadn't forgotten and she didn't have to give a great long winded explanation.

"Oh, that's a shame, love." Eve was disappointed too, Louisa had been a good worker, very conscientious and if she could just fill the vacancies with people who knew the work it would be much easier for her, less time consuming if there was no training to do.

"Got no aunties about or kindly neighbours? All got to pull together these days, love."

"Oh, of course." Louisa felt a fool. "My neighbour Penny has no family either and she has a young daughter I know it's a lot to ask but is there any chance we could share the work and wages?" Louisa was gazing at Eve with her big brown eyes, she really wanted to do this.

"Errrr, well," Eve was stumped, she'd never had two people sharing one wage before, she rubbed her chin, "Errrr, well." She was trying to think, "Errrr, well, I don't see why we can't give it a try," she eventually responded. "Errr, I'll have to check with John Heart, I'm sure he will be fine about it though, he will just be glad I managed to get some of the old hands back, means less training and I will have to check with the Town Hall about two people doing the same job but I won't do that for a few weeks.

Beggars can't be choosers, if they want me to employ women they will just have to agree with whoever I can get hold of!" Eve fell backwards, sniggering, "Cripes, sorry, love! Don't mean any offence." Eve was obviously relieved she had filled one position.

"I will have to meet your neighbour first, Penny you say her name is?" She looked at Louisa.

"Is she trustworthy and clean like you and Rosie?" they both had a big grin on their faces.

Tell her to pop in and see me at Rosie's tomorrow and you can both start next week, God willing the Jerries don't get us first! And you can even have a new hairnet!" she patted Louisa on the shoulder.

"They've moved the ovens and are just setting everything up now, it's bigger than the old place but that's all right, probably make it cooler."

"Actually," Louisa stopped in her tracks and looked back towards Eve, "I think Rosie's sister could help you and maybe even her mum Betty too?" Louisa suggested smiling, she turned and waved at Eve.

"I will go and see Rosie straight away Eve, see you tomorrow."

"Brilliant, see you tomorrow, Louisa."

Eve and Louisa rushed off in different directions full of optimism. Harry had fallen fast asleep.

On the return journey, the newspaper stand had a new poster'

'VICTORY AS GERMAN BATTLESHIP TORPEDOED AND SUNK BY ROYAL NAVY SHIPS AND PLANES ENDING ONE OF THE MOST INTENSIVE NAVAL BATTLE'S EVER!'

Louisa sailed past with her nose in the air trundling Harry along fast asleep in his pram, she was oblivious to everything except telling Rosie and Penny about her lucky encounter with Eve.

Chapter Twenty-Eight

Rosie was sitting on the sofa knitting. She had decided to try and make Louisa a matinee coat for the new baby. Betty had a footstool beside the sofa where she stored all her craft needs, it contained balls of different coloured wool, threads and sewing needles, knitting needles, all types of buttons, hooks and eyes, press studs and a couple of pairs of scissors. When Rosie and Caren were younger they loved their mum's craft box so much as if it were overflowing with expensive jewels from pirate ships and the Tower of London.

Betty would let them feel the silky ribbons she had coiled neatly on the lower tray and show them all the different coloured threads she had collected for years and some had even come from her mum, their Nana, who was long gone to the angels now.

The box had round bun shaped feet and a tapestry cover across the top so you could also use it to rest your weary feet on if you had had a particularly hard day at work. Rosie chose some lime green wool because she intelligently thought that would be suitable for either a baby girl or baby boy. The only problem was she hated knitting, she hated anything crafty and was just no good at it. She kept dropping stitches and Betty helped her correct the matinee coat time after time. Caren had inherited their mum's flair for needlework but it had passed Rosie by. She had to do something though, the post lady had walked straight past their front door today so there was no letter of an employment offer today. Betty was humming in the kitchen whilst preparing their evening meal. It suddenly dawned on Rosie that her mum sounded happy. Yes, happy! Puzzled Rosie called out,

"You okay, Mum? Do you want me to come and help you with the vegetables or anything?"

After a few seconds of silence, her mum appeared at the open kitchen door.

"Yes, I'm great, love, why are you offering to help?" Betty was smirking. "You gone wrong again on that knitting?"

"Not as far as I know!" Rosie replied as Betty walked towards her and nodded her head.

"Looks grand, does that Rosie, we'll make a seamstress of you yet my, darling daughter."

Rosie was definitely flummoxed now, 'darling daughter', her mum had never called her that in her life. Something strange was happening.

"I was thinking, love, do you reckon we should start making your wedding dress? Because I was in the butcher's today and the lady in front of me said her son was allowed home for two days leave and he got a special licence and married his childhood sweetheart then went back to fight, apparently they're allowing that so say Frank turns up and proposes you won't have a dress to wear." Betty lit a cigarette as there was a knock on the window.

"Who's that, I wonder," Betty blew out the smoke and walked towards the door.

"Hello, love, Rosie, it's Louisa."

Rosie hid the knitting needles and ball of wool down the side of the sofa and stood up.

"She's got Harry in the pram, leave him there, Lou, I'll leave the door open so we can keep an eye on him, by the way have you got that pattern your mum used for your wedding dress while I think of it?"

"Errr, I'll have a look for it," Louisa replied but didn't ask who it was for as she was bursting to tell them the good news.

"We've got our jobs back! I just saw Eve! She said she was coming to see you, well, after she had been to the Heart's Bakers bombsite, but well, anyway, they've got new premises just over Tower Bridge and they're kitting them out now as we speak and it should be up and running by next week and we can all go back to work."

Louisa danced around the little sitting room, Rosie clasped her arms and joined in. Betty roared with laughter.

"Eve says you and Caren can join them too if you fancy a job."

"Hooray!" screamed Betty, stubbed out her cigarette and joined in the dancing.

"And I am going to ask Penny to share the job with me and we can look after each other's little ones while we're not at work."

"Hooray!" screamed Betty again, they all waved their arms in the air and sang.

"Hooray, Hooray, Hooray, Hooray!"

Louisa walked briskly from Rosie's house and banged on Penny's door, luckily no strange men were there, well as far as she could tell. She stood at the front door, she wanted to be quick Harry hadn't eaten for hours now and she was sure he would soon wake up starving. He must have been so tired from all the walking earlier and the River Thames air, he hadn't even stirred when Louisa, Rosie and Betty were dancing about like lunatics in Rosie's sitting room.

She had been fretting all the way home wondering if she had done the right thing and hoping with all her heart that they could work this out between them. Penny was as delighted as everybody else, Louisa gave a big sigh of relief.

"Oh, that's just brilliant news!" Penny flung her arms around Louisa and squeezed her tight. "Thank you so much, when shall I go and see her? Now I can give up…" Penny abruptly stopped mid-sentence.

"Do you want a cup of tea," Penny offered.

"No, I won't stop, thanks for offering but I must go in and feed Little Harry. Eve, the manageress, she is lovely, you will like her, well, she wants to meet you tomorrow she is going to Rosie's at 10 o'clock so I'll give you a knock about ten to ten in the morning and we can go and see her together. We can take Harry and Violet with us, I'm sure Betty won't mind and I doubt we will be there for long."

"By the way," Louisa said as she pushed the heavy pram across the pavement to her house.

"Where did Violet get that hat from that she gave to Harry? He loves dressing up in it."

"Oh, gosh, I can't remember one of the men that's been around here, they didn't give it to her someone just left it here and she tried it on after they'd gone," Penny replied looking ashamed.

Louisa and Penny were both so excited and Louisa later listened to her favourite wireless programme *Women's Hour*, that night they broadcast how to create 'Lord Woolton's pie' a recipe using turnips, carrots and swedes, or you could add any vegetables you had left in your kitchen. Gloria the presenter on *Women's Hour* said with her purring voice that it was taking the nation by storm, everybody was eating it. It did sound delicious and Louisa had been meaning to get the recipe for ages. She jotted it down whilst Gloria explained over the wireless, it had been created at the Savoy Hotel in London by their maître chef de cuisine. Louisa promised to make the posh nosh for her and Harry next time she had been to the greengrocers. Now she had' a job she would be able to buy more food. That night, she and Little Harry enjoyed the best night's sleep they had had since Harry was born.

The following morning Penny had drawn up a rota already, with Louisa working Monday, Wednesday and Friday the first week and Penny covering the Tuesday and Thursday, then the next week it was opposite. Whoever was working would drop Harry or Violet off to the other at whatever time they had to leave and they could lay in bed with them.

"Well, we can only try." They both agreed thinking about the lack of sleep!

The sheet of paper Penny had written the rota on had a little PS at the bottom saying,

"From now on you can share Violet's pushchair!"

"Oh, well done," smiled Louisa, "That's really good of you! Thanks." Life was getting better every day!

Louisa and Rosie were ten minutes early and Betty made them all a cup of tea. Betty had lipstick on and the house was spotless.

"Oh, I forgot to look for that dress pattern," Louisa suddenly remembered, "I'll go and look for it as soon as I get home, who is it for?"

"Oh, no, this is embarrassing," Rosie said looking at her mum, "She said I should make my wedding dress now so when Frank asks me to marry him I'm ready! But do you think that's putting a jinx on it? Do you? It feels a bit funny to me."

Louisa and Penny politely laughed but did silently agree with Rosie. Say he doesn't ask her to marry him? Louisa was thinking.

"Well, if he doesn't ask you, someone will," laughed Caren, "and I can have the bedroom all to myself!"

"What will your name be when you marry Frank," enquired Louisa while they all looked out the window hoping to see Eve.

"Mrs Butcher."

Eve arrived and the children were so quiet and well behaved and Eve seemed to approve of Penny and liked Betty and Caren and it all went swimmingly.

"See you Monday then, girlies, not 4 anymore but a 5 am start so you all get a lay in!" Eve dashed to the door.

"Sorry to rush off but places to go, people to see! Take care."

Chapter Twenty-Nine

As it happened the children didn't even wake up, they went to sleep in one bed and woke up in the morning in a bed next door unaware they had been moved. Harry was getting a right heavy lump now, he would be three next birthday, Louisa tried to have a nap in the afternoons, after getting in from work she would put Harry down and give him a bottle of juice then just try to grab thirty minutes quite time. Sometimes it was successful sometimes not but there was a war going on and they all had to muddle through together.

One Friday evening, a war warden knocked on the door. *Bang, bang, bang, bang, bang.*

"Excuse me, ma'am," he had a lisp and sprayed his words at her, "do you mind if we search your house, we have an escaped convict missing 'bout these streets? Have you noticed or heard anything odd sweetheart?"

"Oh, my gosh, really? How scary, yes, of course, come in, no I haven't noticed anything, oh, my God, can you check upstairs as well? I'm scared now," Louisa pleaded.

Of course, sweetheart, that's what we're here for," as another warden, whom she recognised, followed him in, they tried to bounce up the stairs but it was more like a crawl.

"Oooooggghhhh, my blinking back's killing me," the first warden groaned spitting everywhere.

"Aghhh, my knee," then, "Ouch, aghhh, ouch," on every other step complained the second warden.

Louisa stepped into the front room containing her laughter, "Oh, please, don't let there be an escaped convict up there! Because those two will never overpower him!"

"Ouch, Oooooggghhh." They limped back down the stairs, "All safe upstairs we'll just check your back for you." The second warden clasped Louisa's hands, "Sorry about your Ma and sister, God always takes the best first."

"Oh, thank you, I thought I knew your face, do you live in the Peabody Buildings? I've had a letter from the Ministry of Defence and I've lost my dad too," Louisa confided in him.

"Oh, you poor poppet, no! Gosh, I'm so sorry to hear that, if there's ever anything we can do, I'm Derek and me Missus is called Muriel, I'm sure you would know her if you see her, she's always laughing, my Muriel, never see her without a smile on her face. Anyway, honestly, just give us a shout, I mean it if you need anything just ask poppet, we live in the third block, number seven."

The lisping warden limped in from the backyard.

"No convicts hereabouts, sweetheart, checked your shelter, and outside lavatory, just make sure you keeps your doors and windows secure and we'll let everyone know when we've nabbed him."

"Oh, and don't you go worrying yourself," they both called cheerily as they left.

Harry was sitting on the rug playing with a spoon in front of the fire, he loved spoons, give him a spoon and he was happy for hours. "Don't go worrying yourself," Louisa repeated, that's all she did, worry all night long, she kept hearing creaks and noises and doors opening and windows opening and imagining escaped convicts walking up the stairs to get her and Little Harry in their beds.

Rat-a-tat-tat.

Rat-a-tat-tat.

Louisa sat bolt upright in bed, it was daylight, she ran down the stairs, still half asleep, it was Penny.

"Have I woken you up, lazy bones?" Penny teased.

Louisa walked through to the kitchen to get the kettle on, what time was it?

"Have you heard they caught the escaped convict?" Penny couldn't wait to spill the beans.

"He was in Joey's air raid shelter with a great big knife to slit someone's throat."

"No! Is that what he was going to do!" Louisa was so shocked. "How do you know that Penny?"

"Well, I don't actually know but I can guess, can't I? Have you got that kettle on yet?" Penny replied.

Louisa had written to James and told him their happy nappy news many weeks ago now and she had today at last received back from him the most beautiful emotional letter he had ever sent her. He sounded really homesick, she had no idea where he was as he couldn't say, they weren't allowed to give any information, in case the Germans got hold of any letters and could gather information from them. They weren't allowed to put any date on any correspondence so Louisa didn't know how old it was or how long ago it had been written and really Louisa was just grateful that they were able to deliver all the post it must have taken a massive amount of organisation. James only mentioned they were experiencing treacherous conditions and that there were many enemy vessels around them She sat down and wrote a letter to Sylvia straight away, hopefully James had written to his mum at the same time as he written Louisa's letter, but you obviously couldn't guarantee when letters were delivered or if they would ever be delivered at all, there were more important matters to deal with at the moment. Louisa told Sylvia the happy news and thank God James was all right. She told her about her new job and said to say hello to June, Mark, Cyril and the Land girls, Maureen and Carol, finishing with 'oh, and give the cats a stroke from me and Harry!'

After writing the letters it made her think about Stevie, it wasn't right, she had not had one letter from him, he wouldn't do that to them. He would know they would worry and he would want to let them know he was okay, if he was okay. If he had sent her a letter or two that had not been delivered that was understandable, but to have received nothing in four years was grave. Louisa didn't know how she could find out about him but decided she would ask about if there was any way of tracing a missing seaman.

Chapter Thirty

One Saturday, Louisa got two buses all the way to Dagenham. She had written to Ma Pritchard twice and had no word back. She wasn't really surprised as she didn't think Ma Pritchard had time to write letters and as much as Louisa loved her she knew she was really bad at keeping in touch and she wasn't even sure if she could read and write! Anyway, she thought she'd get the bus and go and see if this 'Darling Dagenham' was as nice as they were all saying. They had started to build the new town of Dagenham just before the war started but all the construction work had then drawn to a halt. Apparently, it was a huge area of old chalk quarries out to the east of London on the border of Essex. They were going to have new shops and schools and even a motor car factory owned by an American called Henry Ford that would give employment to hundreds of men in the new town.

Well, it took hours and it was no better, definitely no better than Bermondsey, white, greyish houses like boxes stuck on a drafts board. No dark bricks like Bermondsey. Beautiful Bermondsey beats darling Dagenham Louisa told Harry.

She kept stopping and asking people for Ma Pritchard's street. after going backwards and forwards, everybody was friendly and wanted to help but sent her in wrong direction. *They probably don't know themselves as its all fairly new,* Louisa thought; she did notice that there weren't as much bomb damage there as where she lived. She also spotted a newspaper stand like the one near her home and the poster displayed,

'MEETING BETWEEN WINSTON CHURCHILL AND
FRANKLIN D. ROSEVELT.'

Finally, after what felt like hours she found the street, quite neat, just plain houses really, she quickened her pace to get to Ma Pritchard's door number and you guessed it! No one there!

Louisa peered through the window to the left of the front door, There was no furniture just an empty room with a tiled fire place!

But, thought Louisa to herself, *that didn't mean Ma Pritchard didn't live there, she'd probably sold any furniture that she had owned or broke it up and put it on the fire! That is if she had any in the first place!*

Louisa tried to look through the letter box but it wouldn't open. She stood at the door tapping for a couple of minutes.

"What shall we do now, handsome?" She pulled a face at Harry lazing in the pushchair.

Louisa then decided to knock at the house next door. A lovely chubby lady with no teeth answered the door. She had a half smoked cigarette stuck to her lips like Ma Pritchard, a squashy round belly straining against a maroon jumper and grey woolly hat on her head with some jet black hair poking out the sides. Louisa explained she had come to see Ma Pritchard and had next door as their address but there appeared to be no one in. Did she know if they lived there? Or did she have the wrong door number or address maybe.

Mrs Chubby stared at Louisa.

"Ayyyyeeee," Mrs Chubby shouted, "speak up, love, you talk too quiet can't hear a word you saying."

Harry was getting inpatient, Louisa let him out of Violet's pushchair holding his hand and again went through the whole story about Ma Pritchard whilst hoisting Harry onto her hip.

"Oh, my dear," Mrs Chubby exclaimed really loudly.

"Ma Pritchard sold her daughter. Well, she said she had her adopted to a Canadian couple but I think she sold her and then flitted off with her black boyfriend back to London without paying the rent. Do you want to come in take the weight off your feet for a minute, love? Have you come far?" Mrs Chubby kindly offered.

Louisa nearly fainted.

Sold her?

Which daughter? June is nearly grown up! Phyllis and Joan had left home ages ago? How would she get to Canada? Canada was in the war too, on our side. Black boyfriend? What is she talking about? Louisa thought to herself. It was all too much to take in.

"Well, I think the daughter was glad to go really, between you and me." Louisa walked into the house with Harry leaving his pushchair outside the front door.

"I won't stop, I've come from London myself all the way on two buses, Ma Pritchard's been a good friend to my family all my life," Louisa protested, "but do you think I could use your lavatory please?"

The lavatory was gorgeous, downstairs not out in the backyard like Louisa's. But that was the only good thing about 'Darling Dagenham'.

"By the way, love," Mrs Chubby bellowed after Louisa as she was walking back down the road towards the bus stop, "If she owes you any money you'd better join the queue!"

"Don't worry, handsome Harry," Louisa cooed to Harry on the bus back, "we won't be coming back to 'Darling Dagenham' again anytime soon!

Chapter Thirty-One

Penny, Rosie and Louisa sat at the table drinking tea and gossiping. Their favourite hobby these days when they weren't at work. Frank had written a letter and proposed to Rosie and they were going to marry as soon as he was home from his service in the Royal Air Force. Louisa did wonder to herself why Frank hadn't insisted they marry before he went but didn't voice her thoughts to anyone as it may make Rosie wonder too. Many couples were getting married in haste, there was no time to waste while this war was raging, you have to live for the day. Anyway, the girls had planned Rosie's wedding, written a 'jobs-to-do' list, a shopping list and decided on the wedding dress they would all try to help Betty make for Rosie's big day. Louisa had found the pattern in her mum's drawer where she kept spare remnants of fabric and old zips and Louisa had cried. One good thing about the war was they all had to learn needlework. Clothes were rationed so it was make, do and mend. Darning, making clothes out of any fabric you could lay your hands on, making blackout curtains. Alice had a big sewing box and she had shown Louisa and Gladys how to sew on a button and mend a hole in a sock. Luckily, Louisa had been able to look through her mum's work box and work out what did what! As Louisa brewed another pot of tea the subject changed to Clara who had also gone back to work at Heart's Bakers and her antics and they laughed so much their sides ached. Louisa was now so large she had to sit sideways on the kitchen chair.

"What happened to Violet's dad?" Louisa whispered to Penny. She had wanted to ask for ages but Penny was always so happy and bubbly Louisa didn't want to depress her. They'd had so much doom in their lives. Penny didn't speak with the same accent as her and Rosie and Louisa wondered where exactly she lived before she moved next door but couldn't ask too many questions at once, it would have been rude.

"Well, I hardly remember him to be quite honest!" She stood to close the door between the kitchen and front room where Harry and Violet were playing so they couldn't hear.

"He was a bloke I met one night at the Greenwich Palais brought me a couple of Cinzanos and we went out for a cigarette," Penny paused unsure whether to continue or not.

"Next thing I know I'm up against a wall having a great time with him in my knickers! Never seen him since, not sure I would know him if I fell over him," Penny was giggling.

Louisa's mouth was wide open and she was speechless, her and Rosie collapsed into hysterical giggles as Penny opened the door and blew a kiss to Violet and Harry.

"No! Oh, my gosh! No!" Louisa screamed, "You and I are just complete opposites! How on earth do we get on so well?!"

They were all screeching with laughter.

"How did you pay for your food and rent before you were working at Heart's Bakers?" Rosie asked seriously.

"Well I'm sure you've guessed – haven't you?" Penny enquired looking from Louisa to Rosie.

"Or are you two as slow as snails?" she laughed, "If I do tell you then you must promise never to say a word to anybody.

Louisa and Rosie sat frozen staring at Penny.

"Do you promise? Do I have your word?" coaxed Penny raising one eyebrow.

Louisa and Penny slowly shook their heads with their eyes wide open waiting in anticipation of the next confession.

"Those men that come a knocking on my front door reward me for my services. Now you must swear never to say anything otherwise I might get evicted. Then who would look after Little Harry for you while you go to work?"

"No," screamed Louisa. Her and Rosie were still a bit puzzled but just fell about laughing again. "What a scream we've had this afternoon!"

A bit later after they'd calmed down the girls went upstairs to check through all the bits for the new baby, Louisa was completely organized , twelve terry towelling nappies, Vaseline petroleum oil, clean baby clothing that had been Harry's, towels, and some old rags, washed ready for the birth. Harry's crib was all spotless and made up with a tiny crocheted blanket. Harry had gone into Gladys's old bed about three months previous. Louisa was worried at first he might fall out of the bed, he looked so grown-up being in a proper bed. Sometimes she went and gently picked him up and put him in bed with her but he was getting so heavy now and she really should not be carrying him. She could imagine her mum saying, 'Don't you dare pick that big bruiser up!' If they had to go to the shelter she would let him come back into her bed after they'd been given the 'all clear' siren. But she knew she had to put a stop to it in case he gave her a boisterous kick in her tummy while he was asleep. He really was turning into a stocky little chap. Louisa was such a worrier always anxious about something. But then again she had a lot to be anxious about.

There was a group of midwives, nurses and doctors who held a baby clinic in the Seaman's Mission Hut by Hayes Wharf. Louisa had been around there twice, the first time she registered and they asked her to lay flat on a bed and they felt all over her belly. The doctor placed a metal trumpet shaped instrument on her bump and listened to her baby's heart beat through it. Simply genius! Whoever was clever enough to invent that? Louisa was very impressed They were all very caring and kind and said when her time came to send word and they would visit the house to assist with the birth, so that was a relief. Joey the nurse who lived in Acacia Court had gone to work in a hospital in Liverpool to help with the wounded soldiers so Louisa couldn't call on her for help. She returned to the baby clinic about four weeks later as they had asked her to and they repeated all their checks again and said baby sounded fine. It was amazing and Louisa wasn't really worried about the impending birth because for some mad reason she thought she'd done it all easily and by herself when she'd had Harry! For the first time in years she wasn't worried!

Not long after Penny and Rosie had left after the 'confessions' afternoon. Louisa's waters broke gushing everywhere soaking her dress and slippers, she really started to panic and blaming all the laughter on starting her labour off, she waddled in her squelchy slippers to Penny's front door with her dress stuck to her legs.

"Oh, thank God, you're not busy earning money! Louisa exclaimed, took a deep breath and bent over holding her baby bump, "Can you nip to the Seaman's Mission Hut for me see if they can assist please," Louisa panted, "If it's not shut for the night?"

Penny grabbed Violet's hand and together they made a bolt for Louisa's door, Violet started laughing, thought it was a game, Penny parked Violet down next to Harry in the front room, Louisa was still walking with her legs wide open back to her own house when Penny sprinted past her. "See you in a minute." Penny ran off all excited down the street.

"Breath slowly," Louisa kept repeating, she hoisted one foot up the small door step, then the next and collapsed onto the small sofa in the front room making it all damp but feeling beyond care. "I want my mum," she wailed.

The birth of their gorgeous second son Johnny went on forever. Oh, it was so painful she must have kept the whole street awake. She thought the second one was supposed to be easier. He was an enormous boy! Seven and half pounds! Harry had been six pounds. She couldn't believe it when the lovely nurse called Doreen said she had a son. She was sure it would be a girl this time she had actually been talking to her bump calling it 'Dolly'!

Chapter Thirty-Two

Stevie had been walking for three days, every bone in his body ached, it was freezing cold and he was soaked to the skin, right through his boots, every item of clothing he adorned was sodden. He was with his new mate, Fergus, they had clicked as soon as they met. Fergus was from Northern Ireland, shorter and lighter in weight than Stevie, he was a fiery character and very witty. He reminded Stevie of a greyhound dog. Between them they were bearing a wooden crate containing medical supplies belonging to the German Army. They were prisoners of war. They had been captured when the German battleship Bismarck sunk the Royal Naval vessel they were on, HMS Hood. Stevie had survived by somehow managing to clamber onto a floating pallet with two of his comrades, goodness knows what he thought he would do on a pallet but his survival instinct just took over. It was get on the pallet or drown. All around him in the sea were screams and flashes of light from gunfire and torpedo's exploding. The sea was freezing and very choppy. They had been picked up almost immediately and thrown in the gallows of a German cruiser ship. Not a huge battleship, the Germans had probably sent it out to collect up all the allied Forces they could lay their hands on so they could glean information from them. What else would they save enemy's lives for? Bomb them to kill them then go out save them? It didn't make any sense to Stevie.

After his capture he was taken to a prisoner-of-war camp called Milag in Germany, where there were thousands of other captives and it didn't seem at first to be as bad as he had envisaged. The German soldiers were not too bad but the Gestapo and the SS were evil little weasels though and seemed to enjoy in inflicting pain and mental torture. Stevie was sure his Allied Forces soldiers would not have behaved as nastily as that towards any German prisoners of war. He was interrogated for three days with little sleep and nothing to eat to try and get him to talk. He revealed his name, number and rank but beyond that just repeated what he had been trained to say,

"I know nothing."

They gave him a few aggressive whacks across the head, minimum sips of water and asked him his religion. He was eventually thrown into a room with forty other prisoners of war. Germany, like the United Kingdom, was part of the United Nations and had signed and therefore had to comply by The Geneva Convention in 1929 which laid down strict rules outlining what was and was not acceptable treatment of a prisoner of war. Stevie saw many cases of this being violated and doubted that he would ever see good old England again.

He was held in that squalid stinking hovel for three months. There were many rooms in the camp all the same. They got one meal a day and had use in shifts of a block containing ice-cold showers and lavatories. Occasionally, the Nazi soldiers would enter the rooms, call out a name and drag that person out. Sometimes that person came back sometimes they didn't.

The Red Cross visited a few times. On those days the prisoners of war received three portions of rice with some unrecognisable meat in the dish served at mid-day. The Red Cross left parcels for each prisoner of war containing luxuries such as soap, jam and tinned meat.

One morning in winter, the soldiers entered Stevie's room and they were all told to stand. It was still dark. Stevie thought that was it, they were all going to be taken outside and shot, but they were ordered to collect their belongings and were marched seven miles where they were all crammed onto a one train which was also laden with probably one hundred wooden crates.

Stevie had by then got to know some of his fellow inmates and Fergus was his favourite, although they were all a pretty decent bunch of chaps. During their training with the British Military, it was drummed into them that if they were taken as prisoners of war then they should attempt to escape. Fergus wanted to and was always trying to get Stevie to dig a tunnel with him. Some of their cellmates told them stories about past prisoners of war whom had attempted to escape. They were always caught, interrogated for days again then beaten. Stevie couldn't see the point, he felt a bit of a coward but weighed up that if he stayed put he may survive, if he tried to escape he would get caught and either shot or if he was lucky punished and put back in the camp. It just wasn't worth the risk. But Fergus would hear none of it. He pined for his green fields and freckly fair-skinned wife he had left at home and was desperate to be a free man.

On the train, they were all crushed in to the carriages and informed they were being transported to Poland. They were on the train two days with no food or water. There was not enough room in the carriage for them all to sit so they took it in turns for half the prisoners to sit whilst the other half stood. There were no facilities and before long the carriage was stinking. After two days and nearly dead, the train stopped and they spewed into the snow-laden terrain and were ordered, although they could hardly carry themselves, to lug a crate per pair of prisoners. The medical supplies were needed in Poland where the injured German servicemen were being taken from all over Northern Europe.

After the two days on the train, Stevie, Fergus and all the other men had to carry the crates for three more days, through freezing conditions, sleeping at night on the bare ground. They received one bowl of soup every evening and many fell, dehydrated, exhausted or victims of frostbite, never to stand again.

They reached Belaria in Poland five days after leaving the prisoner-of-war camp they had been held at in Germany.

Chapter Thirty-Three

Johnny was so different to little Harry, he was a very active and alert baby.

"I wonder if that makes you more intelligent," Louisa asked him while dressing him one morning, "Or maybe you'll just have a bit of a wild or naughty streak in you like Rosie's dad when you're grown up?"

He was always kicking his legs about and waving his arms. He never seem to settle down all content like Harry did when he had been a little, Johnny seemed raring to go from the minute he woke up, forever gurgling and thrusting his little arms and legs out. She couldn't keep any blankets on him. The first few days were a haze, washing nappies, feeding Johnny and Harry, sleeping, cleaning, washing more nappies, feeding, it just went on day into night into day! But she was very happy even though exhausted, she still felt like she was drained from the birth and she'd just had to get on with it. No mum, no sister. She was only getting a couple of hours sleep at a time, when Harry was asleep Johnny wanted feeding, when Johnny fell asleep Harry was awake and when they were both asleep Louisa felt wide awake! The sirens had calmed down a bit and they didn't have to go into the shelters every night now. There was no mention of this on the radio and Louisa wondered why.

There wasn't one day go by without Louisa gazing wistfully out the window in the direction of the River Thames. She hoped to see James walking towards the house. James, looking handsome, with maybe a gift in his arms for her. Daydreaming. The ship did berth but it was secret where. Louisa heard on the radio one evening that it was very dangerous for vessels crossing the Atlantic Ocean, it did alarm her because she didn't know where James was but suspected it might be in the Atlantic, the radio presenter said that Germany was trying to eradicate all the

British Navy vessels, wanted to stop them bringing food into the United Kingdom hoping to starve everyone to death. Gosh, it was all so terrifying. Italy was on Germany's side, Japan was on Germany's side, America was at war with Japan, Germany had invaded Russia or somewhere or something like that it was all too horrifying to listen to.

Anyway, Louisa wrote James a very happy, chatty letter straight away after Johnny's birth she wanted to cheer him up and remind him how funny she could be. Penny had posted it for her. There was no guarantee that he would get it. She really wanted him home. It was all so hard and she felt angry that her mum and sister weren't there to help her, then she felt really annoyed at herself for feeling angry towards them. She knew they all wanted to be there with her. She would have done anything to turn the clock back and have the house full again.

There was one thought that had been niggling at her for months now, why no word from her brother Stevie. He really wouldn't do that intentionally, he would write, he would know they'd be worried about him, he may not even know his parents and sister are dead. One or two letters from him may not have arrived but no word at all, she was very concerned.

Louisa had received something through the post though it was a ration book for Harry. He was allowed blackcurrant tablets so he gets all his vitamin C and cod liver oil and orange juice to keep him healthy too. Something for nothing she could do with that. Going shopping was a chore, and she had to do it with three children as on her days off she had Violet. Harry held onto one side of the pram and Violet the other. Her usual routine was to go to the greengrocers first as that was the heaviest items and they went in first to the metal basket that stretched across the bottom of her pram just above the wheels. She brought whatever was cheapest and would fill them up, always potatoes, Harry loved his potatoes. Lately, she had been using the green beans from the backyard, they were very tough and stringy but she boiled them for as long as possible and disguised them with a bit of gravy. Louisa had also come across some tall green shoots waving about poking through some old bricks that were still scattered about the backyard from the bomb blast. When she tugged at the green shoots, she was delighted to see an onion on the end quite a large onion it was as well.

After the greengrocers where she had also brought two carrots, they brought some liver from the butcher's and Eric the butcher chucked in a sausage for free.

She didn't have to buy any bread as she had brought a loaf home the day before from work. They would have a cheese sandwich for lunch using the tiniest bit of cheese she could get away with and a lettuce leaf in each sandwich to bulk it up. Tonight for dinner, they would have the liver, mashed potatoes with green beans, carrots and gravy. They stopped at the chemist and Louisa left Violet and Harry outside guarding Johnny in his pram as she nipped in and brought a bar of cold cream soap. She would have to use it to wash not only their faces and bodies but it would have to double up as shampoo as the chemist hadn't been able to get any shampoo for months now. She was very proud of herself! "What a wonderful housewife I've turned out to be!" she told Johnny, Violet and Harry.

When they got back to Louisa's house, it was school time as all the schools were bombed or closed the radio presenter who was on *Women's Hour* last night said everybody should be trying to teach their children what they would be learning at school. There was talk of the authorities finding another venue for the children still in London to attend but there had been no official announcement yet.

Well, Violet and Harry had never been to school so she assumed she should try to teach them to read and write.

They thought that was enormous fun, scribbling on a tiny piece of paper each, that's all Louisa had and she certainly didn't have spare money to buy paper, with a coloured pencil each which had originally belonged to Stevie, Louisa and Gladys.

Louisa left Johnny in his pram so she knew he was okay and brought it into the sitting room, he kicked and thrashed about in his normal boisterous manner while she tried to show them both how to write their names. They scribbled and giggled and stuck the pencil in each other's arms and in their own ears, tried to eat it and eventually realised they were supposed to be copying Louisa's example of their names.

"Well, I may be a wonderful housewife but I'm a lousy teacher," she announced as she got up to start making the sandwiches.

"I can't even get you to hold a pencil properly never mind teaching you how to read and write!"

That night, the air raid siren sounded about 8 o'clock in the evening, just after *Women's Hour*, Louisa was taken aback at first, it hadn't sounded for ages, she waited a second to see if it was a mistake and would stop, but it didn't and she grabbed Johnny, told Harry to run for it and they all made the shelter just before a huge, thundering noise went over head. It was so loud she thought the shelter was going to collapse.

"That wasn't very nice, was it boys?" she tried to keep light' hearted but decided it was best if they slept in the Anderson shelter all night. She actually had a decent night's sleep which was rare, just before she nodded off she heard the 'all clear' siren sound and as far as she knew there were no more air raid sirens sounded that night.

When she got up at 4 o'clock the next morning to get ready for work, she was shocked at the blazing red sky across what she thought was North London.

"Oh, dear, they must have been badly hit during the night," she spoke to herself whilst going into the kitchen to put the kettle on.

On the cold and frosty walk to work with Rosie, they noticed the previous day's poster at the newspaper stand, it was a bit soggy but you could still make out the headlines of the day,

'ENGLAND SATURATE GERMANY.'

"Oh, brilliant!" the girls giggled together and clasped hands.
"Please end this war!"

Chapter Thirty-Four

One snowy afternoon in February 1942, Penny came home from work straight to Louisa's as usual all flustered. She had snow on her scarf and coat and was rubbing her gloved hands together.

"Gosh, it's cold enough to freeze a brass monkey out there." She was shivering as she walked into Louisa's sitting room.

"I've just been chatted up!" Penny announced incredulously.

"Well, that's nothing new to you, you've always got men around you," Louisa commented.

"No, I really have been chatted up, I think so, anyway, Hank the Yank." Penny was laughing. She did look a bit flushed but that could have been the cold.

"He asked me to a dance on Saturday night at The Seamaster's Arms. He assured me the dances are excellent, really good, no fights or rowdiness, they've only just started up, Oh, I would really love to go with him! He was gorgeous and I could really do with a spin around a dance floor! I don't suppose you would you consider watching Violet for me? I know it's a really big favour to ask but I promise I won't be late back and I do let you use my pushchair!" Penny giggled.

"Honestly, he was so nice, he's just arrived from America, well, he said he had been here just a month, and he gave me some American candy! Look Harry, look Violet, I have some sweets for you. He said he will call for me about 7 o'clock on Saturday night, he was standing outside Heart's Bakers with a friend, another American soldier called Bruce, when Rosie and I left work. He looked so handsome, his accent is lovely and he asked me if I had a light for his cigarette and offered me one! Oh please, Louisa, please say yes, I'll do anything for you to reciprocate."

"You do talk posh sometimes, Penny," Louisa laughed. Penny could speak the same as them one minute then come out with all posh words another minute.

"Gosh, I'm shattered but of course, I'll mind Violet for you," Louisa smiled as she slumped onto the sofa.

"Violet's no trouble, are you poppet? But you had better come in your thick pyjamas because it's freezing."

Violet and Harry were just staring at the candy Penny was holding out to them. They both looked at her suspiciously as if it were some sort of trick.

"They're sweets," Penny explained, "Sweeties, you can have one each after your tea tonight if you've both been very good children today and mummy says it's okay, Harry, have you been good children for Louisa today?"

Their little faces were priceless. They actually looked scared of the candy.

Louisa and Penny doubled up with laughter.

"Well, we can always burn them to keep us warm if Harry and Violet don't like them," Louisa laughed as she tore some cardboard into strips and threw onto the open fire in the sitting room. Eric the butcher gave me a couple of cardboard boxes this morning and Harry and Violet very kindly carried them home for me, they did really well, didn't you kids?"

Coal was rationed like nearly everything else and you had to burn whatever you could get hold off. Louisa had picked up lots of bits from the bombsites she passed and brought home to burn. She had seen children playing on the bomb sites and they looked like had been sent there by their parents to scour for rubbish for the fire. It was the coldest winter anybody could remember.

"I'm going to listen to the radio tonight, apparently the fighting is really bad in Italy have you heard?"

Penny enquired as she left for her own house holding Violet's hand.

"Brrrr, it's freezing, night, night, and thank you again, I'm so excited! What shall I wear?"

Louisa was happy for Penny but it made her miss James even more.

"Chin up, Lou Lou, time to get tea started."

On the Saturday 'date' night, Rosie came to sit with Louisa and keep her company while she babysat Violet. Louisa didn't need any help as she was a 'wonderful housewife' but was glad of Rosie's company.

Penny looked stunning. Her lustrous copper hair was curled into ringlets then piled up loosely on the crown of her head in a bun. She had left a ringlet cascading down each side which softened her face. She donned black pointed toe shoes and a matching black pencil dress with shoulder pads which were the latest craze, Louisa guessed it must be new as she not seen her in before but didn't have a chance to enquire as Penny was in such a breezy fluster. She had drawn a line up the back of each of her legs with her eyebrow pencil and couldn't sit down because she said the line might rub off. She had her poppy red lipstick on and she had rubbed some into her cheeks to give her a rosy glow. Louisa had lent her Alice's mink coloured fur cape and Penny looked like a film star. The temperature had warmed up a teeny bit but she was still nervous of slipping on the icy pavement in her high heeled shoes.

"You'll just have to take his arm to steady you!" advised Louisa with a cheeky smile.

"I really do hope you have a fabulous evening," Louisa blew Penny a kiss as she walked back her own front door.

"Thank you so much for being such a darling," Penny walked sheepishly across the path.

"Rosie, Rosie, Rosie," Harry bellowed bumping about on the sofa.

"Do you like my hat? I'm in the navy," Harry was squashing the hat as far onto his head as it would go.

"That's not a navy hat Harry, that's a Royal Air Force hat, dear," Rosie explained.

"No, no, no, it's a navy hat, I'm in the navy," Harry insisted.

Louisa and Rosie listened to *Women's Hour* on the radio and watched the children trying to write their names on some paper Rosie had brought from her house.

"My dad's given up drinking again!" Rosie whispered during a boring bit on the radio.

"He's actually been given up for about two months now, but I just ignored it at first because I thought it wouldn't last but he's been really good and him and my mum are like they're on honeymoon! All lovey-dovey and laughing and being nice to each other, it's right weird!"

"Awww, that so lovely, that's really great, I hope they can make it last," sighed Louisa.

"I really miss my mum and dad, well, I miss everyone it's like I've got no one left."

"You can share my mum and dad," Rosie tenderly patted Louisa's hand, "Now they're normal they might be worth sharing." Rosie and Louisa laughed and concentrated again on the radio presenter telling them more ways to serve up vegetables.

The following Saturday Louisa was just putting her coat and scarf on ready to go out, Harry was so wrapped up he couldn't move and Johnny was drowning under blankets in his pram. Louisa wanted to go for a little walk whilst it was light and see if she could pick up anything to burn on the fire, when there was a knock at the door.

"Who can that be?" Rosie looked from Harry to Johnny with her eyebrows raised.

Her jaw nearly hit the floor when she opened the door.

"Ma Pritchard!" Louisa was amazed.

"Ma Pritchard! Oh, my gosh, I don't believe, come in, come in." Louisa made way for her to come into the warm.

She hugged Ma Pritchard and Ma Pritchard was laughing and shivering at the same time.

"I went to Dagenham to see you and your neighbour said you'd sold June!" Louisa was shouting at the top of her voice.

"And that you'd run off with a black man and June had gone to Canada!"

Ma Pritchard was slapping her thighs laughing.

"No! She never did! She's as nutty as a fruitcake old Mrs Greenbaum," Ma Pritchard continued, "is that the neighbour you mean? Bit chubby with black hair lives to the left of my house?"

Louisa nodded her head in agreement.

"Well, I wish she had told me you'd been to see me! When was this? She never said a dicky bird. You wait till I see her! Anyway, Lou Lou, how are you and is this the new addition to the family?" admiring Johnny.

Louisa took all their coats, hats, scarves and gloves off and took Johnny out of his pram, collecting rubbish for the fire would have to wait. Ma Pritchard had brought a cake with raisins in it, it was made with cold tea and was so delicious and moist they all wolfed it down like animals from London Zoo. Ma Pritchard stayed for ages and they didn't stop talking. Apparently, the new Fords Factory at Dagenham had been bombed and the Germans were now in control of Jersey too. Now that did worry Louisa, she was sure she had heard it before but didn't know where Jersey was. When Ma Pritchard explained it was an island just off England, a cold shiver ran down Louisa's back. That is a bit too close to home.

"Why do they not give us more information in those radio broadcasts?" Louisa asked Ma Pritchard.

"Because I think they think the Jerry Germans are listening and they want to pretend we are all fine and dandy in England. That's what I think, anyway, but they tell you things in the newspapers so why do they think they can't find out that way?" Ma Pritchard pondered.

"Well, how's a German soldier going to walk past us and go and buy a newspaper at an English paper stall?" laughed Louisa! Honestly! Ma Pritchard was daft as a brush sometimes.

"And also they've shot thousands and thousands of Russian Jews, just marched into Russia and shot them all."

Louisa felt really bad because her first thought when she heard about stories like this were 'Thank God, it wasn't James or Stevie'.

"And we've got prisoner-of-war camps going up everywhere with all the Jerry Germans and Italians in them, and even Japanese as well I think, all living in our country so it must be true, we must be nearly winning or how else would we get all these prisoners-of-war?"

"There's even one at Ashford so I heard near your mother-in-law."

Ma Pritchard quickly changed the subject.

"Our June is one of them Land Army girl's now gone and got a job in Surrey, very posh, is that where your neighbour Penny comes from she sounds a bit posh? Anyway, June wrote me a letter that I got me mate in the East End Docks to read to me and she is loving it , so I'm free now, they've all buggered off and left me and I can do whatever I like's," Ma Pritchard threw her head back and laughed.

"Oh, I do love you," Louisa said and as she hugged her. Harry wrapped his arms around their legs and joined in.

Chapter Thirty-Five

Betty was humming to herself a song she had heard on the radio the previous evening and she couldn't get it out of her head.

Dum de dum, dum de dum, oooggghhh.

She would have sung it if she could have remembered any of the words.

She was in her kitchen preparing Lord Woolton's pie with turnips, carrots, swede and potatoes. Ed's number one favourite since food rationing began. *He'll be pleased as punch when he gets in from work,* she smiled to herself. *How funny,* Betty thought, *this time last year I wanted to kill him.* Could not stand the sight of him, but now, he was all right again, been really decent and happy and not pawing her, even being gentle and loving in bed. They say marriage has to be worked at and she was so glad she had struggled on with it now. Well she'd had no choice, didn't have anywhere else to go and no money either. She mashed all the vegetables together, which was tough going, splashed in a dash of Worchester sauce and popped the casserole dish into the gas oven. Taking her apron off as she walked she took the stairs two at a time and popped her head in the girls bedroom. They were late home from work she realised and walked into her own bedroom where she patted her hair to give it a bit of volume and applied a new coat of bright red lipstick. She checked her teeth in the mirror and went down the stairs humming her song again.

Dum de dum, dum de dum, oooggghhh.

Not a million miles away in Biddenden, Kent there was another noise being created.

Cyril sat in his shed at the bottom of the garden.

Click, click, click-click, click, tap.

He loved his shed, he hated being indoors with all those women. Why on earth he had ever agreed to let the Land Army

129

girls lodge with them he would never know. Right morons they were, talking about stupid girl stuff all the time, driving him mad. Still at least it kept June occupied and he didn't have to suffer another drab conversation with her. And if he had refused them a room it may have drawn the authorities to be suspicious of him. No, he did the right thing letting them lodge and it was all more money for him to spend when the war was over, he would be able to buy whatever he liked.

His shed was his and his only. From the early days of their marriage he had said it was men only. June didn't seem to mind, was too sweet to complain about anything anyway she was. Stupid insipid female.

Click, *click-click*, *tap, tap*.

He moved his head closer to the Morse code machine to ensure his message had been transmitted. He was in for a nice reward when Germany won the war and he couldn't wait. More money, he would move away, abroad, be able to go wherever he wanted in Europe he would.

"Hello," Rosie and Caren called out together as they entered the sitting room and smelt the lovely cooking aromas.

"Hello, girls," called Betty.

"I was getting worried about you both, you're a bit late tonight."

"Yes, well, Penny's new man, Hank the Yank, was waiting outside work with some of his friends so we stopped for a bit of chat with them. They're quite nice really, aren't they Caren?" Rosie said looking towards her sister.

"Oh, yes, I'll say they're nice, gave us some nylon stockings Mum look."

"No really! Oh, my gosh they're lovely," exclaimed Betty taking the packets and inspecting them.

"Only two packets where's one for your poor mum?" Betty teased.

"We'll get you a packet next time we see them, they talk so funny though but they are very good looking and smart."

"Now you two be careful, can't have rumours spread about especially as all our poor boys have been away for years fighting the war and the yanks have just arrived trying to seduce all our girls who are missing their fellas."

Rosie and Caren laughed all the way upstairs 'seduce' they both repeated and sniggered to each other. Their mum was good company now.

Ed brought a newspaper home that evening that someone had left behind at work. They all read it from cover to cover. Money was so tight they never brought a newspaper. Louisa sometimes treated herself to one on a Saturday as she was trying to find out everything she could about the war in the hope she could discover any clues about where James and Stevie might be. When she had finished it she always gave to Rosie or Penny whoever she saw first but with the strict instructions she wanted it back. After they had both read it she would use it on the fire. Louisa burned everything. Anything that would burn she kept for the fire. Potato peelings, carrot tops, anything they couldn't eat and believe me that wasn't much, she kept for burning. Sometimes she had to open the door because the smoke was so bad, tea leaves especially caused lots of smoke, there wasn't really much point having the fire roaring to warm the house then having to open the door to clear the smoke she chided herself.

Anyway, in the newspaper were pictures of Princess Elizabeth and Princess Margaret all dressed in army clothes posing by an army wagon looking really glamorous.

"Look at those two," Ed said, "that's grand they're getting stuck in too."

Rosie and Caren studied the pictures. Rosie wanted to copy Princess Elizabeth's hair style for her wedding day and Caren suggested they go upstairs and practise it.

Chapter Thirty-Six

Penny was practising hair styles as well in her bedroom a few doors down Acacia Court. Violet was sitting beside her on the double bed gazing in awe at her beautiful Mummy. Penny twisted her naturally wavy hair into an elegant chignon and secured her silky locks in place with some small elegant hair grips. Violet twisted her hair around her fingers trying to copy her mummy. Penny smiled to herself, life was great at the moment. She had the loveliest friends, she had taken the red light bulb out from outside her front door and totally refused to accommodate any men there as soon as she had started to work at Heart's Bakers factory. She secretly hoped that Violet will never remember any of the men visitors, surely as she got older any memories she may have had would have disappeared? Penny hoped she was right. Anyway, she had to keep herself and Violet and that was the only way she had known how. Her family had disowned her when she revealed she was expecting a baby, they said she was the black sheep of the family and they wanted to send her to Cornwall, to some rich old aunties cottage where she could hide away until the baby was born and then have it adopted. Taken away never to be seen again. Penny hugged Violet as she recalled the decision she had been forced to make. Penny left her parents' home about a week later with all her belongings and had never been back. Sometimes she wanted to go there and knock on their front door and ask them to accept her but had never had the nerve, her parents had always been distant with her. Penny imagined they would snatch Violet and not give her back. No Penny was not willing to take the chance.

Penny was an only child and suspected that she was deemed a nuisance to them. Her parents never showed her any affection or to each other really, she had never seen them holding hands or being soft with each other. It was a mystery really, why did they get together in the first place and how? Penny was determined to have her baby, someone for Penny to love and someone to love Penny. It had been very hard and Penny had often laid in bed in the middle of the night wondering if she had taken the right path. But one look at Violet and her heart melted. Penny would do anything for her little princess. Anyway, today was good and it was all going to get better. Once the war was over everything would be *A Wonderful Life* just like the title of an American film Hank the Yank had been telling her about.

Yes, Penny was counting her blessings, not looking at past disappointments, she loved her new job at Heart's Bakers and the banter they all had together, she had a beautiful daughter, she was so lucky and she was going out with Hank the Yank again on Saturday and was quite smitten. He was so gentlemanly and generous. He smelt lovely and wore expensive looking suits. The previous two Saturdays he had taken her to The Seamaster's Arms dance and tried to teach her the latest American dance called the Jive, he said she had natural rhythm and Penny was putty in his hands. He was calling again for her this Saturday. There was one blot on the landscape though. Penny had told him Violet's dad had been killed at the beginning of the war. *Oh dear, she thought to herself, how am I going to get out of that whopping lie?*

Rosie and Caren entered the sitting room to be greeted by their parents cuddling each other.

Stunned they both burst out laughing and gave Betty and Ed a twirl each to display their stylish hair creations.

"Oh, behave yourself, you two, you're like a couple of teenagers," Rosie teased, "Mum we've got a wedding dress to sew."

Ed sat on the sofa with a very smug look on his face reading his free paper. The headline on the front page was

'CHURCHILL'S UNEXPECTED GUESTS.'

A story about all the prisoners-of-war now captured and held all over the United Kingdom.

Chapter Thirty-Seven

Winter ended finally and the fire was left to go out in Louisa's sitting room.

Thank goodness for that she said to herself, really time consuming job that is.

One Saturday, she gave the house a really thorough spring clean, Johnny was walking now and into everything so she had one eye on the duster and one eye on him.

Louisa had opened the front door to let some fresh air in and Harry was sitting on the door step watching some boys further down the road playing on the bombsite where houses had once stood until that dreadful night when Alice and Gladys had lost their lives.

Anyway, Harry was watching them and he asked, "Mum can I go and see those boys? They're playing with a football."

Louisa went out of the front door and looked down the road.

"No, Harry you're too young to go out on your own, love, come inside and we'll read that book Ma Pritchard left for you,"

"Oh, please, Mum, please," Harry started jumping up and down.

"No," Louisa tried to steer him back through the front door.

"No," Harry yelled, he was so angry his face had gone all red he brushed her arm away from him.

"I want to go, please, please, please, they're the same size as me why can they play out and not me it's not fair."

Louisa had never seen little Harry like this before and didn't really know what to do. She glanced up the street to see if any of the neighbours were out watching.

"Let me go, please, Mum, please."

"No, now get indoors or you'll get a smack," Louisa grabbed hold of Harry and pushed him into the sitting room slamming the door behind her. She felt scared. How should she handle this?

Gosh she missed her mum or anyone who could advise her really, boys need a man around the house.

Harry stomped up the stairs as loudly as he could crying and screaming.

"It's not fair, I hate you, I'm going to run away and find my dad."

Louisa sat down on the sofa completely stunned. There had been no lead up to this behaviour, it hadn't been happening gradually, he had always been a kind little angel, now this was new to her and she was concerned.

Louisa stood up and continued with her cleaning, her heart wasn't in it now and she just did as little as possible to make it look acceptable. Violet was coming in again tonight and she didn't want Harry to start making trouble again later. She thought she'd leave him to calm down then take him up a cup of Horlicks. He loved his Horlicks that might sooth his temper she hoped.

Rosie had been so good at making flowers for Louisa's wedding she felt she should do the same for Rosie's wedding. She knew Rosie didn't like any sewing or crafts so that made the flowers even more special that she had gone to all that effort. When the cleaning was over, she made the cup of Horlicks and a small one for Johnny too and took Harry's upstairs, he was fast asleep on his bed and his face was all puffy from the crying.

"Awww, he looks like a peaceful angel now." Louisa's heart melted.

She went into Alice and Tom's old bedroom and opened her dad's wardrobe. She had never got rid of one single item of their clothing. She had intended to move into there herself but couldn't bear to clear their possessions away. She would have to get rid of them soon they had so much stuff. The Town Hall didn't like people living in houses that were too large for their families and she was expecting a letter from them at some point. Although she was sure they had more than enough to do re housing people who had lost their homes in The Blitz. Anyway, she planned to make lots of outfits for Harry and Johnny with the fabric she could re-use from her parents clothes and James and Steve may want a pick of their dad's clobber first. He owned some smart stuff. She opened her mum's wardrobe. She could smell her. She pulled a blouse towards her and kissed it. On the floor of the wardrobe lay her mums jewellery box. Louisa opened it and a little mechanical ballerina starting pirouetting inside. She was about two inches tall and had a white, which was now faded, lace skirt on, Louisa and Gladys had loved this jewellery box. She recalled sitting on her mum's bed with Gladys and they kept asking her to make the ballerina dance again. She thought the jewellery box was a Christmas gift from her dad. There was only her wedding ring in it that was of any value and Louisa knew one day she may have to take it to the pawn brokers in Commercial Road and get some money for it, but that would be only if she was so desperate she had no money for food. There were some little black and white photographs all crinkly around the edges. Louisa smiled, they were of her, Gladys and Stevie. There was one of her dad when he was young and slim with a full head of hair and a larger photograph of their wedding day, they looked so young. There was a couple of different coloured buttons, a metal cigarette lighter and a raffle ticket.

"Wonder what that was for?" Louisa asked herself.

She looked up again at the clothes, one of her mum's favourite outfits was a cream blouse with pink lilies on it, Louisa took it down and pondered. Could she make something with this for Rosie's wedding?

"Something borrowed, something blue, something old, something new," she said to herself turning back to the rail of clothes and selecting a blue blouse. It had small silver coloured heart buttons.

"Perfect," Louisa decided, "Now what shall I create?"

When Penny looking gorgeous again, dropped Violet in later that day Louisa asked her,

"Penny, if you get a chance can you ask Hank if he has any idea how I can find my brother Stevie for me, please? Only if it's not awkward for you and you don't mind."

"Of course, I will, angel, thank you so much for having Violet again, promise you can be my bridesmaid in America as a reward," she laughed as she nipped back to her own house.

Louisa stood behind her blackout curtains to wait so she could get a glimpse of Hank the Yank. Then looked at Violet who was watching her and hoped she didn't tell her mum Louisa had been spying. She also hoped Hank didn't see her he would think she was a crazy nosy neighbour. When he arrived he did look very dapper, and confident, he had a swagger like a movie star and as they walked down Acacia Court they made a very attractive couple. Louisa smiled, "Good luck to her," she felt proud.

Harry started to sing,
"My daddy is out on the ocean
My daddy is out on the sea
My daddy is out on the ocean
Oh, bring back my daddy to me, to me
Please bring back my daddy to me."

Louisa was stumped, Violet was giggling uncontrollably. Harry started to sing the verse again, after the first line Violet joined in. At the end they were in hysterics. When Harry repeated for a third time Louisa and Violet both joined in. They sang it on and off all night. It somehow made them all so happy, how strange, doesn't cost anything and it had a real feel good effect on them all. Harry was very well-behaved the whole evening and Penny got home before 10.30 and took Violet straight in to bed. Louisa was exhausted.

"Come and tell me all about it tomorrow, I want to hear every last detail!" she ordered as she waved goodnight to Violet and Penny singing,

"My daddy is out on the ocean…"

Stevie slumped in the corner of the rancid room.

"You must be mad, they'll shoot you, you'll never make it over the fence, they're everywhere the evil little gits. And even if you do get out then where you going to go? You'll stick out like a sore thumb, we don't even know where we are. If we get out how do we eat or even know where Britain is? We have no weapons, we can't swim across the channel, we'll freeze, starve to death or get shot."

"I'd rather die trying to escape than waiting in here to get murdered by these nasty Gestapo bastards," Fergus hissed back in his rich Irish brogue. "You in or out? Make your mind up big man it's tomorrow or never."

Chapter Thirty-Eight

Rosie banged on Louisa's door, eventually it was opened by Harry wearing his favourite hat.

"Good morning, handsome Harry, can I come in its pouring down? Where's Mummy?"

Rosie followed Harry into the sitting room as Louisa was coming from the kitchen.

"Oh, hello, bride to be, how are you this wet morning?" enquired Louisa.

"Well, actually I'm panicking now, can you go over my 'to-do' list with me if you're not too busy?" Rosie pleaded.

"Course, I will, let's get the kettle on and we can sit down with a nice cup of cha as my good old dad used to call it!" Louisa laughed. There was another bang on the door and Harry skipped to answer it. This time it was Penny and Violet.

"I had better put another spoonful of tea leaves in the pot," Louisa announced.

"I was wondering if you wanted to go and visit the graves sometime I could return the favours you keep doing me by minding my Violet. I could watch Harry and Johnnie whilst you go to Greenwich Graveyard?" Penny offered.

"Oh that's so kind of you… thank you… I would love to visit them, I'll work out a day when we're not working and both have nothing going on, oh, thank you so much, Penny, that is so thoughtful of you," Louisa felt blessed.

"Also," continued Penny as she bent down and looked under Harry's hat into his face, "Hank said he can get you tickets to go and watch a football match with him or with him and Mummy if she wants to go! How would you like that young man?"

"Harry's eyes widened and he just looked at his mum quizzingly.

"Oh fantastic! A football match! Wow! Harry that will be great, won't it?" Louisa felt doubled blessed.

They all sat down at the kitchen table, organized Rosie's wedding and gossiped about Clara's life. Penny left after about an hour and Rosie confided to Louisa that she was feeling nervous about her upcoming nuptials.

"That's natural to feel nerves, I did too but I'm sure everything will go according to plan and you'll have an amazing day. Louisa comforted Rosie as she pulled her coat around her shoulders and stood to leave. Harry put his hat on Rosie's head giggling and Rosie good naturedly tickled his tummy.

"Does this mean I can have your beloved hat, little Harry," Rosie enquired as she pulled it from her head.

"No, it's Harry's hat," he demanded with a cheeky grin.

Rosie studied the inside of the hat.

"When did Frank give this to Harry," she enquired looking shocked.

"Oh, Frank didn't give it to Harry, one of Penny's customers gave it to Violet, but Violet didn't like it and passed it on to Harry,' not really Violet's cup of tea is it? She's such a feminine little girl," Louisa explained.

Rosie's face turned to stone and she sat back down with a thud on the chair she had just risen from.

Instantly Louisa realised something was very amiss.

"What do you mean Frank's hat?" asked Louisa taking it from Rosie's hand and looking at it.

Inside was written 'Frank Butcher', Louisa's heart stopped, she looked at Rosie who had put her head between her hands and leant on the table.

Harry grabbed his hat back and ran off to show Johnny some wooden spoons.

"I knew I knew that name," was all Louisa could think to say.

She sat beside Rosie and patted her back,

"There must be loads of Frank Butchers," Louisa commented not really believing herself.

"There must be an explanation, let's not jump to conclusions, I mean he could have dropped it in the street, or lost it ages ago," Louisa continued, her mind was racing, there was no possible explanation she could think of.

"He said he hasn't been home for ages how can he drop his hat in the street?" Rosie mumbled still holding her head.

Rosie stood angrily, "I'm going to ask Penny," and marched towards the door.

"Oh, no! What are you going to say? " Louisa followed her.

Rosie was shaking the hat right in front of Penny's face. "How did you get my Frank's hat," she screamed.

"Who's Frank?" Penny looked stunned. Oh dear, what had been a good day so far had suddenly turned sour.

"My Frank, my Frank, the man I'm about to marry." Rosie was spluttering and waving the hat in the air.

Penny looked up and down the street.

"Shhh, Oh my God! Shut up! Please keep your voice down, come in, quick, come in."

Penny hissed as she grabbed Rosie's wet sleeve and pulled her through the front door with Louisa following.

"Who told you it was Frank's hat?" Penny enquired as she closed the door behind her.

"It could be any bloke's hat."

"It has got his bloody name in it, look." Rosie was stabbing her fingers at the name in the hat and getting angrier by the minute.

"He must have been around here, I can't bloody believe it! You're supposed to be my friend."

Penny led Violet into the kitchen.

"You sit there and practise writing you name, sweetness." she instructed Violet as she pulled Violet's piece of paper in front of her and put a pencil in her fingers.

"Mummy won't be a minute and she shut the door to the kitchen.

"Please keep your voice down," Penny pleaded.

"I've never seen your Frank, I don't know who he is or what he looks like."

Penny was shaking her head at Rosie.

"I have never met him, have I? If he's been around here that's him that's wrong not me, I didn't ask him to come around. I am your friend."

Penny put her arms out to reach Rosie.

Rosie flinched away.

"I would never, you know, well, I would never do anything with him if I knew who he was, they don't tell me their names," Penny was pleading.

Rosie slumped into Penny's armchair and started to cry. Penny pulled a handkerchief from up her sleeve and handed it to Rosie. Rosie took the handkerchief and put it across her face, she was really sobbing now and couldn't get her breath. Louisa and Penny looked at each other, gosh, what a mess, what should they do now?

Louisa went to the front door.

"Look, I've got to go, I'm really sorry but Harry's indoors' on his own with Johnny and Harry keeps wanting to go out and play in the street so I've got to keep my eyes on him."

The atmosphere at work was very uncomfortable for the next few weeks. It must have been even worse on Louisa's days off when Penny would be there with Rosie, Betty and Caren. Every day Louisa asked Penny if anything more had been said and Penny did the same when Louisa returned from work. Louisa really wanted to talk to Rosie but they hadn't been alone and Rosie hadn't called round to Louisa's house. Life carried on as normal as possible, Penny continued to go out with Hank on Saturday evenings, they seemed to be getting quite serious and Louisa hoped he wouldn't break her heart. Violet came in with her and the boys and was growing into a lovely young lady. She was a good calming influence on Harry and Louisa spent every Saturday evening reading books with them. Books from her and Gladys childhood and also some Penny had brought. Penny had recently introduced Violet to Hank but Violet never mentioned him. Hank was very generous lavishing Penny with gifts for her and Violet. He had been here in England months now and was still waiting to be drafted to the continent somewhere which Louisa was sure must happen soon.

One Sunday, Penny looked after the boys and Louisa visited the graves. She would have to get them a headstone when the war was over, if ever, for the time being they just had a little wooden cross each, two crosses on one grave, her mum was buried beneath with Gladys on the top. Louisa wished that her dad could be buried with them too. Not washing about in a freezing sea. The tears streamed down her face but she felt peaceful. There were hundreds of new graves, all those people lost their lives in such a short space of time. And that was the ones that could be buried that wasn't counting all the bodies lost under the bombsites, probably never to be recovered or recognised by loved ones and also people reported missing. Just gone into thin air. Disappeared. There must have been thousands of lives lost during this war.

Later that day, Louisa sat on the sofa pondering what to do. She had been friends with Rosie all her life and her loyalty lay with her. But she could see Penny's point of view, if Frank had been using Penny's services then he's to blame. Would you believe it, sneaky pig, nipping in next door which is only four doors down from his fiancée. What's the matter with him, couldn't he have gone somewhere else, somewhere where he's not likely to get caught out. Or did he just not care, well, he couldn't have cared about Rosie much anyway or he wouldn't be visiting Penny. *Oh dear*, thought Louisa, *poor Rosie*. Or maybe there is an innocent explanation, perhaps somebody took his hat by mistake, she was dying to ask Rosie so many questions but couldn't go trundling up to Rosie's house with the boys it's not fair on Betty and Ed and even if she did go up there, there was nowhere they could talk privately and Louisa wasn't sure if even Betty and Ed knew anything yet. *Oh, gosh, so many questions*, Louisa's head was spinning with it all, *only God knows how Rosie was feeling. Why hasn't she been to see me? Surely, she can't think I'm to blame as well, I don't want to lose her friendship, does she think I've taken Penny's side?*

Harry jumped on his mum's lap.

"Mummy I'm hungry, can I go out and play in the street with the other children?"

"Give us a hug, handsome, and we'll go and get dinner on," she smiled as she cuddled him.

Johnny jumped onto her lap too and she sat there feeling blessed again.

Chapter Thirty-Nine

"Rosie," Louisa screamed as she opened her front door, she was just so pleased to see her standing there.

They hugged for a long time both obviously comforted to be together.

"I'm sorry I haven't been around I just didn't feel like talking to anyone," Rosie explained.

"That is totally understandable, darling, let's get the kettle on." Louisa walked into the kitchen clapping her dainty hands together and Rosie sat at the kitchen table where Harry and Johnnie were trying to complete a jig saw puzzle.

"I've been dying to talk to you, see how you were, see what Frank had said, did you write to him but I just never got a chance to be alone with you, does your mum know? Or Caren or don't you want to talk about it," Louisa enquired while filling the kettle with water at the sink.

"Well, yes to all really, I'm okay now, thanks, just a shock at first really, I wrote to Frank straight away, Louisa I was just so sure he wouldn't do that to me, couldn't do that, I feel so stupid," Rosie paused, "I convinced myself that it must all be a complete mix up, but no, he didn't even deny it, Lou, he wrote back saying he was sorry and maybe it was for the best, I feel so embarrassed."

Rosie slumped forward and tears dripped from her eyes on to the kitchen floor.

"No," Louisa was stunned. "Gosh, you poor thing." She embraced Rosie and wiped her wet cheeks with a tea towel.

Rosie attempted a feeble smile

"So I told my mum and dad, and Caren everybody's been really quiet at home, not said much at all, I think they're in disbelief, my mum has put the wedding dress away somewhere, God knows where, probably thinks it will upset me and so now all we do is talk about the war or food or work really."

"Aww, I feel so sorry for you, Rosie, what a pig! I can't believe it, I thought he really loved you."

Rosie cried some more.

"So did I," she blew her nose on her handkerchief.

Louisa then felt bad and added quickly.

"I'm sure he really did love you, I mean we don't know what being away fighting does to you, do we? It must change your outlook on life, make you have a devil may care attitude."

Louisa patted Rosie's hand.

"I feel such a failure, look at me twenty years old and not even a boyfriend now. I think everyone thinks I'll just end up a lonely old spinster," Rosie wailed as she dabbed her eyes.

"Now come on you! Don't go talking like that! You're a beautiful girl, you can have any man, well, any man when they get back from the war! You'll meet someone else and you'll look back and be glad you didn't marry Frank, I mean say you hadn't found out until after you married him! Just look at it as a lucky escape."

The girls laughed and Louisa felt confident Rosie would recover from this heart breaking situation.

That evening the air raid sirens went off.

"Oh, for God's sake," Louisa called.

She and the boys slept in the air raid shelter all night.

The Seamaster's Arms had offered their saloon and public bars to the authorities to use as a temporary school. It was available every week day morning up until lunch time. Harry and Violet were both offered a place three mornings a week. They loved it, they looked so cute going into the pub holding hands. Louisa was really glad as she felt Harry needed other company he was just stuck indoors with her and Johnny all the time, no grandmothers or grandfathers around to stimulate or spoil him. She felt really guilty that she couldn't carry out activities with him that she had enjoyed with her dad, just like walking through the park or digging the garden. Their garden was full up with the Anderson Shelter and debris from the bombings, God knows when that would ever be dug again. The green beans she grew just climbed out from beneath a pile of smashed old bricks, they must just keep re seeding themselves every year. She did water them occasionally though so liked to think it was her green fingers making them flourish.

Anyway, they both loved the school, practised their handwriting and reading at home, they got free milk at school so that was good, more help from the government to make them grow stronger. Louisa liked talking to the other mums when she took them to and from school and Penny took them on Louisa's work days. Initially, the comments were that it wasn't going to work, trying to teach children in a smoky old pub, 'they'll come home drunk on the beer fumes' and 'at least they'll know how to be a landlord when they grow up!' were the sort of comments bandied about. But luckily, it did seem to be successful and everybody soon got into a routine.

Louisa even decided Harry was now mature enough to go out in the street with the other boys and play football or whatever. She did read him a great list of 'cans and cant's' before though.

'No fighting with the other children,

No spitting,

No swearing,

He must not go out of sight of his front door,

If anybody hits him he must hit them straight back, unless it's a girl, then come and tell Mummy,

No climbing on any bomb sites, they could collapse and crush him to death,

No tearing any clothing or touching anything with ash on, try to stay clean,

And he is only allowed out for one hour at the most if he is a good boy then maybe as time goes by he may be allowed to stay out for a bit longer.'

Phew, he was out the door like a rocket. Louisa stood by the window and watched him. It was right, he needed to learn how to get on with other children on his own, not with a mother or teacher watching him. And funnily enough, Louisa enjoyed it as it gave her precious time to dote on Johnny. They had never had time together just the two of them, when Harry was little it was just her and him but she had never had that privilege with Johnny. Louisa wondered if she would ever have any more children. She switched the radio on to listen to Winston Churchill addressing the nation and leant over Johnny.

"Just think, Johnny," Louise murmured into his warm little ear, "One day Daddy will come home, you might have another brother or sister and we might all live in a splendid house with a bright red door out in the beautiful countryside of Kent."

Johnny ran around the sitting room obviously relishing the attention he was receiving.

The following Saturday, Hank took Harry to watch the promised football match, Crystal Palace versus Millwall. Louisa was worried if James would approve. She had to make the decisions now and he would have to stand by them. How could she stop him going, it is such a treat for Harry and he doesn't have any grown up male company. Louisa had so many hesitations does James even like American people? Has he ever met any? Would he be angry she had trusted their son to a stranger really, a foreign stranger at that. Perhaps they had Americans on his ships now or would the Americans just stay on their own navy vessels. It was just, well she wasn't sure, she didn't really know Hank the Yank, say he lost Harry? Was he used to children, would he keep hold of his hand? Oh, she was such a worrier, why did she always fret about everything, she was sure she never used to feel like this before she had children, or was it the war? Did it make everybody anxious and tense? Well, she trusted Penny's instinct and Harry was so excited. Louisa couldn't concentrate on anything else for the whole afternoon. She just plodded on with all her housework chores and read to Johnny, like a zombie she was, not really aware of what she was doing. All that worrying and they came back safe and well and elated that Millwall had won the match 2-0 and Harry was now a devoted Millwall football fan.

"Oh, honestly, Hank, I can't say how grateful I am, really, it's so kind of you." Louisa was looking at Hank close up, he really was a very good looking man, his skin was so healthy.

Hank was smiling.

"No problem, we had a great day, didn't we, little chap," he drawled in his American accent which was so charming.

"You must let me repay your kindness and you can come here for dinner sometime with Penny and Violet of course."

"Well, that would be grand, ma'am, I sure do look forward to that." Hank tipped his hat as he left and smiled with perfect white straight teeth.

Chapter Forty

The post lady was at the door.

"Good morning," Louisa cheerily greeted her. She had just taken Harry and Violet to school and was busy preparing some vegetables for their meal later that day.

"Two for you today, love, how you doing?"

They chit chatted for a few minutes and Louisa looked at the letters with trepidation. Her heart always beat faster with anxiety when she saw the post lady.

But all good today a letter from James. It was very short, not in his usual beautiful script and didn't give much away, which gave Louisa a bit of cause for concern, but she brushed that aside and continued to absorb his scrawly handwriting. He said he loved her more than words could ever say, that they were having a hard time but was sure they would dock soon as he had been away so long and the ships supplies had to be running out soon. He wasn't getting any sleep and couldn't wait to be back in London holding her, Harry and Johnny. Louisa's eyes filled with tears and she clasped the wafer thin piece of paper to her chest.

The second letter was from Sylvia, saying that Canterbury, a city about twenty miles away from Biddenden had recently taken a massive battering by the Luftwaffe, the German Air Force. But they hadn't seen any German planes for a long time now, the British Air Force planes were still flying back and forth nonstop to Headcorn, they were really busy they were, so hopefully they were giving the Germans double what they have dished out to us! The Land Army girls were still lodging with them and whilst Sylvia was writing the letter Mark had brought into the kitchen two rabbits and said to say hello to Louisa.

Louisa had to read the next sentence over and over again.

Sylvia had written Cyril hung himself in his shed.

No, Louisa couldn't take it in. Cyril hung himself in his shed.

Sylvia wasn't sure of the details but Mark had discovered that he was a spy. Sylvia didn't say how Mark knew but that Cyril knew the authorities were on the brink of coming to arrest him. He would have been sentenced to capital punishment which meant he would have been hung anyway and so he took the coward's way out. Those were her words. She didn't say if Mark had informed on him or even if Mark had told Cyril that he knew. He had been telling the Germans that roads were blocked, bridges closed and spying on the activity at Headcorn Air Strip. Louisa couldn't believe it.

"The snidey bugger," Louisa exclaimed, "And I was living in his house, Sylvia's been there for years, my brave strong husband is away risking his life for his country and that scum bag's giving away all Britain's secrets." Louisa felt livid.

Sylvia's letter continued that since his death it had come to light that Cyril's father was German, he had fought for Germany in the First World War but he too fell to Nazi Germany as he was Jewish. He had managed to flee to London, change his surname to 'French', met Cyril's mother, got married and they then of course they had Cyril.

Louisa was gobsmacked. Why on earth, if Cyril's father had been forced to flee Nazi Germany would he then take Germany's side in the war? Louisa wondered if June had known? It all started to make sense now, his aloofness, asking Louisa to go back to London, he probably knew London was going to be the target of a massive bombing onslaught. He probably wanted her and her baby to die. It made her shiver.

"Well, you just can't trust anyone." She continued to read Sylvia's letter.

June was coping well and they were all just waiting for someone to explain it all really.

Sylvia finished the letter sending her love to them all and praying the war would be over soon.

"My God," Louisa said to herself. "Whoever would believe it? A spy? How come?

"Whatever next? How would he have any information that was useful to the enemy? It was all a mystery! This life of mine has certainly turned out eventful."

Louisa couldn't wait to write to James and tell him all about it, he like her would be gobsmacked.

Chapter Forty-One

Harry and Violet were taught in school what to do in the event of an air raid. Harry was turning out to be a little leader and all afternoon they practised air raid drills in Louisa's sitting room with Harry giving out all the instructions.

Penny came home from work all excited that day, they had all been given the day off on Thursday as Winston Churchill was coming to tour the estate, visit the school and chat to the public.

"Oh, brilliant!" squealed Louisa.

Louisa looked through her wardrobe contemplating what to wear.

Posters were everywhere the next day,

'WINSTON CHURCHILL TO VISIT BERMONDSEY.'

That Thursday was a bright clear day and they were all up, washed, dressed and eaten their breakfast really early. Louisa, Rosie, Penny, Violet, Harry and Johnny all walked slowly to The Seamaster's Arms. They wanted to get to a good spot so hopefully they had a good chance of seeing the prime minister close up and in case the newspapers came to photograph the event!

"We might make the front page!" Rosie bubbled.

All the girls had poppy red lipstick on and had made an extra special effort with their clothes that day. There were hundreds of people out and about all ready. Lots of police, Louisa noticed, and air wardens were handing out little triangular shaped union jack flags.

Harry, Violet and Johnny waved the flags like mad.

Betty, Ed and Caren joined them after about thirty minutes and Rosie nudged Louisa in the ribs and pointed across the road to them. Ma Pritchard was standing there with a dark skinned chap. She looked quite attractive and blew them a kiss. There was such a crowd it would have been impossible to barge through the gathered mass to reach her.

Winston Churchill came, he was just so lovely, walking about, shaking people's hands including Harry and Violet's, saying we will win the war, thanking everybody for their contributions to the war effort. The flash bulbs were going off constantly on the newspaper photographer's cameras and it was a thoroughly enjoyable day.

"Harry and Violet will remember that forever," Penny quipped.

"So will we all," blubbered Betty.

Louisa looked around the retreating crowds for Ma Pritchard but she had couldn't see her face anywhere. On the way back home, the streets were covered in litter and Penny said quietly to Louisa that she had something to tell her when they were on their own.

Louisa didn't want to know what it was, *Oh, no* she thought to herself, *I hope it's not anything about Frank, I'm fed up with all this malarkey, Good riddance to him.*

Hours later when they were finally alone, Penny blurted out obviously bursting with excitement

"Hank has asked me to marry him."

"Oh, my gosh, No! That's wonderful, blimey, he didn't take long, well, I never, I wasn't expecting that, Oh I'm so pleased for you Penny, have you told Violet? What did she say? But hang on a minute where will you live? Here? Will he be allowed to live here? Are you sure you know he's right for you? You haven't met his family or anything! You don't really know each other that well surely."

Louisa couldn't stop rambling on.

Penny interrupted.

"Well, Hank's been conscripted to Norwich in Norfolk to help build a runway for the American Air Force to use and we just clicked straight away really Louisa, I felt like he was the one after the first date really. We can talk about anything, we agree about everything, sometimes he finishes my sentences for me and I often know what he's thinking without him even saying. I do love him dearly. We probably wouldn't have got married so soon if he wasn't going to Norwich but that's just brought it forward. He said he wanted to marry me after the first time he met me."

"Awww, how sweet," Louisa had a warm glowing feeling and wrinkled her nose.

"Oh, no! You are not going to move to Norwich though are you? I love you living next door, I will miss you so much," Louisa felt selfish as soon as she had spoken.

"I'm sorry, I am really happy for you darling and for Violet, I think he'll make a brilliant daddy for her."

"Yes, so do I, well he is going to see if he can get accommodation by the air field and for exactly how long he will be up there for, it's not worth us moving all that way and taking Violet away from school and Harry and you and everything that is familiar to her and also my job, and I'd miss you too of course; well, it's not worth it if its only for a few months but…"

Louisa waited.

"Yes," pressed Louisa, "Yes, but what?

"Well," continued Penny, "We will of course be going back with him to America when the war finally ends."

Louisa's face was a picture, her mouth was wide open her eyes were nearly popping out of her head

Before Louisa could comment Penny continued.

"Hank said Violet will have a much better life out there, I have no family and he has four sisters who all can't wait to meet us, and they have really nice big houses, much grander than English houses, and lovely schools and parks, and so much more money to spend on everyday items."

Penny felt like she was pleading with Louisa to let her go and Louisa realised this.

"Oh, my darling, I'm so happy for you, I really am. America! Gosh! It's just such a shock, I like Hank and I think he will make a wonderful husband. Congratulations, my darling!"

The girls hugged and Johnny, Harry and Violet all hugged too.

"There's just one problem," Penny added.

Louisa looked into her eyes enquiringly.

"I told him I am a war widow."

Chapter Forty-Two

Princess Elizabeth looked so beautiful. She was wearing overalls and standing by a green truck. Louisa studied the photograph in the Daily Mirror that she had treated herself to. She was always watching the pennies but when she saw the princess on the front page of the newspaper she just couldn't stop herself splashing out the one penny to the newspaper stand owner. Princess Elizabeth had joined the Women's Auxiliary Territorial Service and was training as a car mechanic. *How fantastic was that,* thought Louisa, *the same job as Mark.* All the women in the country were now working, it was amazing how this little nation had coped so well. There was more food in the shops and even though all the women were working hours and hours everybody looked more glamorous than they had before the war. There was no room for idleness every female was doing their bit. Well the men were too to be fair. The wardens, the train station staff, men whose jobs were protected like members of parliament they were not allowed to go into combat they had to stay here and run the country but the whole country had come together and been quick learners.

Louisa was making two shirts for Harry and Johnny out of her dad's best shirt. He would be pleased and proud of her. After she put Harry and Johnny to bed the previous evening she had spent the whole night sewing, staying up until about midnight and her fingers were sore. About 11 o'clock the previous evening, there was a gentle tapping on the window and Louisa nearly jumped out of her skin. She peeped out of the front door but it was only the air raid warden telling her off because one of her blackout curtains wasn't shut properly.

"You have a gap, and I can swee some wight," the warden chided her with his lisped vocabulary.

Louisa giggled to herself, she felt like saying,

"I'm weally sowwy," but behaved herself very well and apologised politely before going back into the sitting room and correcting the offending blackout curtain.

She enjoyed a big mug of Horlicks made with boiling water and tip toed to bed.

Sleepily on the way to work the next morning she bravely broached Rosie with Penny's news. She had been dreading telling her but hoped Rosie was over her betrayal by Frank now and she would be pleased for Penny. But she may have read the situation wrong because all Rosie said was,

"Oh," and her chin set very firmly.

Louisa offered Rosie a piece of chewing gum from a pack which Hank the Yank had given to Harry, which with hindsight may be wasn't a very tactful thing to do. Rosie declined and they walked to work in silence.

Betty and Caren worked different hours to Louisa, Penny and Rosie, they worked a later shift which had been introduced when they started at their new premises by Tower Bridge. They did the cleaning of the apparatus and ovens, it all had to be totally spotless and in preparation for the next day's produce. It did mean though that Louisa, Penny and Rosie never got any leftovers like the sausage rollies that her Stevie adored, all those goodies went to the staff on the later shift. Louisa was usually glad it was only her and Rosie as it gave them a chance to chat on their own about matters they wouldn't usually share with Betty and Caren. But there wasn't much said that day.

Instead Louisa thought about Stevie, she made a mental note to herself to go to the air wardens and ask their advice. Surely, if he was dead or had been injured she would have heard? Received one of those dreaded letters?

"We've set a date!" Penny's grin stretched from ear to ear. She waved an official looking document at Louisa when she arrived at Penny's house from work later that day.

"Oh, brilliant!" smiled Louisa. "How exciting! When's the big day to be?"

"December 18th! Hank's due in Norwich on the 20th, so we want to get married before he leaves. Oh, I'm so excited."

"December 18th? But that's only next week, oh, my gosh I'm excited for you too."

Louisa steered Penny to the front door away from children and whispered,

"Did you explain about Violet's dad?"

Penny glanced over at her daughter, and whispered in reply,

"No, I'm leaving that until after Christmas."

Louisa's raised her eyebrows in astonishment. They obviously couldn't talk here and it was probably nothing to do with Louisa but how could she get married on the 18th of December and not tell Hank she was not a widow until after Christmas.

Louisa took the boys indoors, she must stop getting involved in everybody else's problems she told herself, she had enough of her own to do and must get more focused. Louisa felt a little fed up with it all. It was about time the children started to help. Harry wanted to go out and play but Louisa asked him politely to set the table for dinner. Harry glared at her like she had asked him to fly to the moon.

"You are getting a big boy now and Mummy works long hours and I have to do all the washing, cooking, shopping, cleaning and I am getting tired," Louisa explained as gently as she could, her son was a strong willed little fellow and she felt she was gradually losing the ability to control him. *Please, James, hurry up and come back! I need help*, she thought to herself. But Harry did as he was asked although he did slam the cutlery onto the table and bang the chairs about a bit.

Louisa had eventually finished the shirts, they looked all right from a distance but if you got up close the button holes were a bit scruffy. She would press them and then hopefully they would look better. They would have to do, there was no money for new clothes and even if you had lots of money you would have had a hard job finding anything to buy. Everything was running out or had long run out. It was use what you've got or go without. Harry had two jumpers that Sylvia had knitted him and posted last Christmas. Johnny wore two jumpers that had once been Harry's and in the warmer weather they both wore vests. Also Harry and Johnny seemed to tear or rip everything they wore, they were such rough and tumble boys. Louisa was forever darning shorts and socks for them. Louisa would wear the dress she had created for Rosie's wedding with a pink flower in her hair and the fur wrap that was hanging in her mum's wardrobe.

At school the next morning, there was a big poster on the salon door saying,

'INVITE A G. I. FOR CHRISTMAS DAY.'

Awww, great, thought Louisa and immediately felt all happy. The instructions were that the American's helping us were a long way from home and it would be a great idea to invite them into our homes and celebrate Christmas day with us."

Louisa couldn't wait to invite Hank, Penny and Violet. They would have a fun day, she would make sure. She planned to clean the house and try and get a chicken. She would get Harry and Johnny to help put decorations up, just like her and Gladys used to do when they were little and may be hopefully they could even get a teeny Christmas tree from somewhere.

Rosie came around after her work day had finished. Louisa was pleased to see her but decided she had to stop waiting on everyone and asked Rosie to put the kettle on. Also, she felt a bit ashamed of the way she was thinking, but it did occur to her that Rosie earnt more than Louisa as she worked five days and only had to keep herself and yet was always in Louisa's house drinking tea yet she had never once even offered Louisa a box of tea leaves or a bottle of milk.

"I'm not very happy about her getting married."

Louisa was shocked, she thought Rosie was going to say she wasn't very happy about putting the kettle on. Louisa bit her lip and Rosie continued,

"If it weren't for her I'd be married now and I'm not."

There was a bang on the front door, Gosh Louisa's heart dropped, she just knew that was Penny come to collect Violet after work.

"Don't you two walk home from work together anymore," Louisa enquired as Harry went to let Penny in.

"No ,we do not," barked Rosie.

Penny entered the house all smiles but her face soon dropped when she saw Louisa's guest.

Penny nodded politely to them both looking a little embarrassed, Violet run into her mother's arms and Louisa offered Penny a cup of tea.

"No, thanks, thank you for offering but I've got a lot to do this evening so I'd better get indoors, hadn't we Violet?"

Penny took her daughters hand and they strolled gently towards the front of the house.

"See you bright and early tomorrow," Penny said cheerily as she left.

"I'm going to tell Hank the Yank exactly what he's getting for a bride," Rosie shouted.

Louisa had never her seen her like this

"He ought to know the truth he won't want to marry an old slapper, he needs to be told."

Rosie demanded looking at Louisa.

"Oh, no! Rosie! Please don't do that, You mustn't do that, it's not her fault it's Frank's, if he wasn't visiting Penny he probably would have only gone to someone else. There is absolutely nothing to gain from telling Hank, you will just feel so bad with yourself. Honestly, you will." Louisa felt so weary.

"She's turned over a new leaf now, she has a job and she only did all that because she was so desperate for money, she had to feed Violet no one else would, she has no family to help her," Louisa was pleading with her now.

Rosie slammed the kettle down onto the wooden draining board,

"I don't fancy a cup of tea now I'm going home."

"Oh, Rosie, don't be like that," Louisa begged.

As Rosie reached the door she turned and emotionally added, "How come everybody thinks she's so beautiful? Why should we all keep her sordid secrets quiet? I should have known you would take her side."

Chapter Forty-Three

Harry screamed and shook Mark's hand, his little face was beaming.

"Oh, my gosh, Mark what a wonderful surprise what you doing here? I mean I'm so pleased to see you but it's so far, oh, my gosh, is Sylvia all right?" Louisa's heart suddenly stopped.

"Yes, Yes, Yes," Mark nodded shaking Harry's outstretched hand and holding out his hand to Johnny.

Louisa was surprised Harry remembered Mark, but Johnny wasn't sure of this large male looming in his sitting room, he wanted to copy his big brother but was hesitant.

Mark sat on the sofa and continued.

"Just thought I'd pop up and see you are all well and surviving. Sylvia has given me some Christmas parcels for you all and I couldn't come empty handed could I so I've got you all a little something as well." Mark handed Louisa a big red paper bag.

"Oh, I'm so touched, really, that is so very thoughtful of you and you've driven all this way, I feel guilty you using all your petrol, when it is so rationed, just to come and see us. And it's dangerous as well, being out so far from home. You are a love, let me get the kettle on."

"Had any news from James lately?" Mark casually enquired.

Mark ended up staying and sharing their vegetable stew, which Louisa had made for last night's tea, there wasn't a huge amount left so she made some suet dumplings to add to the stew and left it to simmer on her stove for about forty five minutes. While they were waiting they caught up with each other's news enjoying the hunger inducing smells.

Mark explained all about Cyril, what a traitor he was, how he banned Mark from the house as he probably suspected that Mark had cottoned on to what he was up to. Cyril had been sending secret messages somehow from his shed to German intelligence telling them the plans of the British forces, information he had gleaned from newspapers, local knowledge, the position of Headcorn airfield. It was all beyond belief, Cyril had been putting his own life in danger as well.

"I just don't get it," Louisa shook her head, "Why on earth did he do that? He had a lovely life, a beautiful wife, gorgeous home and no money worries, why would he sympathise with the German's after they'd hounded his own dad out of the country?"

"God only knows," Mark shrugged his shoulders.

Louisa told Mark that Penny next door was to marry an American G.I. and she confided that she was worried what would happen to her job when Penny did eventually move to America.

"If she goes soon I won't be able to work as I have nobody to mind Johnny, nor Harry really, although he goes to school that doesn't open until 9 o'clock and I have to start at five!"

"Oh, sorry, Louisa, I'm not thinking, I had better make tracks, you've got to be up early and I've got a long drive home with dimmed headlights," Mark laughed as he rose to leave.

Louisa didn't want him to go but she was shattered and did have an early start as usual in the morning. They had been talking for hours, the boys had put themselves to bed, but it was so nice just to have some male company.

Rosie was so polite and sweet to Louisa and Penny every day Louisa was puzzled. First of all, she was relieved but then she became a little bit suspicious, what had made her have a change of character? Rosie was behaving like her normal self.

Hank had arranged for one of his comrades, Bruce and his English girlfriend Rosemarie to be the witness's at their wedding. Penny had met Bruce a few times and Rosemarie once. There would be no family, as Penny never saw hers and Hank's were in America, it was to be a small quick service and then they would go to the 'Seamaster's Arms' for a few drinks afterwards to celebrate. Ted the landlord had promised to lay on a couple of plates of sizzling hot roast potatoes on the house as a wedding gift. Louisa and the boys were invited although Harry and Johnny would have to stay in the back yard of the 'Seamaster's Arms' along with Violet as children were not allowed in. Hank and his comrade had to go to Norwich the next morning to begin their service for the American Air Force. Penny also invited

Rosie, Caren, Betty and Ed. Louisa hoped with all her heart Rosie wasn't planning any nasty surprises as revenge. Penny told Louisa that she could invite Ma Pritchard if she wanted but Louisa thought the chances were any letter Louisa wrote to her now wouldn't get there in time, it was only a week away. Harry and Johnny both had coats each which Louisa had brought the previous winter and they luckily still fitted, as she had brought them especially large so they could hopefully last a few years, she hoped that they would keep them warm enough, she didn't want to have to put a jumper over their new shirts. Louisa wasn't sure if they would be standing around much outside the registry office, she knew she would only be able to stay for a short while, maybe one drink to toast the bridge and groom at The Seamaster's Arms as she couldn't leave the boys outside for long. But all in all it was something to look forward to and she was feeling blessed again.

"So will Hank go all the way to Norwich on the 19th then come all the way back for Christmas dinner at my house?" Louisa asked Penny one morning.

"Well, he said he's coming for Christmas dinner with us, I haven't really asked him how he's getting back, to tell you the truth, I've had so much else to think about."

Louisa hoped she got the chicken she had begged and begged Eric the butcher for. He had said he would do his best but couldn't promise.

Chapter Forty-Four

"Oh, don't you just love a good old sing song, Louisa?

Ma Pritchard had been shouting not singing as far as Louisa was concerned, shouting out the Christmas carols at the top of her voice. She was so funny, Louisa loved her. They were at the Seaman's Mission Hut attending the Christmas carol service which before the war was on every year but this was the first one since Christmas 1940, must be a good sign decided Louisa.

It was packed full, all the seats were taken and Louisa, Ma Pritchard, Harry and Johnny were standing squashed at the back of the hall. The children from the school (well school in a pub!) had opened the evening's entertainment with 'Away in a Manger', it was so cute. They had been rehearsing for weeks, Harry and Violet had been practising at home and Harry being so bossy kept telling Violet when she was going wrong. Violet kept singing,

"Away in a Manger, no sheep for a bed
The little Lord Jesus lay down his sweet bed."

"Not sheep," bellowed Harry in an authoritative voice, "you are meant to sing 'place'."

"No place for a bed."

Violet listened intently and they tried again.

"Away in a Manger, no sleep for a bed
The little Lord Jesus lay down his sweet bed."

"No, it's not sleep! It's place," Harry was exasperated, "and it's not bed its head."

Violet nodded, and they tried again.

"Away in a Manger no sheep for a bed
The little Lord Jesus lay down his sweet head."

"Hooray!" Harry threw his arms in the air, at last, right let's just have one more try and its 'place' not 'sheep'.

Violet nodded again.

160

"Away in a Manger no sleep for a bed
The little Lord Jesus lay down his sweet bed."

"Aggghh." Harry held his head in his hands as if it was the end of the world. Louisa couldn't stop laughing and wondered if Violet was singing the wrong words on purpose just to annoy Harry, he really didn't have any patience at all.

"Mum, please tell her," Harry pleaded.

Anyway, on the night of the concert, it was so funny, all the little ones looked adorable, so innocent, Miss Evans stood to the front of them with her back to the audience and waved her arms as if conducting a large orchestra. You could just about make out the words, they were all singing them at the wrong time, one little girl ran off the stage holding herself as if she was about to have an accident. Everybody was in stitches laughing but the children just seemed to think they were happy due to their marvellous performance. At the end of the performance, the audience trying to compose themselves, clapped, cheered and yelled whoops of delight and the children joined their parents to continue the evening's festivities.

"They're something magical about Christmas, isn't there, Lou Lou? Makes a change to be doing something special instead of worrying about them Jerry Germans."

Louisa had received a mysterious hand written note through the post saying Ma Pritchard would knock at her door on the 16th of December as she had heard about the Christmas concert and would love to come and see her old muckers. Louisa didn't mention to her about Penny's wedding nor Christmas day as she wasn't sure what Hank would make of Ma Pritchard. Hank had never said anything she would class as stuck up but Louisa felt he must come from a pretty rich family in America as he always dressed so smart and was so generous to them all. Ma Pritchard could be a bit outrageous sometimes, like this evening and Louisa was a bit ashamed to think it, but just hoped that if there were any people attending the Christmas concert that didn't know Louisa, well, she hoped they didn't think Ma Pritchard was her mum.

Anyway, Ma Pritchard had probably arranged to spend Christmas Day with her mysterious man friend from the East End Docks. If Louisa's Christmas lunch was a success this year, she promised herself she would invite Ma Pritchard next year and she could bring with her whomever she liked!

Chapter Forty-Five

The big day, the 18th of December arrived and it was not dark or raining but very cold. Louisa felt very emotional because the last wedding she had been to was her own. Hers and her wonderful James's. Her mind was racing with memories and it made Louisa wonder, *What is this life all about?* Anyway the boys struggled into their shirts and it took Louisa ages to do the odd buttons up. They didn't like the collars and kept fiddling with them. They looked so grown up though and Louisa hoped someone would have a camera and maybe she would be able to send a photograph of them all to James. She felt attractive herself and looking forward to doing something different. They all went together on the bus and Hank's friend was going to meet them all at Greenwich registry office at 11 o'clock along with his girlfriend. Penny looked beautiful and Louisa told her she even looked a bit American, like a younger Wallace Simpson whom the last King of England, Edward VIII had even abdicated his Royal Throne to marry as he was so in love with her! Hank looked handsome and expensively dressed and put Penny's arm into his. Violet was a flower girl and had a red velvet cape on like Little Red Riding Hood.

Louisa and the other guests stood in the small room and watched the smart Americans, she prayed Hank would look after Penny and that he wouldn't see or question anything that said 'Spinster'. The certificate was right in front of them laid across a brown shiny wooden desk. There is no way he is going to miss that it's not even small, and in a minute they're going sit down and be even nearer the certificate. She was holding her breath staring at the certificate when Rosie stood up.

No, Louisa closed her eyes, No this can't be happening, Louisa waited for Rosie to speak. Small beads of perspiration were gathering above her perfectly pencilled eyebrows, she was going to faint, her wrists were clammy. There was nothing but silence, Louisa opened her eyes, Rosie smoothed both hands down the underneath of her skirt and took her seat again. Louisa took a huge breath, Hank lifted the ink pen from its well and leant over the certificate, Louisa's heart thumped so hard her chest was hurting, he signed the certificate and looked leftwards at Penny. He was smiling, Penny took the pen from his hand and scrawled it across the Certificate of Marriage. They embraced and Bruce along with Rosemarie signed the Wedding Certificate as witnesses.

Oh, my gosh! thought Louisa, *I don't believe it! It's done.* She was so relieved.

The actual ceremony only took about six minutes but to Louisa felt like six months. The chaplain pronounced them Mr and Mrs Bailey. Everybody cheered and even Rosie seemed genuinely pleased. Betty and Ed held hands and exchanged warm romantic looks with each other and Louisa couldn't believe how totally calm she felt. It was as if a huge weight had been lifted from her shoulders. She vowed to get some lavender smelling salts like her mum used to carry around with her and to do something about her nervous disposition.

"It's a wonder all this aggravation I've had over the last few years hasn't sent my hair grey," she chuckled to herself.

Hank's dashing friend Bruce had been courting a beautiful dark-haired English girl called Rosemarie for one month, they also seemed very in love and Louisa wondered why the American G.I.s all seemed to be so smitten with the English girls. Bruce called her his 'English Rose' and Louisa guessed they wouldn't be far behind Hank and Penny getting married. She had heard of so many English girls going out with the American G.I.s and felt sorry for all the poor, brave English lads, like her brother Stevie, been away fighting for all these years for their country and when they eventually do come back, please God, they wouldn't be able to find any single girls as all the American's would have taken them!

Eve in Heart's Bakers called all the Americans G.I.s 'Johnny come latelys', and so Penny said, "I was going to invite her to my wedding but now I refuse to."

The rain kept off and they all went to The Seamaster's Arms, the boys had been very well-behaved all day. Violet and Harry said they would watch Johnny and make sure they all stayed in the in the minute backyard, although she did think they all looked a little bored, it must have been a bit tedious for them. Louisa took them all back to her house about 3 o'clock in the afternoon, she wanted to get indoors before it got dark and left everybody else to continue the merriment.

"Don't worry getting Violet tonight, she can sleep with us," Louisa offered the bride and groom and Hank thanked her with a very mischievous look on his face.

Louisa went to sleep with a huge sigh of relief that night, it was all over with no disasters and Bruce had even taken some photographs.

"Thank you, God," she said, looking up towards the ceiling, "and please look after Harry, Johnny and James and Stevie and keep us all safe. Amen."

Chapter Forty-Six

So much excitement in such a short space of time. Christmas Day already and the wedding seemed only like yesterday. The days in between had whizzed by, Louisa only had to go to work two days that week, it was actually her turn to work three, but her third day was 24th of December, Christmas Eve, and Heart's Bakers would be closed from 23rd until Monday 27th of December. They weren't paid for the days they didn't work but they did all get a small box containing some of the delicacies they had all tried to make for the Christmas customers. The boxes contained a fig pudding, which Louisa knew was a bit sparse on the figs but it saved her buying one for her Christmas feast, a loaf, and a sausage pie. Louisa confessed to Rosie on the way to work that she had been so worried about the wedding and who would say what and she was really proud that Rosie had done the right thing and kept her thoughts to herself.

"I know," Rosie smiled, "You were right, what would I have got out of opening my big mouth? And Yes, I would have felt a right bitch for the rest of my life so I'm glad you told me bluntly and thank you for being my best friend."

They hugged in the middle of Acacia Court.

Louisa had filled Harry and Johnny's stockings with a tangerine each, a pencil, some paper, a jumper and a pair of socks each (which Sylvia had knitted) and a can of coca cola too which Penny had given her as a donation from Hank. She kept the presents from Mark out of the stocking and put them under the tiny Christmas tree she had picked up at the greengrocers and dragged all the way home. There was a present already there wrapped in old newspaper and string with a bit of torn paper threaded through the string signed by Harry and Johnny. Louisa laughed to herself and didn't dare imagine what on earth it could be. The boys woke up about 5 o'clock in the morning and bounced around on Louisa's bed showing her their gifts from Santa. Louisa had to pretend to be in awe of them all and wearily sat on the bed over exaggerating her surprise and delight.

"Oh, my gosh! Harry! How did Santa Clause know you needed paper to practise your handwriting on?"

"Oh, my gosh! Johnny! How did Santa Clause know you needed a new pair of socks?"

The boys were ecstatic. Louisa missed James.

Mark had given Harry and Johnny each a pack of playing cards with 'Old Holborn Tobacco' printed on the reverse of each card and he had also a given Louisa a sweet gift, a new apron in pink with a little pattern on the fabric, she loved it.

"Wow," Louisa said to the boys, "Mummy has a new apron to wear for Christmas day dinner!" The boys couldn't wait to play snap.

Good old Eric the butcher had got Louisa a great fat chicken already plucked, (she was sure he had a bit of a soft spot for her even though he was married) and it was all stuffed with chopped onion saved from the garden in October and stale bread and smelling absolutely mouth-watering slowly roasting in a big tin spitting with lard in the oven. Louisa had peeled some potatoes and even managed to get three parsnips from the greengrocers. She couldn't remember the last time she had eaten parsnips. They definitely hadn't been cooked by her, but by Alice. Louisa just wanted her Christmas day dinner to be as happy as the Foster Family's Christmas Day dinners of the past. She knew she couldn't buy half the food her mum used to miraculously produce but if there was no cross words and everybody felt full up at the end then she would be feeling extremely pleased.

The American Air Force had taken all the G.I.s that wanted to could go back to their original base by Streatham in London free of charge. They were to be back at Streatham at 7 o'clock in the evening at the latest for their return journey to Norwich. Hank could walk to and from Louisa's house from Streatham, he would probably have to leave about six in the evening to be sure he made it back to the bus and Louisa planned to serve Christmas day lunch about two thirty which gave them plenty of time, and also she thought he and Penny may like to go into Penny's after dinner for a spell of time alone together. Louisa was all organised, the sliced carrots and green beans were on the stove in cold water ready to go on, she had boiled the giblets from the chicken in some water and would thicken it up with some flour to make gravy later. All she needed to do now was open the bottle of sherry she had found in the cupboard that her mum and Dad must have hidden away years ago. It had a crystallised sugar substance around the lid and when she opened it the smell made her eyes water, it was so strong. Louisa puffed her chest out, wait until James sees what a talented, capable wife he has she laughed to herself. If only he was here, she needed to cuddle him, to feel his strong arms around her, to smell him.

Hank the Yank lived up to his reputation and brought an amazing cardboard box containing

Fruit Juice, a can of evaporated milk, some bacon rashers wrapped in greaseproof paper, a box of coffee, a packet of sugar, a packet of rice, some fresh peas and a pack of lard.

She couldn't believe it

"Oh, my gosh, Hank, I won't have to go shopping for two weeks." Louisa was so grateful. Harry and Johnny had never eaten bacon and none of them had ever tasted fruit juice.

"I'm glad I invited you now," she laughed.

Penny mentioned that Hank had received fifty invitations to Christmas day lunch with families in Norwich and East Anglia.

"Never! Fifty invitations – blimey, you are popular!" Louisa exclaimed, "Now I do feel very honoured you chose us out of all that lot!"

He then gave to Harry, Johnny and Violet a pack of building blocks each and wished them 'Merry Christmas'.

The building blocks were tipped out immediately on top of the playing cards on the sitting room floor which was also strewn with string and tissue paper. The children were so engrossed in their new possessions there was not a peep out of them for at least an hour which left Louisa, Penny and Hank to enjoy some sherry in her mum's posh glasses at the kitchen table and have an adult conversation and listened to Bing Crosby singing 'White Christmas' on the wireless.

When they all finally did sit down to eat the meal, Hank insisted on saying 'Grace' which was quaint, Violet and Louisa shared one chair, Harry and Johnny shared another, which made Violet giggle and Harry bossily instructed Johnny exactly how to sit properly. Louisa bestowed Hank and Penny their own chairs as they were guests and apart from the gravy being a bit watery and bland Louisa felt the meal was a success. Everybody said they enjoyed it anyway. She poured some Sherry on the miniscule fig pudding but was too scared to light it like her dad used to in case she burnt the house down and they all had a teeny amount and sat back holding their bloated tummies.

Chapter Forty-Seven

Betty was straddled across Ed's back. He was lying on their double bed completely naked resting his head sideways on his folded arms. Betty pressed firmly with her palms into his muscled back with slow sweeping motions upwards towards his shoulders. His eyes were closed and his breathing was heavy. He had put on some weight over the last year or so, not a lot and it suited him. She was surprised really because he only had the odd pint of beer now and then so she would have thought that would have made him lose weight and she definitely didn't recall him eating anymore because he had no chance of that with all the food shortages and rationing. For Ed's Christmas present she had created some homemade coupons, she wrote them in her best handwriting and used a different coloured pencil for each one. She daydreamed for weeks at work about what she could get him for a gift. They had no money for frivolities but she was so totally in love with him again, like a teenager, she wanted to spoil him. The coupons had been an idea on *Women's Hour* on the radio one evening. The presenter, Gloria, had suggested 'cleaning your husband's shoes' or 'polishing his chisel collection'. Betty had raised her eyebrows it wasn't hard imagining what services she could offer her husband and it had nothing to do with shoes! Gloria suggested a different experience for each coupon. The first three coupons read,

'I will make you Lord Woolton's pie – your favourite dinner.'
'I will roll you ten cigarettes from your tobacco pouch.'
'I will cook you a delicious cottage pie.'

The other coupons were very private and Bettys only dilemma was making sure Rosie and Caren never laid eyes on them.

Betty's request to Ed for her Christmas present was a sturdy lock on their bedroom door which he had brought and fixed up no problem within two days.

Ed groaned and slid his right leg upwards slightly shifting his body to accommodate his obvious appreciation. Betty smiled and settled down onto his back wiggling and giggling as she did so.

They were both thoroughly enjoying today's voucher 'A sensual massage'.

Louisa felt really flat after Christmas, everything seemed flat, the last few weeks had been a whirlwind of excitement, the Carol Service at the Seaman's Hut, Mark coming up to London to visit them, Penny and Hank's wedding culminating in Louisa's first attempt at a big family Christmas dinner there now seemed nothing to look forward to except dark damp evenings and Louisa voiced these thoughts one day walking to work with Rosie.

The wind blasting up the River Thames felt like something from Russia. Louisa had seen pictures of a Soviet winter in the Daily Mirror before, they told an horrific story about Adolph Hitler's Nazi troops shooting Soviet Jews, thousands of them and although the pictures were in black and white you could see the blood staining the high piles of snow.

"Brrrrrrr," the girls pushed their heads down and held arms as they battled across Tower Bridge.

"It's funny you should say that I'm feeling a bit the same, I heard there's a British Legion Club in Russell Square, up the West End and they have dances on every Saturday night, if I asked my mum to look after Harry and Johnny would you like to come with me and Caren? I haven't asked her yet I only want to go if you say yes, I just think it will do both of us good to get a bit dressed up and have a night out and I'm sure my mum won't mind looking after the boys. We can even ask Penny if you think she would like to join us, she is on her own with Hank away working."

Louisa was horrified.

"No," she mumbled through her grey woollen scarf, "I can't. possibly come, I would just feel so bad with my poor James stuck out in an ocean somewhere encountering God knows what and me out dancing and what not, don't seem right, I just couldn't."

"Oh, please, Louisa, please come," Rosie stopped in her tracks, Louisa tugged at her coat to get her to carry on walking, it was far too cold to stand here talking.

"We could all get killed tomorrow, blown to bits by a great big bomb, please come, just once, I don't want to go to The Seamaster's Arms, my mum and dad keep trying to get me to go to one of the Saturday night dances there but I know too many people there and I don't want them all asking me all about Frank, please, please Louisa at least say you'll think about it? Please, Please, you are my best friend! And you can't make any difference to what James is going through whether you stay in or go out."

Louisa agreed to think about it, Oh dear, she would feel so dreadfully guilty about going, it would feel like she was being unfaithful, surely James wouldn't like it one bit, her in a dance up the West End, with other men around her. What would she say if one of them asked her to dance or even offered to buy her a drink? No, how could she go, it would be really out of order. But she did feel sorry for Rosie, she was having no fun at all since Frank had done the dirty and her wedding had been called off. If only she would start going out with Clara, then she could meet another boyfriend. But Clara and Rosie were as different as chalk and cheese and that was never going to happen.

"Let me sleep on it," Louisa sighed as they walked into the warmth of Heart's Bakers. Rosie beamed and Louisa instantly regretted yielding to her proposal.

On the return journey that day the headlines were 'PARIS RECAPTURED AFTER FOUR YEARS OF NAZI RULE.'

Chapter Forty-Eight

Penny was having none of it.

"No way is Betty looking after little Harry and Johnny, after all the times you've had Violet for me when me and Hank were courting, No way, I'll have them. I think it's a jolly good idea, you need to get out and enjoy yourself, darling, you're always slaving away after these two horrors," Penny wailed pointing towards the insulted boys.

"But surely you want to come too, oh gosh, how do I get myself into these situations, I don't even want to go, I love sitting indoors all warm and cosy with my dressing gown on and a big cup of Horlicks, I can't even keep my eyes open after 9 o'clock these days."

"You go, I'll come in and help you get ready, we can have some of that lovely sherry we had Christmas day if you've got any left over and I'll paint your nails for you, what are you going to wear?"

Louisa grimaced, she knew when she was beaten, she would just have to go, get it over with and then Rosie will think she's a fabulous friend and everybody will stop nagging her.

As it happened, Louisa had one of the best times of her life. They left the house about 6 o'clock. Penny had given Louisa and Rosie a manicure each with her bright crimson nail varnish which smelt disgusting and took ages to dry but did look so glamorous and matched their lipstick. Louisa couldn't stop holding her hands out in front of her and admiring her film star nails.

It took the bus about an hour to get to Russell Square, it was stop and start all the way and was full of young people all about the same ages as Rosie, Louisa and Caren. Everybody was in a party mood and looked dressed to impress. There were some

G.I.s at the back being really loud, the conductor yelled, "Russell Square," and nearly everyone stood to disembark.

"Wow!" Rosie squeezed Caren's arm. "This is going to be some night!" The streets were swarming with happy, boisterous revellers.

The Red X Club was owned by the British Legion and was gigantic, there were hundreds of people in there jostling to get to the bar and an enormous queue for 'the ladies'. The girls grabbed three seats around a table just inside the door where about fifteen other people were already standing and sitting. Caren said she would go and get them all a Babycham each and Louisa and Rosie placed their coats on the back of two vacant chairs and stood there taking it all in. They had never been anywhere like it and felt very conscious that they looked 'new'. There were a few people dancing on the dance floor and crowds still piling through the doors. A couple of the men on their table started chatting and turned out to be G.I.s. They weren't rude or pushy and Louisa immediately relaxed. Caren and Rosie had a few dances with various men but Louisa declined the only offer to dance that she received which was from a tall blond gentleman saying she had twisted her ankle. He had laughed when she told him that and Louisa thought he knew she was pretending, but he hung around and they had a respectable chat. He was from Boston in America, his grandparents were originally from Ireland and had sailed to America in search of a better life. He had one sister and was obviously wealthy as he had been to college. Louisa was really glad she had come, it was nice to hear about a different way of life and hopefully Rosie and Caren could come on their own next time and they were good looking girls so should easily be able to attract some nice boyfriends, with good hearts and backgrounds that could eventually become nice husbands! She really did want to go home now and get in bed but Rosie and Caren were laughing hysterically with some G.I.s and Louisa pined for her Horlicks.

Chapter Forty-Nine

Fourteen nights on the trot they had been sleeping in the air rad shelter.

"I thought this was all over with," Penny complained, "what's going on?"

"Me too, I can't believe it, thought it was all coming to an end. Well, I hoped anyway, I can't stand this much longer it's too cramped in that Anderson Shelter, now the boys are getting bigger and it's so hot too. I don't know how we survived all those nights during the Blitz, seems a life time ago now!"

Enormous airships just like giant balloons that really made a racket had been going over every night from the Jerry Germans, as Ma Pritchard liked to call them. These airships or planes or whatever they were had obviously been able to trick the British Forces out because no air raid sirens were being sounded. The airships really made a deafening noise, but the radar obviously wasn't picking them up. And they were huge, gigantic. After the first few nights, the air wardens had called everybody to a meeting in the Seaman's Mission Hut, this was serious they said. The airships were called V1 and V2 and many lives had been lost already in just three days. These new bombs just made you disappear, they left massive empty craters in the ground with no sign of what had been there ten minutes before.

Most people had got out of the habit of using the air raid shelter, the bombing had really dwindled over the last year or two. If you heard the siren and you were out in the day time most people ran for an underground station or a large communal shelter. Louisa held her hands up to this, but recently if she heard the air raid siren in the day time and she was at home she usually ignored it and got on with her housework chores. She did listen out to see if she could hear any airplanes getting nearer. On the odd occasion that she did then, she would take herself into the shelter but nowhere near as urgently as she did in the first days of the war. The danger passed every time and she ended up moaning to herself about it all wasting her valuable time. They were all becoming very blasé about this Second World War. The Town Hall had sectioned off the bombed warehouse site at Hayes Wharf and erected a huge round tin hut on it to be used as an air raid shelter for the school children, it was only one minute's walk for them. Also Miss Evans had an air raid drill every Monday and Tuesday morning to make sure the children knew it inside out.

The United Kingdom definitely seemed to be Adolph Hitler's favourite place to bomb.

At the meeting, the air wardens went over again and again what had to been done if you heard one of these monsters heading your way, what to listen for and generally recapping all the safety measures they had learnt six years ago. It was like a school revision test. There was a drawing of one of the V2 airships, it looked as big as the Peabody Buildings. *How on earth does that stay up in the sky*? wondered Louisa.

They were told that the airship would make the deafening droning sound until it was ready to unload its bomb then it would be completely silent. Now that was scary. It didn't have a pilot was just aimed off in the direction of the United Kingdom. Louisa didn't tell Harry and Johnny that bit of information as she just couldn't see the point, there was nothing you could do about it, you wouldn't be able to run away, you would be dead before you knew it.

So every night Louisa, Betty, Rosie, Caren and Penny would lie in their air raid shelters, squeezing their hands tight and willing the roaring objects to go past them.

"Please don't stop above us," they all begged silently.

It was so terrifying and all the mums at school spoke of and the only topic of conversations in the shops was of 'doodlebugs'.

Two weeks they lasted, then they just stopped as suddenly as they had started. The Daily Mirror called it 'A Mini Blitz', they hadn't only targeted London. Ireland, Manchester, Liverpool, they had all got a bombarding too. Six thousand people died. After the two weeks of crashing them into London, they started sending them to Norwich. The Germans must have known the American Air Force were there. Louisa read about it in the Daily

Mirror. She never said anything to Penny about it and Penny never mentioned it so, if she knew she was being very brave. Not a constant worrier like Louisa.

Louisa, Penny, Violet and the boys listened to a speech on the radio by the President of The United States of America, Franklin Roosevelt. He had the most purring, charismatic voice, just like Hank. Penny was missing Hank immensely. He had written to her twice only but said he was working sixty to seventy hours per week and when he was not toiling away he was sleeping. She hadn't seen him since Christmas. Although he did send her a parcel which contained some very odd looking, uncomfortable shoes, two pairs one for her and one for Violet. They were called clogs and were rock hard, made of wood and were pretty impossible to walk in. Violet loved them but Penny said they looked like something Louisa would throw on her fire. Louisa tried clomping around Penny's sitting room in them, they were so difficult to keep on your feet.

"How you supposed to look like a lady in these?" Penny exclaimed.

"Can you imagine me going to meet his parents and sisters for the first time and turning up in those?"

Penny and Louisa went into hysterical giggles. Louisa kept laughing all day thinking about the clogs.

Louisa was a bit concerned about the Hank situation, she knew that Penny hadn't ended up telling him the truth about Violet's dad after Christmas as she had planned to and was worried he may have found out Penny had lied to him, maybe he had heard some gossip from somewhere, who knows? Maybe somebody had made a snide comment about Penny, she didn't know what to think, but Louisa kept her fears to herself.

"Clara's coming with us next week!" Rosie was like a new woman. Her and Caren had not wanted to leave the Red X club and had been in buzzy moods ever since. Clara really like the sound of it all and wanted to meet some 'rich blokes'.

"I think it's about time we got married," she asserted to Rosie and Caren one day during their break.

"I wouldn't mind a life in America, heard they treat you really good those G.I.s, got a bob or two and we can't wait around for ever for our boys to come home we might be too old and wrinkly for any man to want us then, No I'm sorry we have just got to look after ourselves and get a handsome yank, like Penny's Hank the Yank."

They all laughed but knew every word Clara said was unfortunately right.

A couple of months later, they had an unwanted visitor, a deadly doodlebug hovered over Heart's Bakers factory during the day. Eve came screaming through the heavy doors,

"Get under the benches," she screeched throwing herself across the floor, everybody panicked, it was terrifying, they hadn't heard a thing but now it was deafening, good job she had seen it, Clara and Rosie held hands, Louisa was at the other end of room under the bread table. For what seemed like an age the sound stayed the same, it didn't get louder or quieter, just sat up in the sky over them, it was even more scary than when they were in their shelters. Then is ceased. Louisa looked down the room towards Clara and Rosie, she closed her eyes, she could hear crying and people shouting,

"Nooooo, please, God. Nooooo!"

"This is it." Louisa felt unexpectedly calm, her mind flashed back to being with her mum and sister in Greenwich Park when she was very little, she thought of her dad bouncing her on his knee, of skipping up Bermondsey Walk holding Stevie' s hand and it being very sunny.

The explosion blasted through the two windows in the Baker's factory. The doors blew open and a deafening silence followed. Dark grey heavy smoke roared into the room like a dragon's breath. Debris fell from everywhere, everybody screamed, a natural instinct, they were just screaming without knowing they were. But then it receded, the smoke slowed down but you could hear the din from outside the building. Sirens, yells, people running, bangs, crashes.

"Quick," yelled Eve, dragging herself up from under the table, she beckoned everybody to follow her from the building, Louisa was hesitant. "What are we running in to? It could be worse outside; surely, we're running into the danger?"

The dust felt warm and was so thick they all covered their mouths with cupped hands, Clara felt the grit going into her eyes, Rosie looked for Louisa and Eve but couldn't see anybody through the smoke.

Woolworths Store down the road at New Cross, South London had taken the direct hit from the V2 doodlebug bomb, every member of the staff had been killed and all the customers in the store. A total of one hundred and sixty eight people.

"That could have been us," Louisa cried. She was just so grateful it wasn't them, who would have looked after little Harry and Johnny.

President Franklin D. Roosevelt threatened to drop something called a nuclear bomb on Japan because Japan had annihilated America's main Naval Base at Pearl Harbour out in the Pacific Ocean in a place called Hawaii.

"What a pretty name," Penny commented, "Like Acacia Court really, when I first moved here I thought what a pretty name for a street."

At Pearl Harbour two thousand, four hundred and three people had been killed. They had lost three hundred and sixty aircraft and about eight great destroyers. It only lasted an hour and fifty minutes yet they had carried out all that devastation. It must have been a simply massive attack, taken weeks to plan, how did America not have an inkling?

They were all shocked. For some silly reason, Louisa thought as soon as the Americans had joined with Britain and France the war would be over within weeks. That Saturday she brought the Daily Mirror, let Johnny go out to play with Harry in the street poured herself a sherry and read the newspaper from cover to cover. She was hoping that James was nowhere near Hawaii.

"Mrs Louisa scared of everything should be my name not Mrs Louisa Bishop," she tipsily murmured to herself.

Chapter Fifty

She just knew James was dead before anyone told her.

She knew it. Call it 'sixth sense', 'women's intuition', anything you want, Louisa thought but she just knew it. She felt so scared, terrified, she was shaking looking out of the window she just had this feeling that doom was upon her. Six weeks had gone by with no word from James, everyone kept asking, Sylvia had written twice but had received nothing in return from James. Louisa knew it was not right.

Louisa was sitting on her threadbare sofa, Johnny had fallen asleep which was very unusual for him. Harry was at the kitchen table with his building blocks. Louisa walked over to him and stroked his hair, he was getting tall.

Bang, Bang. There it was, she knew it was coming.

She opened the door slowly with a big sigh, it was Penny!

Penny steered Louisa back into the sitting, in her hand she held a letter.

"The post lady delivered this to me by mistake." Her voice was bubbly but her face was grave.

The white, rectangle shaped envelope from the War Office was all too familiar to Louisa.

This time it was addressed to her, Mrs James Bishop.

When Louisa thinks back now she is so proud of herself for coping so well. She liked to think James would have been proud of her too. Before his death she was always scared, nervous, anxious about something. In a strange way all the years of worrying, of the fretting had been just as bad as actually receiving the news that James was dead, 'Lost at Sea' was the official explanation. Louisa must have cried for probably six weeks solid. She cried when she woke up and was still sobbing when she went to bed. She wailed because Harry wouldn't see his daddy again. She broke down because Johnny had never seen his daddy. She sobbed because she wouldn't see their daddy again. Everything made her weep. But most of all, what made her very saddest out of everything was that her handsome, kind, wonderful James was floating lost in a dark, cold sea somewhere all on his own. Now that was just too painful to comprehend.

Every day it was like she had been hypnotised. They would all wake up, have a wash, get dressed, have breakfast, brush their teeth, open the curtains, she was like a zombie, doing the washing, preparing meals, shopping, looking after Johnny and Harry everything she did was automatic like a wound up toy. Even talking, she would have a conversation then five minutes later wonder what she had spoken about. It was usual to hear her voice talking to James without her realising she was. Now there was only her and her boys left, she hadn't heard from Stevie for years and shrugging her shoulders thought he was probably gone too. Only her left. For now anyway who knows they might all be dead this time tomorrow. She wanted to die, to be with her mum, her darling daddy, Gladys and James but she couldn't, she would have if she could have, she really would but who would look after Harry and Johnny?

Sylvia came to visit her staying two days and nights and sleeping in Harry's bed. Harry and Johnny shared Johnny's bed they were such good boys. They didn't know any different, they had only really ever had Louisa in their lives but knew that their dad dying was very serious and Mummy was very sad. Louisa cuddled James's underpants every night in bed, they were like a comfort blanket, they smelt of him and good times.

Sylvia took the boys and Violet to school, she made endless cups of tea, cried with Louisa, cleaned the windows. Really there was nothing anybody could do to ease the pain. Sylvia was suffering probably more than Louisa, James had been in her life twenty five years, Louisa had only had him for seven.

During this period poor, old President Franklin Roosevelt, the president of the United States of America passed away. More tears were shed by Louisa she had loved listening to his warm voice on her wireless.

Sylvia gave Louisa £35. She said she had to get back to Laburnham Farm in Biddenden, Kent. It wasn't an option for her to be away for too long as June depended on her entirely since Cyril's death and she fondly wittered that Maureen and Carol,

181

the Land girl lodgers, couldn't cook or do the laundry, all they were capable of was working on the Hop Farm or going into Tenterden to enjoy themselves. Secretly Louisa thought they were paying June money every week so why should the poor things also cook and clean on top of fifty hours solid graft on the Kent countryside!

Heart's Bakers factory managed without her for six weeks, Penny covered a lot of Louisa's shifts, it made no difference to Louisa if she had Violet or not, her brain had switched off, thinking was just too painful. The girls at Heart's Bakers even had a whip-round for her and Clara came with Rosie and Penny one afternoon and gave her a huge bag containing fruit, vegetables and even some biscuits they had baked. That made her cry, she was so touched, they didn't earn much money how very sweet of them. But she had no appetite at all, she just couldn't eat, everything made her nauseous. Harry, Violet and Johnny polished off the biscuits in one week. Penny gave her £1 a week as well for looking after Violet which was totally unnecessary, Louisa didn't care about the money she was numb with grief but didn't have the energy to protest to Penny so took it and placed it into her purse.

Her first day back at work was a shock, she couldn't seem to walk at her usual speed, not only walking, everything she did she felt like she was in slow motion.

The strangest realisation occurred to Louisa one evening while she was dishing up their evening meal. She didn't worry any more, how odd, not once since she had received that letter saying James was dead had she felt anxious, afraid or fretted about anything. How can that be? Or why? She was so devoid of emotion now that she wouldn't even be able to worry about something if she tried to.

Then to top it all, on the 8th of May 1945, Britain declared the end in the Second World War in Europe.

Chapter Fifty-One

Since the DD landings of 1944 the whole scenario of Second World War altered.

Great Britain at one point was so close to being invaded by Germany and taken over and having them rule for ever. The whole world has to be grateful for all those poor men that gave or risked their lives to halt the Nazis.

The Allied forces invaded Normandy in France on the 6th of June 1944 and over one hundred and fifty five thousand Allied troops fearlessly battled the Germans by air, sea and land all the way back into Germany. Some of the countries the Allied forces freed had been under German rule for years by then. What absolute heroes were the Allied Forces? It was a truly amazing feat.

Adolph Hitler's last chance attempt to win was in December 1944 in the snow-covered forest of Ardennes. He believed he could halt the Allied advance by driving them back to Antwerp in Belgium. It didn't work.

The Allied Forces harrowingly uncovered German concentration camps during their advance through Europe. Since before the outbreak of World War Two, the Germans had been gathering up as many as they could of people they deemed to be undesirable. Gypsies, Jewish people, convicts were used for slave labour, starved, executed. They even allowed medical practise to be carried out on them. Adolph Hitler's vision was one for a pure race for the whole of Europe. He dreamt of a great day when all of Europe would have blonde hair and was actually convinced the world would thank him for it. Thousands of these barbaric camps were discovered and millions of poor souls lost their lives.

Millions of people were held in the concentration camps. Just imagine for a start how totally terrified they were, in the first place, that they were going to be captured by the Gestapo, their days and nights must have been unbearable living in fear and hiding. To have no choice but to leave your homes, your friends, your careers and attempt to escape to just anywhere you could get to, with your children and probably very little money or possessions.

Many of them didn't make it and died on route. The unlucky ones that were caught and rounded up lived in the concentration camps in total squalor and freezing conditions, the Germans tried to starve them to death, the poor blighters had no clothing, no food or water, no heat. Thousands were sent to shower blocks thinking they were going to bathe but instead of water being emitted poisonous gases were pumped through the shower heads and the people dropped dead.

When the Allied Forces discovered these concentration camps, they found hundreds of naked bodies, like skeletons, still sitting where they had passed away, starved to death. There were huge mounds of bodies all slung on top of each other, having been murdered in the gas chambers, lost to untreated diseases or starved to death. Human waste was everywhere. It was beyond belief.

In an underground bunker in Berlin, the then-capital of Germany, on the 1st of May 1945, Adolph Hitler, who knew he was being defeated, committed suicide and the world was rid of a monster.

Chapter Fifty-Two

London was in the midst of the hugest celebrations. The whole population of the United Kingdom was ecstatic. Day and night the so happy people cheered, partied, blew paper trumpets, sounded car horns. So proud of themselves and the Allied Forces. Probably in disbelief a tiny bit, they had come so close to losing World War Two and Winston Churchill, their Bulldog, had been a strong and wise leader and now the whole of Europe was free to re build. New beginnings. New outlooks.

Muriel and Derek arranged a street party for Acacia Court. Louisa and all her neighbours lugged their tables and chairs and any other furniture item of any use out into the middle of the road. The tables were lined up next to each other from one end of the street to the other end resembling one gigantic table. Everyone was in high spirits. Any slight happening was classed as a cause to cheer again, to celebrate around the clock. The tables were draped with the now un needed blackout curtains, they were ripped down with glee from the houses at the realisation there would be no more air raids, no more cramped and uncomfortable nights trying to sleep in air raid shelters or down underground stations. No more waking up in the middle of the night or running for your life when an air raid siren bellowed.

Food although still in shortage was miraculously discovered was piled high on the tables and everybody had such a fantastic day, like twenty five Christmas days all squashed into eight hours. Photographs were taken, best outfits were worn with pride, hugs and cuddles were enjoyed by every neighbour of every age. Dancing and singing and cheering was the order of the day and Acacia Court obeyed with a vengeance.

From Land's End at the very bottom of Great Britain to John o' Groats at the top of Great Britain, Street parties were embraced everywhere, the day was called V-E Day, Victory in Europe Day.

King George VI, Queen Elizabeth, Princess Elizabeth and Princess Margaret all appeared on the balcony at Buckingham Palace to wave and join in the celebratory mood with the thousands who had thronged down Pall Mall. People for as far as the eye could see. Princess Elizabeth, the future queen, even went onto the street and mingled with her public.

After the street parties, many adults carried on celebrating and swarmed into the bombed towns and cities to continue the frivolity. Rosie, Caren and Clara travelled to Nelson's Column at Trafalgar Square and then onto the Houses of Parliament for more hugs under the shadows of Big Ben with complete strangers, flag waving and cheering. They travelled home on the first bus of the next morning in daylight after being awake for twenty four hours. VE day would never be forgotten.

Events didn't finish overnight though, thousands of Allied service men were spread all over Europe, starving and living in hope of getting back to their homes before it was too late for them. Depending on where they had ended up made a huge difference to how they were treated. It was a massive operation to transport these young boys, who had suffered so much, many not even officially men, back to their homes and waiting families.

Japan was still battling America hoping they could have a bigger slice of world domination. Japan's dream was for one united Asia continent. In the United States of America, Harry Truman became the new president and continued with his predecessor, Franklin Roosevelt's plans to drop atomic bombs on Japan.

On the 6th of August 1945, the first atomic bomb was dropped and between ninety thousand and one hundred and forty six thousand human beings perished in a city in Japan called Hiroshima. Three days later, on the 9th of August 1945, between thirty nine thousand and eighty thousand further deaths were caused by another atomic bomb dropped on a city called Nagasaki. The after effects of these lasted decades.

Chapter Fifty-Three

A whole year had passed since she had received the telegram informing Louisa she was now a widow. Louisa asked Penny if she could get her 'some work'? Penny was flabbergasted.

"If you know what I mean?!" Louisa added sniggering nervously.

Penny's mouth was wide open, she was speechless.

"I don't want to but I need money to feed mouths, what I'm earning at Heart's Bakers is just not enough, there's talk of war widows receiving pensions from the government but nothing's official yet, it's got to be approved by the new labour government apparently and the boys are just eating so much, they must have hollow bellies,' Louisa gingerly explained pointing at Harry and Johnny.

"Really? Little miss goody two shoes? Honestly?" whispered Penny, she just wasn't sure about this.

"I need money, I can do anything, I have to do anything to support them," Louisa whispered, "Do you have any contacts from the past or ever bump into any one, you know like who might want a service?"

Louisa laughed, not through humour, through nerves really. She realised she was asking a lot from Penny. Penny had distanced herself from that part of her life long ago, she had buried it totally when she had met Hank, pretended to herself it had never happened, it was tucked away at the back of her memories never to be thought of again, for her to re visit it could cause her trouble, if Hank ever found out, if he didn't suspect already, bang goes her new promised future in America.

The following week, a dark, cold, windy, early October evening, Penny had arranged for Louisa to meet a man called Lawrence for thirty minutes outside The Seamaster's Arms at 6.30 pm. It was a bit odd really Louisa actually enjoyed getting dressed up and ready to go out. She put the boys to bed and told Harry she was popping next door for half an hour.

"Without us?" he questioned, "Shall we come?"

"No, you and Johnny stay in here, it's cold outside, you practise some reading and you can look after you and Johnny for thirty minutes – it's a test to see how grown up you really are. Then go to sleep. You have school in the morning, and anyway I'll be back before you know it," Louisa kissed them both.

"I want to be a grown up," Harry exclaimed sucking his lips in, "I want to be in the Navy and be in a submarine."

"Now you lie down and go back to sleep," Louisa smoothed his hair, giving him another kiss. She was shaking. As she pulled the front door firmly shut behind her, her heart was thumping ferociously. She nearly never went.

"Oh, my gosh! Say someone sees me, say I know him," Louisa fretted to herself, "Say I've seen him about?"

She felt like she was walking through a cloud it was so damp outside. She pulled the rough scarf around her chin and ears. The wind was roaring across from the River Thames up Acacia Court. The sky was black and sinister looking.

"Oh, my gosh, say he knew James." She was petrified. "Hurry up, girlie, and get this over with, if Penny did it for all those years you can too!"

She would never tell anyone about that night but she approached The Seamaster's Arms shaking, there were three nicely dressed, pretty women whom Louisa didn't recognise standing outside the door which had 'Saloon Bar' painted on it and three men standing at the public bar door smoking cigarettes. She walked towards the men with her head down, she didn't make any eye contact with the women. She may not know them but they may recognise her or worse still know Harry or Johnny. Her heart was pounding.

"Rita," one of the men called. Louisa ignored him for a split second then remembered Penny had told him her name was Rita, Louisa shyly turned around and a really nice looking man was calling her. He had short blond hair and was about 6 foot 4 inches tall, roughly the same height as Stevie. He was slim, very upright in his posture and wearing an expensive looking black suit, with a white shirt combined with a black tie. Louisa felt scruffy.

Louisa was shocked, she hadn't given it much thought what the man would be like but guessed, "It would be some old 'Rum head' scruffily dressed with a huge red bulbous nose!"

Louisa felt very shy and was squirming with embarrassment. Lawrence looked kind and as embarrassed as her.

"I wasn't expecting a lady like you!" he exclaimed as he blew his cigarette smoke away from her.

'A lady' he called Louisa 'a lady', she was chuffed. "Oh, thank you, I've never been called a lady before," she replied coyly smiling. He walked around the side of The Seamaster's Arms and Louisa timidly followed him with her head tucked down dreading seeing anybody familiar. At the side of the pub was a concrete step sticking out under the doorway that only the landlord and landlady used to enter the building. Lawrence sat himself down on it and patted the step inviting Louisa to join him.

"I don't think I can do this," Lawrence muttered looking up into her face with wide eyes. His voice was very high pitched, not low and deep, Louisa was mortified, how embarrassing! Was she that awful to look at? She knew she was a bit heavier than before she had had the children, despite food shortages she still carried a bit more weight around her hips than her younger, pre-children days.

"Rita, I feel so ashamed, I have been away at sea for three years now, not had one woman near me, feel like I'm going to explode but I just can't touch you, I just couldn't, you look like a lady, what on earth are you doing here? Don't you have an old man somewhere, a husband?" Lawrence whispered.

Lawrence reached his hand to her. They sat on the step together and chatted for a while, he came from a place called Merseyside, his ship had docked at London and he had to make his own way back up to Liverpool in the north of England, he would have to catch the train from Marylebone Station in West London and then he could walk to his home from the station when he arrived in Liverpool. He was looking forward to giving his mum a great big surprise when he got home, she didn't know he was coming.

Suddenly Louisa jumped up, she was taking such a big risk sitting here holding hands with a stranger, anybody could see her, the landlord or landlady could open the door, one of her neighbours could walk past, she must be mad and she wasn't even going to get any money out of it,

"Never again," she wailed inside her head, she just had to get back to Harry and Johnny, put this whole shameful experience behind her, Lawrence pushed a five pound note into her hand.

"Awww, thank you! What a gentleman you are," Louisa gasped as she ran off with visions in her head of Harry and Johnny out in the street, looking for her, getting lost in the dark, playing on a bomb site, what would she do without her boys? They were her whole world now, they could even be knocking at Penny's asking for me.

"Oh, my gosh, what did I do this for? I must be mad. How would Penny explain her absence away? Aww, but Lawrence had been a sweetie."

She pulled the woollen shawl tighter under her chin. The freezing Thames mist was so cold it hurt her throat to breath. She had to walk faster. She prayed little Harry wasn't awake. Please god, don't let him be crying, don't let him have woken Johnny. She turned the corner through the fog that was starting to roll in from the Thames she could see her home, quick nearly home.

"Chin up, girlie, you're nearly there."

Chapter Fifty-Four

After her experience with Laurence, Louisa decided that they were just going to have to survive on the meagre income they had. They had no alternative. She had had a lucky escape, Louisa shook her head, waves of shame kept washing over her, *What on earth had she been thinking? Her brain must have disappeared, she had to get with it and toughen up, anyway there is no use crying over spilt milk, she'll just have to forget about it, there's nothing she can do about it now, just put it down to experience and learn from it, Lou Lou.*

She clenched her chin. Her, Johnny and little Harry sat at the kitchen table and with a piece of paper she explained to them that they had,

8 shillings per week for food and soap,

9 shillings per week for rent,

1 shilling per week for clothes,

1 shilling per week to put away for Christmas and days out,

Writing it down for all of them to understand.

It worked out easy to keep to her budget, she didn't know why she hadn't thought of it years ago. For two weeks it was a doddle, easy peasy she commended herself. Then Johnny fell over grazed his poor knees and ripped his school shorts to pieces, and Louisa had to pay three shillings for a new pair. The planned budget hadn't lasted long.

Life went on. Over half of London lay in piles of rubble, Louisa felt sorry that all Harry and Johnny had ever know was bomb sites and hardship but they didn't seem at all affected by it, they made their own entertainment and were happy with life, they had her, friends, food and a bed that was all they were concerned about.

Penny sighed one morning and told Louisa that she had written to Hank confessing. She explained that she was so scared now of him finding out and not wanting her any more that she imagined what it would be like if he didn't find out now but in the future. When they were all safely settled in America. Penny would have given up her house, Violet would have been taken away from all she knew to make a fresh start in a new land and then she would have to up sticks and come back again. Uprooting Violet, no home to come back to, no job, no school for Violet, and if she did have to return to good old England she may get a house miles away where she didn't know a soul.

"Well, you've obviously given it a lot of thought," Louisa agreed with her.

"I've been lying awake at night thinking about it, I don't want to be worried for the rest of my life, it's making me ill, I should have just told him the truth in the first place, nothing's worth this, it's on the back of my mind constantly."

Louisa had never seen Penny looking so forlorn and gave her a great big hug.

"We haven't half been through some stuff in our short lives, haven't we, darling?" Louisa comforted.

"I'm sure it will all work out fine, he loves the ground you walk on and Violet."

Ma Pritchard visited, she brought a great lump of delicious chocolate, oh, it was the best taste Louisa had ever experienced. It just melted on your tongue, it was exquisite.

"It's a wonder you are not twice your size all these goodies your man give's you," Louisa sniggered.

Even June was courting a G.I., she had met him in Surrey and Ma Pritchard hadn't been introduced yet but they seemed to be getting quite serious. Tom was in France hoping to get home, he had been away in the Army for the whole war and Ma Pritchard prayed he would be a survivor. She hadn't seen 'hide or hare' of her Joan for years and Phyllis was in the Military Corps in Edinburgh, Scotland.

"Blimey, how did she get to be stationed up there? I've heard it's even colder up there than London."

Louisa made some tea and they chatted about James, about Louisa's grief, about Little Harry and Johnny and the weather.

Rosie, Caren and Clara were like the Three Musketeers, every Saturday night they were out dancing. Every Monday or Tuesday they enthralled the whole of Heart's Bakers factory with their outrageous stories of being out and about in London Town, they were certainly having fun and accumulating many potential husbands. It was not only Clara's antics that kept them entertained it was all three of them. Louisa couldn't have been happier for Rosie, she wanted her to have a good life.

"I was thinking," she revealed to Rosie one day as they passed the newspaper stand.

I don't know why you don't go down The Seamaster's Arms Dance on the odd Saturday. You could go to the Red X club one week and The Seamaster's Arms dance the next weekend. I know you think everybody's going to be desperate to know what happened with you and Frank, but quite honestly, that was so long ago now it's all water under the bridge, everybody's sure to have forgotten all about it, people have enough going on in their own lives to not be bothered about what went on in yours. A lot has happened to us all."

Louisa was nodding her head hoping Rosie would agree, but she didn't say anything.

"Also, if you go to The Seamaster's Arms dance the weekend your mum and dad go, they may buy you a drink or two, and drinks are probably cheaper there anyway than up the West End and you would save the bus fares too."

Rosie was obviously weighing it all up.

"Yes, I might do," she paused pouting her lips.

"I don't really care what anybody thinks about Frank and I now anyway to tell you the truth," shaking her head.

"But," she retorted smiling, "If I didn't go to the Red X Club one week then what would all my adoring admirers do?"

Rosie threw her arms into the air.

"They would just miss me so much."

The girls walked home laughing.

"Oh, for God's sake," Louisa snatched the envelope from the post lady's hands who looked incredulously at Louisa.

She hadn't meant to snap but she didn't want the letter.

Louisa apologised and closed the door. She knew what this was. She wasn't going to open it. She had had enough.

She stomped into the sitting room and ripped aggressively at the envelope. The War Office had certainly spent a tidy sum on sending letters to her house. She put her right hand to her forehead and tears spouted from her eyes. Louisa had long suspected Stevie was dead but she supposed that deep down there was always a tiny glimmer of hope that she was wrong. No news is good news she kept telling herself. She would have no one, no one at all left from her happy, cherished childhood family. And what life had he, none, no girlfriend, just sent away to fight and experience God knows what all because of some Nazi called Adolph Hitler.

She yanked the stiff white sheet from the ragged envelope.

'The War Office
Pall Mall
Whitehall
London
S.W.1
Dear Mr and Mrs Foster

We have received reliable information that your son Mr Steve Foster was taken as a prisoner of war.

At this time, we can tell you no more than he has been found to be well and uninjured. He is at the moment in France with Allied troops awaiting transportation back to the United Kingdom.

We will write to you again as soon as we are in receipt of further information.

We hope this letter is of comfort to you.

Yours sincerely
W. Skecher'

"No," Louisa gasped out loud.

No, No, oh, my gosh," she jumped up off the sofa and clutched the letter to her heart.

She glanced back at it, was it dated? No.

"Oh, my gosh, oh, my gosh, oh, my gosh," she skipped around the room.

She read it again, had she dreamt it, did it really say he was well? Oh, my gosh!"

Louisa looked out of the window.

"Who can I tell?" She was bursting with excitement.

Chapter Fifty-Five

Three months after the squirmingly embarrassing memory of Laurence and The Seamaster's Arms, Mark arrived on her doorstep. He looked so big and strong when she opened the door he blocked all the light out. Louisa felt faint.

"Mark," she screamed she was over the moon to see him.

"Oh, my gosh! What a wonderful surprise come in, come in." She invited pulling at his arm and nearly dragging him into the house.

He stayed all day, Louisa thought it was so refreshing to have a man around the house again. Harry was quite the little grown up gentleman, asking so many questions about what being a car mechanic entailed, what exactly do you do? Is it a dangerous profession? How much money do you earn? Louisa chided him for that question, but only gently and with a soft look on her face, it was a tad personal, she didn't want Mark to think he was a rude little boy. Louisa was overall very impressed, even though he was her son she did deem him very mature for his age, very bright.

Harry and Johnny went out, they said they were going for a walk along Bermondsey Walk. Louisa watched them proudly from her window ambling down the street, their little arms swinging. It was a good thing that they were so close to each other, she was glad about that. They would always have each other no matter what happened to her.

It was the first fun day she'd had for ages. Anyway, you know what they say you don't get over the loss you just get used to it. Louisa and Mark recalled memories for hours mulling over old stories, pranks Mark and James had got up to as children, stories James had told Mark of life at sea, some Louisa had heard before but it was just so nice to be sitting there talking to a man. She felt guilty and emotional but really enjoyed herself. Mark was very like James, a good man, good morals, good manners, probably why they had been best friends.

Louisa made them a meal of mashed potatoes and corned beef, there was still a food shortage although the choices were gradually improving in the shops. You'd see the odd item that you had never seen before on the vegetable display or in Eric's, the butcher shop and everybody would erupt into an excited frenzy. Mark kept enquiring politely if he was keeping Louisa from somewhere or someone and she retorted cheekily,

"Not at all."

They even listened to the radio together. Louisa thought she had better not bore him with her *Women's Hour* programme, he might not be into Gloria and her knitting or making radish chutney so she twiddled the knob trying to find the B.B.C. news channel. Mark took over and Louisa slumped onto the sofa, she stroked the worn fabric and felt very content.

They sat and listened.

"What's that mean?" Louisa looked doe eyed at Mark.

"Nothing important."

"Oh."

Eventually it was time for Mark to go, it was getting late and he had such a long drive home.

"Well, I have had an absolutely lovely day, Louisa, it's has been marvellous to be in your company and the boys are an absolute treasure.

Mark took her hands in his.

"You should be very proud of yourself, you are doing a fantastic job raising them, I know it couldn't have been easy and I'm sure James is in heaven looking down saying 'Well done, Lou Lou'."

Mark continued, "But I really must be making tracks now."

"Cheerio for now and thanks again for dinner."

Louisa looked down at the floor. She wanted to stand on her tiptoes and kiss him.

He was gone.

196

Chapter Fifty-Six

"Oh, I don't know how I will ever be able to walk down the street again, it's disgusting, how could they, all the neighbours will know I will have to leave home."

Louisa was laughing, not because of Rosie's news but because of Rosie's reaction.

"Well, I never, me and Caren will both have to move out, they need their heads tested, I ask you have you ever heard of anything like it?"

Louisa had to cross her legs she was doubled over chortling and tears of laughter were in her eyes.

Betty had announced to Rosie and Caren the previous evening that they are to have a brother or sister, Betty is expecting a baby.

"It is totally disgusting, they are well old enough to have grandchildren, Yuk, can you imagine, eeerrrr, it's vile and I can't even think about it."

Louisa tried to reason with Rosie but couldn't finish any sentence as she would start sniggering.

Oh, it was a jolly walk to work that day but not for Rosie.

Harry came home with a letter from school in the afternoon.

He had been awarded a 'Certificate of Excellence in Reading, Writing and Arithmetic'.

"Well, I never," Louisa had never heard of this happening before, she looked at Harry who wasn't even smiling.

"Do you know what this is Harry? This is amazing? Well done, my son, that's fantastic, you must be even cleverer than I thought."

Harry smiled slightly and took his jumper off.

"I'm off to play football, coming Johnny?"

They both dashed upstairs to get changed into some old clothes, Louisa wouldn't let them out to play in their day time clothes because they were always falling over or tearing whatever they were wearing. There was not a day went by they didn't come in with a scuffed knee or elbow.

She sat at the kitchen table and stared at the Certificate of Excellence in awe.

Louisa had a bit of a dilemma and didn't know whose advice to ask. Louisa felt she could work more hours now at Heart's Bakery and just assumed that when Hank took Penny to America Louisa would take over Penny's hours. Well, now Louisa didn't know if that was ever going to happen. She desperately wanted to earn more money, every time she went shopping she saw other people buying sausages and pies and just couldn't wait for the day she could too. She wanted to serve great whopping dinners to her sons, plates piled high with solid food drizzled with gravy, to witness their eyes bulging in anticipation of eating such a feast, but she was just not able to.

She thought she could ask Eve if she could do more hours at Heart's Bakers but that would mean she wouldn't be able to keep an eye on Violet while Penny was at work and she was not sure how Penny would feel about that. Also Louisa thought she'd have to be careful here, as this conversation could raise the question about whether Penny was actually going to end up going to America or not. As far as Louisa knew Hank hadn't replied to Penny's 'confessional letter'.

Oh, blinky blimey, thought Louisa, *It's just all too complicated, I wish my mum was here!*

The following Saturday about noon , Mark visited again, Louisa was so thrilled, she had been thinking about Mark every day, she really liked him, really, really liked him but suspected he was just being a good friend to James, watching out for his best friends widow, making sure her and the boys were all right. James probably would have done the same if the boot was on the other foot. But now Mark was here on her doorstep again? Maybe he did have a little soft spot for her after all? Louisa hoped so.

"I've brought this for you from Sylvia," Mark gestured towards an envelope in his hand, "and I got some beef as a 'Thank You' present for mending someone's car and thought maybe you, Little Harry and Johnny might fancy it?"

"Oh, my gosh, that's brilliant, thank you, I'm sure Harry and Johnny would love it! Come in, Mark, that's so kind of you! Thank you! Can I get you a cup of tea?" Louisa tried to act as flippantly as possible, she didn't want to read too much into his visit.

"Yes, please, that would be great."

Louisa put the kettle on to boil and opened the letter, then without looking at it put it to one side, she could read it later when Mark had left, it might seem rude to be reading a letter while you have a guest.

"I know, I've got some carrots and a turnip, shall I make us a beef stew," Louisa enquired excitedly.

"Oh, now, that would be grand, that sounds perfect, just what the doctor ordered, you sure you don't mind like? I'm not interrupting your plans just turning up out of the blue?" Mark laughed, untied his shoe laces, took off his shoes and made himself comfortable on the raggedy sofa.

Louisa thought there was nothing she would rather be doing than sitting with Mark, but just flippantly replied,

"No, of course not."

They played with Harry's pack of cards that day, the ones that Mark had brought him as a Christmas present. Louisa was surprised there were none missing. Louisa hadn't played cards for years, last time she had played was with her mum, dad, Stevie, and Gladys. Happy days they were. Mark taught her how to play a game called Sevens, she loved it and managed to win about one game out of ten!

"You're a novice!" Mark teased, "You'll thrash me next time! You wait and see!"

Louisa warmed inside because he had said 'next time'.

When the boys came in at 5 o'clock all muddy and laughing, Louisa sent them upstairs to wipe themselves clean with a flannel and soap and to hurry up because dinner was nearly ready. It did smell irresistible. The whole house was warm and cosy all because of a beef stew bubbling on the stove. And it tasted as good as it smelt, really tender, the beef melted in their mouths. The boys gobbled it up, Louisa was so thankful to be giving them a substantial meal for once. Mark teased Louisa saying it was so delicious because it was a good cut of meat, from a decent butcher and had nothing to do with Louisa's cooking skills. She whacked him across the head with her tea towel like her mum used to do to her dad. It was fun the four of them together but she mustn't go off into her dream world again. He left without kissing her and she thought she had better get herself out with the 'Three Musketeers', Rosie, Caren and Clara and find a distraction because she was obviously old and lonely and desperate for any attention.

Sylvia's letter said June had died. *Oh, no*, Louisa thought, *that's so sad.* June was a sweet lady, and Louisa guessed that she didn't have much fun as Cyril's wife even though they did socialise a lot before the outbreak of war, but Louisa guessed that was all a show and Cyril probably wasn't that nice to her when they were all alone. Especially now the truth was known about him, he probably was a right old pig to live with.

Sylvia hadn't been able to sleep since discovering June's body. Sylvia had left her what she thought was sleeping until nine thirty in the morning, late for June, and then taken her up a cup of tea. June was stiff and grey. Sylvia had no way of reaching a doctor and had to wait all day with June's body dead upstairs for the Land girls to come home. Maureen walked back to the Hop farm and used their telephone to summon help. The doctor came and said June had died peacefully in her sleep of natural causes.

Louisa tried to work out how old June would have been, she didn't look that old. Sylvia said she didn't know what her future held now but she had just carried on as normal with her housekeeping and looking after Carol and Maureen, the Land girls.

Blimey, thought Louisa, *How's Sylvia going to survive? How is she going to buy food, what will she pay with? Her own money? How will she even get the food in? I had better write her a letter first thing in the morning though I don't know what I can do? Nothing! I can't do anything, can I, I should have read her letter while Mark was here, he would have been able to help or known what to do.* She guessed the Land girls would give Sylvia their rent money but something would have to be sorted out.

A few days later, Louisa was sitting on the sofa having a well-earned tea break. After rising early for work, going to work, coming home, washing some clothes, making the beds, sweeping the floor, watering the green beans and cooking and eating tea she was now shattered. Harry and Johnny were sitting at the kitchen table going over some arithmetic. There was a gentle *rat-a-tat* on the door. It was a second or two before it registered and by then Harry had walked passed her to see who it was.

Penny entered the room,

"What's the matter with you?" Penny asked Louisa.

Louisa had been sitting flopped out on the sofa thinking of Mark, she felt guilty for liking him, for liking him in a womanly way, not as a mate. She felt guilty to James but she just couldn't help her heart fluttering when she saw Mark, she missed James, it had been years since he had held her, she loved their intimate times together. Louisa also felt remorseful that maybe the night she had gone to the Red X club and she had enjoyed herself so much, well maybe James was already dead then.

Louisa raised her eyes to Penny.

"Oh, my gosh! What's the matter with you?" she exclaimed, Penny's eyes were all red and swollen it was obvious she had been crying.

Penny started sobbing uncontrollably, her nose was running, Louisa pulled a handkerchief from her sleeve and offered it to Penny.

"He said he can't forgive me," Penny couldn't breathe properly.

"He said he can't forgive me because I lied, not because of who ever Violet's dad is, he could have forgiven that." Penny was crying, trying to get her breath and wipe her wet nose all at the same time. "But he can't forgive me for lying." Penny was beside herself.

Harry raised his eyebrows and looked at his mum puzzled, Penny was wailing like a baby and Louisa shook her head to Harry and nodded him towards to kitchen. Harry guessed what his mum was meaning him to do and walked into the kitchen and closed the door behind him.

Penny cried for ages, every now and then stammering comments like "he must be going back to America soon" and "I've lost him", which set her off wailing again. Louisa kept rubbing her back, brushing her hair off her wet face and saying, "There, there." She felt so useless, what could she say?

Louisa put the radio on, made some tea and they listened to *Women's Hour*.

Chapter Fifty-Seven

Louisa decided she was going to flirt with Eric the butcher. Of course, it was obvious, that is what she had to do, she was sure that's what all the other women did anyway, get a bit of a bigger loaf, a pat more butter, she would do that from now on with all the shopkeepers. She would get dressed up next time she was going to the butcher's, see if she could get some sausages or even a big chop. He always flirted with her whilst his wife always stood behind looking not impressed. Louisa wanted some decent meals for her boys, they were her priority not Eric's wife. She had to toughen herself up, be more ruthless. The previous evening she had made Harry and Johnny promise on their lives that they never breathe a word about Violet's dad. They did promise but she wanted to reward them with a nice big dinner.

She put her poppy red lipstick on, tied a scarf around her hair creating a knotted bow on top, she pinched her cheeks gently until she looked slightly flushed, pulled her skirt in with one of her mum's belts and trotted off out the door. As she was walking towards Bermondsey Walk, the post lady was walking towards her. The post lady said, "Oh, I've got one for you I think," and delved into the heavy canvas satchel she carried across her shoulder. She handed Louisa a letter. Louisa always tried to be overly polite and friendly now to the post lady after she had snapped at her before. Louisa took the letter, thanked her and continued off to Eric the butcher, she looked at the handwriting and recognised it was from Sylvia, tucking it into her handbag she thought, *Oh, dear, more doom and gloom*, and then immediately felt bad.

Louisa bounced into the butcher's, Eric seemed to be loving the way she pouted her lips and stared at him, requesting some sausages, he was like a wild animal, not a cute fluffy animal like a cat or dog, more like a weasel, thought Louisa as she tucked plump purchase into her shopping bag, *Still, 'never mind it did the trick'*, she continued onto the greengrocers, brought some swede and carrots and trotted off home. All proud of herself. When she was indoors she boiled the kettle to make a cup of tea, patted her scarf like her mum used to and opened Sylvia's letter.

'Laburnham Farm
Biddenden Village
Near Ashford
Kent

Dear Louisa

I have the most amazing news! Your brother Stevie is in Ashford Hospital! I haven't seen him but he is supposed to be well, very quiet and in shock but with no awful injuries like some of the other poor boys! He is alive!

You will never believe this, it is just such a coincidence, the wife of Doctor Watkins (the doctor who attended June's death) is a Matron at Ashford Hospital where they keep bringing the wounded servicemen to. Well, they were telling each other over dinner about what had happened to them during that day and she mentioned Stevie to her husband and that he said that some relative's mother is a housekeeper at a farm at Biddenden. Yesterday morning, Doctor Watkins remembered coming here and said to his wife to find out the patients surname. The Matron couldn't remember it but found out at work and told him last night. Doctor Watkins came this morning and told me all about him. What a small world I was flabbergasted, fancy working out it was me!

And on top of all this last night I had another marvellous surprise! The executor of June's will (I didn't even know she had left a will) called here last night and told me that June has left everything including the Farmhouse to me! All to me!

I am in a daze, I could not sleep a wink last night, I am so grateful, I will write to you again soon when my thoughts have settled as I am in such a whirl! A nice whirl!

I hope yourself, Harry and Johnny are well and enjoying the dreaded war being over. Keep safe my darlings.

Love
Sylvia'

Louisa could not believe it! No doom and gloom! Only the complete opposite!

Louisa slumped on the sofa.

Well, I never.

Would you believe it? A letter with good news in it at last!

Louisa decided she was going to have to wear lipstick all the time from now on because she reckoned that if she looked good then only good things would happen to her.

"I am not looking forward to it." Rosie was still going on every day about Betty's pregnancy. Louisa initially thought Rosie would get used to the idea but Betty was now five months pregnant and Rosie and Caren were still horrified at the idea.

"You can come and live with me if it's going to be that bad," Penny jokingly offered Rosie.

Rosie was aghast.

"Really? What about Hank?"

Penny had only told Louisa about Hank's letter. She was just pretending he was working hard in Norwich and they would one day carry out their plans and go and live in America.

She would keep it up for as long as possible then conjure up a way of explaining why they hadn't gone and why he had disappeared. She would cross that bridge when she came to it, even Violet didn't know.

Louisa just prayed her boys didn't accidently let the cat out of the bag.

"Can Caren come too? Otherwise she'll be stuck on her own with it in our bedroom."

Everybody was laughing but Rosie was serious.

"Well," Penny looked uncomfortable, "I'm not sure I have got room for the both of you."

Rosie tutted and they all carried on with their work.

Chapter Fifty-Eight

Stevie was so thin and gaunt. He looked like a skeleton from the British Museum Tom and Alice had taken them to for a treat when they were all little children. He was so weak he could hardly walk. He looked about forty years old and never smiled.

Mark had driven Stevie all the way up from Ashford Hospital in Kent, Louisa didn't actually recognise Stevie when she opened the door to them both. Mark hadn't stayed long which Louisa felt disappointed about but she had to pay all her attention to Stevie anyway. Louisa was so very glad he was actually alive that she hadn't given much thought to the actual living with him, or rather him living with her and her boys.

Little Harry and Johnny had never met him, it was difficult for them, they obviously didn't remember the handsome, kind, charming chap that he had once been. Now all they saw was someone who resembled a scarecrow taking up space in their sitting room. Stevie was so battle weary that he didn't speak so that didn't endear him to Harry or Johnny either. They never said anything but Louisa could read their thoughts, she was their mum, she knew them better than anyone. Also, she knew Harry was quite an impatient person and he wouldn't like someone who didn't bother to wash or shave.

Louisa was of course more worldly wise and knew it would take weeks, months may be even years for Stevie to regain his strength, to become the fine man that he had once been, to re-gather his sense of humour and ability to chat.

Louisa had asked him gently, "Where he had been? How he was captured? Where he was kept?"

But poor Stevie couldn't bring himself to answer, he screwed up his eyes, grimaced his whiskery face, sometimes even started to tremor. Louisa wouldn't pry anymore, it was obviously too harrowing, she told him light heartedly that there was no rush and he could tell them all about his adventures if and when he was feeling up to it.

One evening, Rosie came banging on Louisa's door crying and in a right panic, Louisa was trying to get some sense out of her.

"Rosie, calm down and tell me what is wrong, whatever is the matter?" Louisa shouted at the top of her voice, she was going to have to slap her across the face soon, she was verging on hysterical.

Rosie abruptly gained some control of herself although still shaking.

"My mum hasn't come home and she went to see her sister my auntie Marlene in Stepney and my dad's just found out that something's happened at Stepney train station and there are loads of casualties caught up in it. A doodlebug dropped on it months ago and it's been unsafe ever since."

Louisa froze.

Stevie enquired, "What's a doodlebug?" and stood up.

"No," was all Louisa could think to say.

Stevie put his arm across Rosie's shoulder.

"I'll get my coat and go to Stepney, you get me her sister's address," he sped upstairs.

Rosie ran back to her house and Louisa felt sick.

Louisa eventually went to bed about two in the morning, she put the radio on quietly in the hope they may mention Stepney but there was only classical music playing. After giving Stevie her Aunties address, Rosie returned to her own house in the hope that Betty returned or anybody came knocking with any information. Ed went with Stevie.

When Louisa woke in the morning, Stevie wasn't home and Louisa feared the worst, but about half past nine he arrived looking shattered. He had been up all night, the bombing had caused a huge crater around Stepney Train Station and the station had just collapsed into it. Betty was in the vicinity, but thank goodness not one of the many fatalities that Stevie had seen. Betty had been very scared and there was a stampede of people panicking to escape. She had eventually arrived back at her sister, Marlene's house and knocked them up about midnight. Stevie and Ed had to fight their way through the emergency services, restricted areas, relatives searching for missing members of their families and injured public being treated at the scene. The whole area was pandemonium. When they eventually arrived at Marlene's house, tears of relief were shed by all. The three of them walked slowly all the way back this morning and then it was Rosie and Caren's turns to break down crying.

Louisa held her chest with relief and whispered, "Thank you, God."

Later on that week, the poster at the newspaper stand said one hundred and thirty four innocent people had lost their lives that day more than had been killed in the original V2 bomb blast.

Chapter Fifty-Nine

Well, every cloud has a silver lining as they say because that devastating situation at Stepney had somehow jolted Stevie out of his traumatised state. He wasn't one hundred per cent better but nearly and went to the labour exchange to see if he could get a job. He was still receiving his income from the Royal Navy but said he was getting bored.

"Surely, that's a good sign," mused Louisa. He and Rosie had become very pally towards each other, constantly laughing and teasing each other and Rosie asked him to accompany her and Caren to The Seamaster's Arms dance on Saturday evening. It affirmed Louisa's theory to herself, that since she wore red lipstick every day her world was getting better!

"I can't believe what I'm seeing," Louisa bubbled to Penny, "Stevie and Rosie are becoming inseparable! Or am I imagining it, reading too much into the situation?"

"I think they make a lovely couple," Penny sighed.

Louisa felt so sorry for her, she was a tough one but knew her heart was aching for Hank, Louisa patted her shoulder.

"Why don't you write Hank another letter spelling out exactly why you said what you did, just explain, saying you liked him so very much you didn't want to put him off you or something like that? It's worth a try, my lovely."

Tears splashed from Penny's thick eyelashes.

"I already have, Louisa, a few weeks ago now, I didn't say anything to you because I feel so desperate and ashamed."

Penny wiped her nose with her handkerchief.

"Anyway, he never even replied."

"Oh, my poor, darling." Louisa was greatly disappointed and hugged her.

But another good thing to came out of that horrific night in Stepney was that Rosie and Caren had now accepted that there would be an addition to their family and had come full circle and now seemed to be excited about a new brother or sister. They must have been so terrified that Betty had been killed, they now pampered her rotten, wouldn't let her do any chores around the house, made her endless cups of tea, insisted she rest and be waited on. Betty was over the moon!

Louisa hadn't seen or heard from Mark for weeks and was feeling mystified. She wrote a letter to Sylvia enquiring about everyone and as casually as she could make it sound asked if Mark was well. Louisa was cross with herself, what was the matter with her? As if an eligible, good looking bachelor like Mark, who had so many appealing qualities would be interested in his best friend's widow. With two children as well, as if he would want to saddle himself with two boys, somebody else's boys at that, even if they are his best friends sons. No he could get any girlfriend, an attractive Land girl or nurse, she betted to herself they were all flocking over him in Biddenden. Hardly any men anywhere so he could have his pick of any females probably. Louisa had made herself thoroughly fed up.

Johnny came rushing in from school one day just ahead of Harry.

"He's only gone and got a scholarship," Johnny nodded his head in Harry's direction.

"Miss Evans said he can go to a posh school in Ipswich." Johnny was panting.

Harry strolled in casually, Johnny was more excited than him.

"What's a scholarship?" Louisa enquired, "I don't think I can afford that."

Both boys doubled up laughing.

"I did an exam in school and I passed it and now they say I can go away to a boarding school in Ipswich and they have, sailing lessons and all sorts. Mum, I don't think you have to pay!"

"Oh, my gosh, you are so clever, where's Ipswich? That's fantastic news, is it or isn't it?" She wasn't sure.

"You are too young to go away, but who does pay? And why didn't you tell me you had sat an exam?"

Louisa knew she was rambling but all these questions were popping into her head. How had they kept that a secret from her?

"Miss Evans would like you to pop in and see her after school so you can discuss it. I don't start until September."

Harry and Johnny went upstairs to change and Louisa just had to boast she was so proud so went and knocked at Penny's door.

Penny was crying, she opened the door slowly, Louisa's heart sunk, is this what she does every day? Louisa asked herself, just come home from work, sit in the house and cry? How could she share her good tidings now with Penny in tears?

Penny opened the door for Louisa to come in, keeping herself hidden behind it so no prying eyes from the street could see her.

"Hank has written to me," Penny waved a letter in front of Louisa.

"He misses me and wants us to stay together."

"Oh, my God, you daft pillock, what are you crying for? I don't believe it."

"Because I'm so happy," Penny snivelled.

Louisa started jumping up and down, Penny joined in, they were like young girls in a children's playground.

Chapter Sixty

Betty had given up her job at Heart's Bakers to rest at home and Louisa asked Eve if she could cover some of her hours. Eve said that was fine and Louisa was due to start the extra shifts next week. She had chosen Tuesday and Thursday only four until six pm. Violet, Harry and Johnny were fine letting themselves indoors after school now, they knew where the spare door keys were kept and Penny said she could cover two extra shifts as well. It wasn't much more money but it all helped. Louisa planned to ask Harry and Johnny to prepare the dinner while she did her extra shifts, not cook it, she didn't want the house burnt down! They could just peel the potatoes or whatever vegetables they were having that evening. Louisa would then finish if off when she got indoors about 6.30 pm, bit later than they normally ate but it was worth it for more money. She also thought it was a good plan because if they had chores to carry out it was less time for them to play out in the street and less chance of getting up to mischief.

Louisa had gone straight round to see Miss Evans after work the day after Harry's announcement, Louisa was worried she would have to buy Harry a school uniform. They were so expensive and knew that no way could she afford it. But that was what the scholarship meant, he would get everything paid for because he was so bright. Twenty boys in the Greater London Area had sat the same exam and Harry had come third out of all of them. Louisa had no idea where he got his brains from and was surprised and so pleased for him. It was a fantastic opportunity and he may have a brilliant life because of it but she was worried he would get all stuck up and look down his nose at her or he would be homesick and bullied by the older pupils. Harry himself seemed to be looking forward to it but the proof would be in the pudding, he would be miles away from his home and family, all on his own with a load of other boys would he be able to look after himself? How much would it cost Louisa for her and Johnny to travel to Ipswich to visit him? Would Louisa have to pay for Harry's travel expenses to come home in the school holidays, and that was another thing Johnny would be so lost without him around. Louisa decided to ask Stevie's advice on how to prepare her eldest son for boarding school.

Hank came one weekend, Louisa had never seen Penny look so happy, Louisa wanted to hang bunting up around the door she was so relieved for her dear friend. Hank just seemed his normal self, very chivalrous and suave. He didn't look one bit depressed so Louisa decided that they have overcome this hurdle in their marriage and everything would be perfect for them from now on.

The same weekend Stevie, Rosie and Caren all went out to the Red X Club in Bloomsbury. Rosie and Caren had been a godsend in Stevie's recovery, Louisa was sure she wouldn't have been able to get him back to normal without them. But also he had helped himself. Louisa had a lot of admiration for him. Now he was a good dancer, Rosie had been teaching him and he was working at the new Woolworth's store part time, he whistled around the house which Louisa thought meant he was happy. Also, he had a lot of grieving to do when he had first got home, Louisa had lost her mum, Gladys, Dad and James not all at once but for him who had already been through a truly terrible ordeal to then be told nearly all his family was dead, well, that would be terrible on its own, without being a prisoner of war as well. Yes, Louisa felt like saluting him, he had made himself better.

They all said Louisa should go out with them but she just declined their kind offer automatically without really thinking about it. Why did she say no? Harry and Johnny would probably be all right on their own and she deserved a good night out. She worked hard all week and should reward herself instead of sitting in daydreaming about a certain car mechanic from Biddenden. Louisa tried to imagine what her mum would say, would she encourage Louisa to go, Louisa thought she would, she could imagine her advising, "Go and have some fun in your life love," so Louisa decided she would absolutely make herself go out the following Saturday evening with Rosie, Caren and Stevie, wherever they were going she would tag along. She chided herself that she was acting like an old lady.

"Ma Pritchard probably goes out more than me," she spoke to her reflection in her mirror.

But on this particular Saturday evening she had treated herself to a Daily Mirror and she sat indoors reading that and thinking about Mark and James.

Louisa had not had any reply from Sylvia and was curious, she had enquired in work if anybody had heard if Kent had suffered any problems recently, everybody shook their heads, No, they hadn't heard about any and she supposed they probably wouldn't have taken any notice anyway, even if they had heard something, she wouldn't have taken much notice either if she didn't know anybody living in Kent. Louisa was standing rolling out pastry in work trying to come up with a solution to contacting Sylvia when she realised Rosie was leaning up against her

"Have you got five minutes for a chat at break time I want to. ask you something? Just between us?"

Louisa nodded, perplexed, Rosie looked scared.

"I'm really nervous about saying this to you, I really have no idea how you are going to react, but I really, really, really like Stevie and wondered if A, you would mind if me and he were boyfriend and girlfriend and B, can you get him to ask me on a date?" Rosie burst out with a nervous snorting laugh.

Louisa smiled far too keenly and said, "Oh, that would be lovely and of course, I'll put in a few hints for you." Her heart was racing, what could the outcome of this be? She knew they were like best pals but how embarrassing, say Stevie doesn't think of Rosie like that, if he liked her wouldn't he have asked her out himself wouldn't he? And oh, gosh, just say they end up getting married, do I want Rosie as my brother's wife? Oh, gosh, I must give this some careful thought."

As it happened Louisa couldn't ask Stevie that night as Betty went into labour and with all the excitement it completely went out of her head. Betty had been having tummy pains since about lunch time. When Rosie and Caren got in from work, they gathered everything together for the birth and Caren went to the Seaman's Mission hut before the baby clinic closed for the day. A midwife would visit in an hour or two. They filled to the brim with water their largest two saucepans, brought them to the boil and kept them both simmering on the stove, collected all the clean towels already put aside for the impending birth from the cupboard and gathered the clean torn rags Betty had been collecting for months. Rosie and Caren had never seen a baby born before and Betty was looking pretty distressed and in so much pain that they secretly decided to themselves that they would never have children.

Louisa called in their house to see how it was all progressing and was shocked to see Betty's faced so screwed up.

"When's the midwife coming?" Louisa asked feeling very grown up and knowledgeable, I mean these two didn't have a clue what to do but Louisa had given birth twice.

"Soon." Caren's eyes were as big as ping pong balls staring at her mum grunting in disbelief.

"Where's your dad, is he due home soon? He'll have to go down to my house with Stevie unless we can get your mum upstairs?"

Betty shook her head, she was holding her back and trying to hoist her huge frame out of the armchair, her nostrils were flared and her eyes had been shut since Louisa arrived. Betty waddled like a duck over to the sofa and lay on it emitting a long, deep gasp.

Rosie and Caren both had huge gazes now as they exchanged frightened looks.

Louisa smiled, "You're all right aren't you, Betty, you've done all this before, now just take slow, deep breaths, you remember?"

Louisa was quite enjoying herself.

Betty's groaning was getting louder and closer together, everything was brought into the sitting room except for the kettle of boiling water. Louisa covered the sofa in some of the towels, the groaning turned into deep wails and puffs and pants, the midwife walked briskly through the door, Betty's face was bright crimson and with an almighty yell Edward Leonard was born.

Chapter Sixty-One

Ed was besotted with his son. He had shared his home with three women for far too long, now it was more equal, he wasn't so outnumbered now, he had a new little mate Edward. Edward Leonard, he would teach him how to play football, ride a bicycle, skim stones on the River Thames, he was so delighted to have him in his life and blessed the day he had cut down on the booze.

Penny was the first visitor, so excited, everybody was excited, it was lovely for Betty and Ed and the girls too, of course. It was not that long ago that the pair of them couldn't even manage to have a civil conversation, now Ed hardly ever drank beer and they were a perfect little family.

Rosie and Caren had the next day off work but on the Wednesday Rosie hugged Louisa on the way to work.

"I'm so grateful, thank you so much I really appreciate it, Lou Lou."

Louisa was very proud of herself and smiling smugly bragged.

"It was nothing, your mum did all the hard work not me."

"Oh, yes, thank you for that as well, sorry, sort of forgot about that already, no, I'm saying thank you for having a word with Stevie," Rosie was whispering so Caren couldn't hear her.

Louisa looked puzzled,

"Oh, my gosh," Louisa grimaced, "I completely forgot, I am so very sorry, I have been in a daze since Edward's arrival, I promise, promise, promise I'll definitely say something to him tonight."

Rosie was shaking her head trying to get Louisa to be quiet, Caren looked at them both suspiciously and they couldn't talk any further.

Eve sat next to Louisa at break time and Rosie was acting very weird. Caren walked home after work with them. And they bumped into Stevie on his way back from Woolworths and they all walked together. Rosie looked really nervous.

Louisa made some polite small talk about Edward and work, she had brought home some left over rock cakes.

She had no idea how she was going to brace this, what should she say? It was 1945, the man is supposed to ask the woman out, not the other way around, she didn't want to make Rosie look desperate but wanted to see if Stevie would open up and tell her if he had any real feelings for Rosie or was it just friendship he felt? She knew he liked Rosie, maybe he did find her attractive and was too worried to suggest anything more than friendship to her. And Louisa did not want a Rosie all broken hearted and miserable again.

"Ermmmm, you and Rosie seem to get on really well, you talk for hours," Louisa slowly murmured later that evening.

Stevie didn't even look up, just sat at the kitchen table reading Saturday's Daily Mirror newspaper.

"Mmmmmmm," he replied.

"Mmmmmmm," Louisa teased, "what does 'mmmmmm' mean?"

Stevie looked up from the newspaper and squinted with a cheeky grin. "Mmmmm means yes she is a lovely girl, why do you ask?"

Oh, Louisa had been working out all day what she was going to say, it had to be dead right, she couldn't be making Rosie look cheap, Men were supposed to do the chasing, oh, why was she doing this, oh, blinking blimey, why do I get myself into these fixes? I'm everybody's helper. Louisa blurted out.

"I think she might have a bit of a thing for you."

"No," she grimaced to herself, "that was not what I was supposed to say, oh, gosh, I could kick myself, you idiot."

Stevie was now laughing, "A bit of a thing? What does that mean?"

Oh, how awkward could she feel, not more awkward than this. Louisa had had enough.

"I think she may be waiting for you to ask her out on a date."

"No," replied Stevie, "what on earth makes you think that we are just friends?" and went back to turning the pages of the newspaper.

Louisa couldn't sleep that night, just kept tossing and turning. Oh, what was she going to say to poor Rosie.

Louisa just got it over and done with the next day. "I'm really sorry, I didn't have a chance to say anything last night, will ask tonight," she whispered to Rosie on the way to work. Louisa promised herself she would try and not be alone with Rosie then Rosie can't interrogate her.

Rosie smiled to herself, maybe she is not that bothered after all pondered Louisa.

Chapter Sixty-Two

The following Saturday came and Louisa spent three luxurious hours getting herself all dolled up. She felt eighteen years old again. She sprayed her hair with water and twisted it into little pin curls secured with some of her mum's hair grips. She soaked in a hot bath with soaped herself all over twice. Hank had come to stay again for the weekend and Penny came in to paint Louisa's nails for her whilst Violet and Hank baked some fairy cakes together in Penny's kitchen. Louisa scrubbed her teeth with bicarbonate of soda as she heard on *Women's Hour* that it was supposed to make them whiter. It tasted disgusting. Penny had generously loaned to her the black dress with the shoulder pads that she had worn on a date with Hank and she swept mascara on to her eyelashes that Stevie had got for her from his Woolworths store. She had to spit on what looked like a small little lump of coal and mix it up, that wasn't very appealing but it was all in the name of beauty. Louisa felt like the Hollywood movie stars she had seen in the newspapers. Stevie took about fifteen minutes to get ready and Johnny and Harry were playing cards at the kitchen table and had promised to be as good as saints staying in the house on their own. Louisa had given them strict instructions to either knock at Penny's or Betty's if they were in the least bit afraid.

Stevie said that Rosie was knocking for them at 7 o'clock, Louisa did think that was odd because they would then have to walk back past Rosie's door to the bus stop but assumed it was something to do with them waking up Edward if they knocked at her door.

Louisa stood in the sitting room waiting, she didn't want to sit down and crease her dress, she would have to sit on the bus that she couldn't avoid, but she didn't have to sit and crease it now. At five past seven, the *rat-a-tat-tat* came at the door. Louisa opened it while pulling her mum's fur wrap around her shoulders, it was Mark.

"Mark." Louisa was dumbstruck, Stevie was behind Louisa laughing and then Rosie appeared as from the darkness. Stevie squeezed past Louisa out of the door and took Rosie's hand.

Louisa was dumbstruck! What are they doing? Where are they going?

"What's going on?"

Mark laughed and walked in. He had a red rose in his hand.

Stevie called, "I'm taking this young lady out on a date, I've got a bit of a thing for her," they both giggled sailing off into the night.

"And I have a table for two booked for dinner and I would be delighted if you would accompany me," Mark beamed as he presented her with the rose and held out his arm.

The evening was like a Cinderella story Louisa and Gladys used to read when they were little girls. Mark took her to an intimate restaurant called Le Escargot which bordered the River Thames and was directly opposite the Tower of London. They sampled strange tasting foreign food, were served by men in bow ties and Louisa drank red wine for the first time ever.

"That's yummy, just like my mum and dad's sherry!" Louisa chuckled.

"Cheers to my mum and dad!"

Mark raised his glass to join her in toasting her beloved parents.

"I hope you don't mind me asking, Lou Lou? And I totally understand if it's too soon, and you really don't have to give me an answer now, but please don't say no!" Louisa started to smile with disbelief.

"I would be most grateful if you would do me the great honour of becoming my wife."

Louisa couldn't stop giggling, Mark's was nearly as tall as her and he was kneeling down. The waiter clapped, the waitress cheered and Louisa cried 'I do'.

Chapter Sixty-Three

They did marry, at Biddenden Registry Office in Kent, the Garden of England, this time the sun was shining and there were no muddy puddles. Mark had a charming old Tudor house right in the middle of Biddenden Village. It had low ceilings and small doors which Mark had to duck under, there were dark beams across the ceilings and a large hearth in the front room. Louisa added her woman's touch to their new abode and Mark was really complimentary about all the tweaks she gave to his manly house. They weren't far away from Sylvia at Laburnham Farm and visited her frequently, sometimes bringing her back to their happy home to eat with them. Harry exceled at boarding school in Ipswich, Suffolk, Johnny settled into his new village school like a duck to water. Stevie and Rosie were engaged to be married. Stevie had worked his way up to be a manager at the Woolworth's Store in Tottenham Court Road, West London. Betty, Ed, Caren and Edward were all thriving. Penny, Hank and Violet went off to live a very privileged life happy ever after in Boston, America and Ma Pritchard made everybody chortle with tales of South London folk at Mark and Louisa's wedding breakfast.

Now standing here looking out across the beautiful trees whose leaves were just turning copper preparing to shed themselves to keep the ground warm for winter, taking in the fields swaying in the sunshine and waiting to be harvested, feeling the sun streaming into her bedroom and the grass on their back lawn looking all dewy she couldn't believe how her life had changed. For a start she was feeling happy again. Ecstatically happy like she did when she was fifteen years old.

World War Two was responsible for a new breed of British women. They had become strong, confident, optimistic and capable. Women had kept the country going. The men may have gone away to fight the war but without the women at home keeping the home fires burning it may have been a different result. *Every cloud has a silver lining*, Louisa thought to herself. Now women were stronger, more confident, excited about their own futures.

Yes, she was anticipating a happy, enjoyable and safe future for herself, Harry, Johnny and Mark. She couldn't wait to embrace the next chapter.